Susan Sizemore takes her readers to a world where a single, smoldering glance can mean as much as a tempting kiss—and a man and a woman discover...

The Price of Passion

Reckless and dangerous, David Evans would do anything to regain Cleopatra Fraser, the beautiful, daring siren he'd once possessed—and been betrayed by. Now he's returned from his adventures to the Highlands, to claim the only treasure he's ever truly desired—Cleopatra.

Cleo had lost her heart, and her innocence, to the devastatingly handsome adventurer, and when he left her life she vowed he would never lay claim on her again. She's suspicious of his sudden reappearance, yet tantalized by his masterful desire for her. Once before, David introduced her to the delights of seduction . . . but is she ready to pay the full price of passion?

SUSAN SIZEMORE

The Price of Passion

An Avon Romantic Treasure

AVON BOOKS

An Imprint of HarperCollinsPublishers

AVON BOOKS
An Imprint of HarperCollins*Publishers*
10 East 53rd Street
New York, New York 10022-5299

Copyright © 2001 by Susan Sizemore
ISBN: 0-380-81651-2
www.avonromance.com

First Avon Books paperback printing: January 2001

Avon Trademark Reg. U.S. Pat. Off. and in Other Countries, Marca Registrada, Hecho en U.S.A.
HarperCollins® is a trademark of HarperCollins Publishers Inc.

Printed in the U.S.A.

10 9 8 7 6 5 4 3 2 1

Prologue

Nile Delta
1868

"I want . . . I want . . ."

Shaking like a leaf, Cleopatra Fraser sank to her knees. Far away from the tents and cookfires, she covered her face with her hands. The sand still held the heat of the day, and as she knelt there that heat began seeping relentlessly through the layers of her skirts and undergarments. The air she drew in with her ragged sobs was hot as a blast furnace. The sun was setting across the river, dyeing the wide swath of delta water blood red. The stars would soon come out to burn gloriously overhead, the wind would blow chill and salty from the sea a few miles away, the tents would glow from within with lamplight, and the

1

campfires would provide warm circles of light and security in this wild, lonely place. There would be food and conversation waiting for her, and duty.

Always duty. She did not mind duty, but—

She *wanted*. She bent forward, full of torment and confusion, full of . . . desire.

Desire.

It was too small a word for this huge, burning anguish rushing through her, trying to drown out every other thought and feeling. The deluge of relief after the long endless hours by her young sister's bedside had destroyed her normal defenses. Worry for Pia was replaced by exhaustion that was somehow transformed to feverish aching. She was dizzy, light-headed. How long had it been since she'd slept? Eaten? Cleo rubbed her tear-streaked face and tried to think. She had acted calm for so long while she held the fear inside. It was hard always being strong, always being responsible—for Pia, for Father, for newly widowed Aunt Saida and her son, for everyone and everything in camp.

But Pia's fever was broken. Cleo's youngest sister would live through this night and Cleo would see that she lived through many more. Cleo sent up a prayer of thanks that her little sister's life had been spared by the sickness that ravaged this harsh, alien land. A land that was beloved to Cleo, a place she called home—but she was hearty, had never been ill a day in her life. Mother had not survived the treks from ruin to ruin to ruin. Mother had not been able to live with Father's burning obsession, while Cleo thrived and grew from touching the bones and bricks of dead civilizations. Her middle sister, Annie, was safe at school back in Scotland. Cleo had won that battle, sending Annie back home to live with Aunt Jenny after Mother died. Pia must return now, too. Cleo could not bear to lose anyone else she loved.

More tears fell as she realized she would indeed lose someone—tomorrow. But losing *him* was inevitable. What a help *he* would be to Father if he stayed—but he was to return to America soon. Besides, he was ambitious; he would never settle for being Father's assistant. She did not know if his ambition was the fatal character flaw Father insisted it was, nor did she care if others thought he was flawed. *He* was the most beautiful man in the world. Handsome. Brilliant. He made her feel . . .

Wanted.

He would look at her with a fire in his dark, dark eyes—look at her from the tips of her toes all the way up to the top of her head—making a slow, bold study of her form and figure in a way that seemed to covet, to promise, to claim. When he looked at her like that, fire followed,

3

leaving her without any air in her lungs, any thoughts in her head. She was aware only of the weakness of her knees, of the fluttering, hot ache deep inside her, of the way her breasts and all her secret places felt that they were somehow being touched by his intense gaze. The first time he had looked at Cleo like that had lit a fuse in her, a thing that sizzled and burned and that she feared would lead to some awful, wonderful explosion.

She couldn't bear the thought of never having him look at her again. Never again making her feel this way.

She'd hoped and prayed to be beside him for every hour of the few weeks that remained of the excavating season. Then Pia had come down with the horrible fever. How long ago had that been? How many days since she'd had a glimpse of—

But what did it matter now?

She was here to take care of others. She had to be reasonable, pragmatic, sensible. But she *wanted*.

She made herself concentrate, to plan. There were important matters she must organize. Pia was so much a miniature version of Mother; the argument with Father to send her back to Scotland would be fierce. Cleo understood his reluctance, his loneliness, his ache for normality in this seductively foreign land. Uncle Walter had succumbed: he'd "gone native," married a foreigner, and his reputation as a scholar had suffered. Father jealously guarded his standing in the academic community. That included having a regular home life with his children around him. Cleo would miss her sister terribly as well, but Pia must live someplace where she could grow healthy and strong. Perhaps she could return when she was older. But Cleo would *not* risk the life of the baby of the family. She would take Pia to Aunt Jenny herself, book passage and go despite Father's protests.

Of course, Angel would be long gone by the time she returned. She started to cry again. Her Angel, with his intense black eyes and silky black hair and long-fingered, fascinating hands. He would never again look at her in that way that made her melt and catch fire at once. She'd known the day would come when she would never see his wide mouth curled in a teasing smile that promised . . . something.

And her life would be empty without the sight of him. Her breath would no longer catch and her heart race at watching him move, long-limbed and sure, graceful and strong. She would never again catch a glimpse of the hard, rippling muscles of his back and shoulders when he stripped to wash at the edge of the river. Or be so painfully aware of the outline of his thighs when he sat a horse or crouched next to her to examine some clue to the past in the sand. Sometimes his thigh brushed against hers. Sometimes his hands inadvertently touched her. And they would glance at each other, touching, their faces within the distance of a kiss as she passed a potsherd or ancient coin into his experienced hands.

She had never been kissed. She secretly hoped he would kiss her just once before he returned to America. Aunt Saida had said that *he* wanted to kiss her, and made a point never to let them be alone if she could help it, which was right and proper, of course. But . . .

It would be too much to hope that he would take her hands in his and declare his undying devotion. How could he, if they never had a private moment together? He had such beautiful hands. Always, her gaze returned to his beautiful hands. She dreamed of those hands on her. She'd wake up not remembering where he'd touched her, or how—but she yearned for . . . something.

Something that would put out the fire he kindled inside her.

She did not want to go to Scotland; she did not want to be where he was not. The pain of loss fueled the burning in her soul. She wanted to beat her fists against the sand and beg the ancient gods of this place for more time. For freedom to do what she wanted rather than what was necessary, just this once.

By the time she returned from Scotland, his touch, his unknown kiss, would be lost to her forever. She would never see his crooked, edgy smile; never hear his deep voice with its easy, teasing Yankee drawl. America was so far away . . .

Did the goddess Isis walk in this place any longer? Isis, who had lost her lover and searched the world over until they were together once more? She would understand. Would an Egyptian goddess grant a Scottish lass a boon?

"Please—I want . . ."

"What is it you want?"

At the unexpected, longed-for sound of his voice behind her a shudder went through Cleo. Fear? Anticipation? Of what?

She lifted her head, unashamed of her tears as she turned slowly to face him. Shame was burned out of her, along with fear and every ounce of sense she'd ever had. They were alone. For the first time ever, they were completely alone. He had found her in the night, when her heart was breaking, when she needed him most.

The last spark of the day's light at his back outlined him in gold and crimson, setting him apart from all that surrounded them. Setting them apart from the world. She could do nothing but stare.

His gaze held hers, dark as midnight. He held his hand out to her. "What do you want?"

She reached for his hand. He drew her up and to him, as strong as he was beautiful. She caught the sharp scent of his skin as he took her into the circle of his embrace. He whispered to her, his lips close to her ear, his breath intimate against her cheek. "What do you want, Cleo?"

Need set her trembling; her knees grew weak. She put her hand on his shoulder, needing his strength. With her lips so close to his, Cleo could do nothing but tell the truth. "You."

Chapter 1

Muirford, Scotland
1878

"All I am saying, Cleo, is that if you don't show a proper decorum I will quite simply *die!*"

"She means she won't find a beau," Pia translated Annie's concern.

"Which is infinitely worse," Annie said to Pia, turning to the fourteen-year-old who sat in a huge wingback leather chair. "You're too young to understand. And Cleo's too old and—"

"Dried up?" Pia teased.

She had a wicked, quick wit, did Pia, and a penchant for telling too much truth. Cleo, unstung by anything either girl said, watched Annie's cheeks go bright pink with embarrassment. Cleo and Annie were blond and fair skinned, while Pia had milky skin and dark hair and uptilted green eyes. She was quite the fairy child. Though sometimes demon seemed more appropriate.

"Cleo is uninterested in anyone who hasn't been dead at least a thousand years," Annie hastened to explain. She turned to face her oldest sister, who sat behind huge piles of papers at the desk. "Cleo, I don't think that you're a dull old spinster or anything, but, well, you are, and . . ." Annie Fraser waved her hands dramatically, encompassing the library and all the boxes of books and artifacts yet to be unpacked. "I care nothing for all this. Scholarship isn't for a proper woman. I want—"

"A husband and children and a nice house with a rose garden," Cleo defined her middle sister's longings. Wanting anything was dangerous, as she well knew, but she had been sixteen once herself. Fortunately, Annie's wants were more modest and mundane than hers had been. Annie would also be seventeen in a few days. Seventeen was not a bad age to begin thinking of home and hearth, and a husband to provide them. "It would be nice if you met someone this summer."

Just as long as you have a long courtship and an even longer engagement, my girl. She wanted her sisters to know and trust the men they fell in love with. She glanced past Annie to Pia, who was still too enamored of dogs, horses, and kittens to care about the male of her own species. Cleo smiled to herself as she looked back at Annie, and she made a mental note not to use words like *species* or bring up Darwinism in company. She was sure Annie could come up with a huge list for her of subjects that ladies shouldn't discuss.

"You do realize, I hope," Cleo said to her nearly-seventeen-year-old sister, "that any eligible young man you are likely to meet here in Muirford will either be teaching at the university or be studying at it."

"No man I marry is going to end up a professor, I assure you," Annie proclaimed. "We've already had way too much of that in the family. Young men are trainable."

Cleo had not found that to be true, though Annie sounded very certain of her ability to manage a man. Perhaps she should have a heart-to-heart talk with her sister about the realities of life. Or perhaps Annie *could* teach her a thing or two about feminine wiles. It really wasn't something Cleo had made a study of. Right now, however, she had no wish to dampen Annie's enthusiasm at the prospect of going out into society.

"You'll have to concentrate your husband hunt away from the history department, then, if you don't want a dusty professor for your mate," she told Annie.

"Mother didn't mind a dusty professor," Pia spoke up. Then she giggled. "But Father doesn't count, I suppose. He's never stayed in one place long enough to get dusty."

"Until now." Annie sighed with relief. "And he *is* the grandson of an earl. Mother married quality as well as brains. I'm so glad he's taken the appointment here in Scotland, where the Fraser name has some cachet. I'm sure to find a beau among the young men who are going to attend Muirford."

"Fortunately for you, Sir Edward intends Muirford University to turn out engineers and other such fine, practical professional men," Cleo said. "I'm sure they'll strike a nice balance between dusty and socially presentable for you."

Sir Edward Muir, newly knighted and rolling in money earned with the sweat of his factory workers' brows, was endowing this new university in the highland village of his birth. He'd bought the estate where the Muir family had toiled for generations as tenant farmers, and put in a railway line to reach the remote town. Beautiful stone-and-brick buildings were going up. A fine teaching staff had been hired. There was even going to be a museum. History scholars from all over the world were arriving for a conference to be held this very week, and there was to be a Highland Ball and many other festivities to celebrate Sir Edward's grand project. Cleo agreed that it was all very exciting, and strove hard to hide her bitterness at being a watcher rather than a participant in these wonderful events.

She had tried, Lord knew she had. Sir Edward had been quite kindly toward her, and very interested in her ideas since they'd first met at the dig he was financing for Father on the island of Amorgis. They'd had many pleasant conversations about the future of the world during afternoon teas with Aunt Saida, but he had not agreed to allow women to attend his new university. Cleo had pointed out that Oxford and Cambridge allowed women to attend classes and had said she hoped that Muirford would do the same. She'd persuaded him to at least glance at Josephine Butler's writings on women's education. She told him about having briefly attended Oxford, which had swayed Sir Edward a bit closer to her point of view. Then Father had reminded Sir Edward that Oxford and Cambridge might allow women to sit in on some classes, but that these great halls of learning certainly would never award "a petticoat" a degree. Sir Edward became convinced that allowing women to study at his fledgling school would ruin any chance of Muirford's gaining prestige and acceptance. It hadn't helped that Aunt Saida had been soothing and agreed with everything the man said. And worst of all, Cleo knew that Sir Edward's fears that the male establishment would not take women students seriously were quite justified.

So Cleo hadn't fought over this injustice. What would be the point? She knew how to work with what she was given.

Which did not discourage her from saying to Annie, "You will be the belle of every party and have hundreds of suitors."

"Fall in love and live happily ever after," Pia added.

"Not unless Cleo cooperates, I shan't," Annie declared, returning to the original subject. She waved an admonishing finger at Cleo. "Talk about the weather. Ask about the fishing. Speak of gardening if anyone brings up digging. Let them drone on and on about every dull subject in the world, and smile while they do it. Don't dance. Don't mention that you've worn trousers. Or been shot at."

"Or killed snakes," Pia spoke up. "Or stolen a prince's favorite stallion."

"Borrowed."

14

"I don't want to know," Annie declared.

"Or slept in a pharaoh's tomb."

"It was that or be found by those awful Turkish slave dealers," Cleo replied.

"You're making this up, aren't you?" Annie demanded. "Please tell me you're only teasing me."

"Or broke anyone out of prison," Pia went on.

"How do you know about that?" Cleo asked her youngest sister.

Pia cackled. "Or done anything at all that a lady shouldn't. You'll be the death of Ariadne Fraser if you do!" Pia declared with a hand clapped melodramatically across her brow.

"Don't tease like that in front of company," Annie said. "And *never* call me Ariadne." She gave a visible shudder. She swept a hand up her slender figure, indicating her quietly fashionable blue dress with only a hint of lace at cuffs and collar, and her simple hairstyle. "Plain Annie is a suitable name."

"What about me? Can't I be Olympias anymore?"

"No one calls you that now," Cleo pointed out. "No one ever calls me Cleopatra, either. You have nothing to fear on that point, Annie, my dear."

Annie gave an emphatic nod. "Good." Then

15

she grew quite serious and twisted her hands together as she spoke. "This isn't a problem for me, but Aunt Jenny is . . . About Saida . . ."

Cleo shot out of her seat at Annie's tone, and Annie backed up a step in reaction. Though Cleo was a woman of intellectual depth, but no great physical height, she could still be formidable. "Saida is our aunt," she said, voice dangerously quiet.

"By marriage. Aunt Jenny said . . ."

"Aunt Jenny can go to the devil."

Annie was nothing if not persistent, even though she paled at Cleo's fierceness and bad language. "But Aunt Jenny says it will be seen as almost scandalous to have a foreign woman living in a widower's household."

"Aunt Jenny is small-minded," Pia spoke up. "Saida helped raise us."

"Not me," Annie reminded her. "Father should never have taken you back to Egypt and then to Greece after you fully recovered from that awful sickness, Pia." She turned back to Cleo. "You shouldn't have kept going back, either. We should have stayed together, been proper sisters instead of just having visits and letters. You shouldn't have run away from Oxford."

"I did not run away. I had to go back to show Father that I'd found the key to translating the Alexandrian papyrus in the Bodleian Library."

"You could have sent the translation by post."

"I wanted to go back, Annie. The papyrus was—"

"I am ever so sick of hearing about that stupid papyrus. Is it more important than family?"

"That document is *very* important to our family." Cleo was completely taken aback by Annie's sudden vehemence, and deeply affected by her younger sister's pain. "I couldn't trust what I learned to a letter. Father needed that information."

"I needed you," Annie said. "I missed you all terribly."

Pia came up to Annie and put her arms around her. "We missed you, too. We're together now. You can come back to Greece with us when we return."

"I want us to be a normal family," Annie said. She sniffed and dashed away a tear.

Cleo didn't regret her years away from her native Scotland. In fact, she could barely wait for Father to persuade Sir Edward to outfit a new archaeological expedition. What she did regret was that Aunt Jenny, mother of four boys, had adamantly insisted on keeping "my little Annie" who was "the daughter I never had" with her. Cleo had been grateful initially, but then the years stretched away, Annie stayed put, and Father let her. Father had needed Uncle Andrew's financial help and academic support, so Aunt Jenny got her way. And now her influence was reaching into their reunited household at Muirford. What a pity Aunt Jenny had chosen to take her summer holiday at the new hotel here.

Well, Cleo would deal with her. And she would try to give Annie what the girl so desperately wanted: a vine-covered cottage with a rose garden in the back and a proper, staid, stay-at-home family to introduce her beaus to.

Cleo came around the desk and joined Pia and Annie in a three-way sisterly embrace. "You're too pretty to cry," she said, passing a handkerchief from her skirt pocket to Annie. "Can't have you all red-eyed if you're to have tea with Lady Alison today, can we?"

Annie dropped the handkerchief and jumped back a step, her hands going to her damp, pink cheeks. "Oh, dear, I forgot!" She looked around for a clock. "What's the time?"

Cleo reached into a capacious pocket and pulled out an elaborately chased gold watch engraved with the initials ADE. She had long ago developed the habit of running her thumb over the lettering as she opened the watch, knew it was foolish, and did it anyway.

"Not yet two," she told Annie. She snapped the watch closed and put it back in her pocket. "You have plenty of time to make yourself pretty. You're not expected at the Dower House until four."

Annie's cheerfulness returned, along with a wicked, teasing grin. "I'm not worried about getting myself together, Cleo." She put her hands on her hips. "I'm not the one who's the absolute fright."

Oh, dear. Cleo pointed from the packed boxes to the nearly empty shelves. "I do have other plans for this afternoon. Father needs his library set up as soon as—"

"We've been invited to have tea with Lady Alison McKay," Annie said slowly, as though Cleo were deaf or slow-witted. "Lady Alison."

Cleo understood that Lady Alison, widow of the late laird McKay of Muirford, was still the social arbiter of the district despite the fact that her husband's ancestral home had been taken over by a rich industrialist. An invitation from Lady Alison was a tacit reminder to the local gentry that they were related to nobility, and opened up a wider range of society to the daughters of Professor Fraser. Or so Aunt Jenny had claimed. Cleo knew for a fact that all the wives and daughters of faculty members had been invited to this gathering, but she wasn't going to dash Annie's excitement with a dose of reality. It was only a party, after all.

"Aunt Jenny will be here to take you to the Dower House at three."

"Take *us*," Annie said. "Though how I shall get you presentable on such short notice, I do not know."

Cleo's gesture took in empty shelves and numerous packing cases. "Father's library—"

"You're not his slave," Annie declared.

"I am his assistant," Cleo told her sister, though, of course, officially she wasn't. Father was quite insistent about her remaining in the background. Over the years she had discovered that the background, where no one paid attention to what she was doing, was a useful place to be. But Cleo had just made a promise to herself to help her sister achieve the "normal" life she craved. "I suppose I really must go." She sighed. "I'd resigned myself to dealing with gown society, but I'm not at all comfortable with townies. Especially townies with titles in front of their names. How do I deal with Lady Alison?"

"Politely," Annie replied firmly. "Deferentially, but remember who *you* are."

"She's been nice to me," Pia spoke up. "She's letting me keep Saladin in her stables. She says I'm welcome at the Dower House any time. She said your thank-you note was some of the finest penmanship she'd ever seen, Cleo."

Annie said, "You don't have any trouble speaking to Sir Edward, Cleo."

That was true, but then she'd been on her

own territory. And he'd certainly been so help-
ful in the aftermath of the accident. No, she did
not want to think of those awful few days. But
the shouts of the men trapped inside the collapsed tomb filled her head for a moment,
ancient dust clogged her throat, and desperate
fear clutched hard at her heart.

Oh, God! Angel!

"Cleo? Cleo? Are you all right?"

Cleo found that she was looking at her
hands, and was surprised to see they were not
covered in dirt and blood from her frantic
effort to dig her way to the blocked burial
chamber. She forced her thoughts away from
that endless moment when she'd wanted to
die, and made herself smile at her sisters. They
looked appalled. "Am I ashen?" she asked.
They nodded. "Oh, dear."

"All I did was ask you to be nice to Lady Alison," Annie said, a half-hearted joke at best.

"She was thinking of Sir Edward," Pia suggested. "Father says she fancies him."

"Really?" Annie managed to look both skep-
tical and excited. "Cleopatra Fraser interested
in a man? And a wealthy, knighted—"

"*Old* man," Pia interrupted.

Annie ignored Pia and looked Cleo over crit-
ically, clearly suspicious that her spinster sister
might exhibit interest in a male. Cleo didn't
bother to point out that *she* had not mentioned

any such interest; Pia was clearly misinterpreting some comment of Father's.

Annie asked, "Wouldn't it be lovely if Sir Edward fancies you as well?"

"Solve all our worries, that would," Pia added.

"Pia, don't be mercenary," Cleo chided.

"Why not?"

Cleo cast a mischievous look at Annie as she said, "Being openly mercenary is not becoming in a young lady."

"I'll mark that down as something I must remember in my journal," Pia replied.

"See that you do," Annie teased.

"I suppose we'd better change before Aunt Jenny arrives." As Cleo rose from behind the desk she glanced out the window and caught a glimpse of Aunt Saida reading on the bench in the lovely walled rose garden behind the house. Saida's nine-year-old daughter, Thena, was close beside her mother, with a paisley shawl draped over her head and shoulders. Cleo smiled at the sight, and said to Annie, "I'll be upstairs in a few minutes. Don't worry, I won't be late," she added reassuringly, and left the library to go to the garden.

Chapter 2

"**Y**ou still have the pelvis of a camel."

The words floated over the garden wall he was passing, along with a heavy, heady scent of roses and a child's giggle. The statement alone, spoken in Arabic, would have been enough to bring Dr. A. David Evans up short, but the combination of all three halted him in his tracks. Professor Duncan continued along the newly laid brick walk without him, still deep in a one-sided conversation about dating Blackware pottery. Evans lingered by the wall, breathed in rose perfume, and cocked his head to listen.

"You really think so, Saida?"

The voice that spoke was sultry, full of delight. Familiar. Not unexpected. Yet the sound of it still shook him down to his bones.

23

Evans caught his breath and took a step closer.

He was a tall man, and the wall was not that high. Nor did he have many qualms about indulging his curiosity. He'd never been strong on having qualms. And he'd made a career of indulging his curiosity, though his excavations and dealings in the Middle East had been given many other names by friends and rivals. It did not take much effort for him to stretch a bit and get a glimpse into the rose garden.

The roses were mostly red, her dress was gray, and her hair shone brighter than the sun in this northern land. She had a paisley shawl tied around her hips, her hips were swaying, and Saida Wallace was right; Cleopatra Fraser moved her body with the sinuous, swaying, rolling rhythm reminiscent of a ship of the desert. But on a camel it wasn't utterly, intensely seductive. The incongruousness of a golden-haired woman belly dancing in a Scottish garden only added to the allure of the moment. Evans couldn't help but smile, though there was a tightness to his expression. And his body couldn't help but respond. And he couldn't help but remember.

The girl shouldn't have run off crying, and he shouldn't be off looking for her. It had been two hours before he could get away from her father's droning prattle. The man paid no attention to the girl, but Evans hadn't stopped thinking about her pretty face and eyes bright with unshed tears throughout the afternoon. She knew about the crocodile and hippos in the river; she'd be safe enough. But—still—

He wanted to be the one to wipe her tears away, and he knew well enough that it wasn't because he sympathized with her pain. He wanted to be alone with her when he wiped her tears away. He smiled. Oh, yes, he knew where the comforting would lead.

Still, idiot though Fraser was, he'd tried to learn something from spending another day in the man's company. Evans had known Fraser wasn't as brilliant as he'd heard from the moment they'd met, but it was too late to leave—besides, there was much he could learn on his own simply by taking part in the excavation. And the daughter was actually interesting to talk to—too smart for her own good. Her father knew it and didn't like it one little bit. Evans liked his women smart. Smart women were better in bed. He liked it even better if they were good-looking. She rated high on looks as well as intelligence, with her big, bright eyes and lush mouth.

He thought about her lips as he hurried down a path that led to a stand of trees and reeds at the water's edge. For a few moments only the sound of the slow, powerful river filled his ears. Then the wind shifted, and a drumbeat accompanied by the bright tinkling of finger cymbals drifted up from the water's edge, followed by the equally bright music of a woman's laughter. Both sounds caught something primal deep inside him. He turned with fresh eagerness and moved cautiously to peer through a break in the thicket of reeds.

He'd heard about a type of erotic ethnic dancing practiced by the native women . . . but he'd never expected to witness it. Yet there on a flat stretch of shore between the river and a wall of reeds were two women dancing as a boy beat time for them on a hand-held drum. They were barefoot, with bells on their ankles, adding to the exotic music as they moved. Their hair flowed freely down their backs and their faces were bright-eyed and rapt with concentration. Though they were covered from neck to ankles in the flowing layers of traditional striped and embroidered garments, the soft clothing enhanced rather than concealed hips and breasts that swayed and quivered like nothing he'd ever seen before. Their gestures were fluid and beckoning; the finger cymbals clashed out a wholly alien rhythm. The sound and sight filled all his senses. And all his senses centered on the taller of the two dancers, a willow-slender girl, lithe-limbed, her slightest movement redolent with seductive promise.

Her unbound hair shone like the gold of the pharaohs in the brilliant afternoon light. He forgot who he was, forgot why he'd come down to the river. She was the most beautiful, wanton thing he'd ever

26

seen. His hands curled into fists at his sides, and he began to burn from a more insistent heat than the desert sun. All he could do was want.

Then the dancing stopped as Cleo Fraser stomped her foot, turning from goddess into girl. She rounded in frustration to Saida Wallace. "I can never get that shoulder roll right, no matter how much I practice it!"

"You're getting better. It's not as if you've been doing this all your life."

"I'm grateful you agreed to teach me."

"The women in my family dance. If I don't have a daughter, who else can I pass it on to?"

"Maybe you'll have a daughter. Does your back still hurt or has the dancing helped like you said it would? And why did Father call me a fool?" she added as young Walter Raschid Wallace put down the drum and ran off to play. "All I did was suggest that he ask the women who've been doing Egyptian laundry for thousands of years how they thought the ancients pleated the clothing shown in tomb paintings. Seems perfectly sensible to me."

Saida Wallace slipped off the finger cymbals and put her hands on the small of her back. Her pregnancy was barely evident beneath her concealing robes. "The dancing helps," the Arab woman told her Scottish niece. "Men are rarely sensible, Cleo; men like your father are rarer than most."

"Angel says—"

27

"Your Angel is no angel," Saida said harshly. *"I don't trust the way he looks at you."*

He almost laughed. Saida Wallace certainly wouldn't like the way he was looking at her Cleopatra right now—but then, the lascivious way she'd been dancing invited looking at, didn't it?

He'd already been attracted to Fraser's eldest daughter, but seeing her like this . . . he yearned to touch the fire her dancing hinted at. Attraction shifted to consuming need, to determination. He would have her before the season was over.

"I really must go."

Cleo's voice brought Evans back to the present and reminded him that he also had somewhere he was supposed to be. But a gathering at Sir Edward Muir's home held no hint of excitement, none of the edgy pleasure of spying on a beautiful woman who was as out of place in this tame setting as one of the *houris* of Paradise would be in the village church.

"I promised Annie I wouldn't dance," Cleo went on. She and Saida shared a secretive smile. "As if I'd ever dance in public."

"You did once," Saida said.

"Don't remind me."

It reminded Evans, and sent cold anger washing through him. Oh, yes, Cleo Fraser had danced in public once. He turned away to catch up with Professor Duncan.

* * *

28

"Foreigners everywhere," Aunt Jenny said. "If you can imagine. I've never met any, and I'm not sure I want to." She fluttered her hand in agitation, then set her teacup on the table beside her so she could clasp her hands together. "I hardly expected a holiday in the Highlands to be so . . . exotic." The hesitation while she chose her last word was quite telling—and disapproving. "The accommodations at the hotel are charming, the service acceptable, and the view quite lovely, but . . . well . . . so many strange types lurking about. And more arriving every day."

Cleo looked at her aunt in confusion, but held her tongue at a warning look from Annie. She sat quietly in her seat on one of many chairs in a room decorated with a mix of shelves full of china figurines and walls crowded with mounted racks of antlers and stuffed animal heads. It seemed incongruous to her, but the decor was probably a perfectly ordinary style for the dower house of a laird's widow. There was a bookcase in one corner, and her gaze wandered longingly to it occasionally, but for the most part Cleo was able to keep her attention on the group of women gathered on the chairs and sofas before the fireplace.

Their hostess, who was seated in a wing-backed chair, presided over the festivities with easy assurance. Lady Alison was curious and genial, a plump, elderly woman with red hair shot liberally with silver, and dressed in pink rather than widow's weeds. She'd told them that her husband had been dead fifteen years this month and she didn't hold with dragging around in black for a lifetime just because the German *hausfrau* who summered at Balmoral tried to make it fashionable. Lady Alison was a vocal Scottish Separatist, and proud to say so. Cleo liked her, though she could tell Aunt Jenny was scandalized by Lady Alison's remarks. Which was probably partly why Cleo liked Lady Alison. Aunt Jenny was the most provincial creature Cleo had ever encountered. Personally, she thought her aunt's encountering foreign guests at the hotel was good for her.

"Well, it is an *international* history symposium," pointed out Mrs. Jackson, the chancellor's wife. "And Sir Edward has granted scholarships to two young men from each of the countries he has business dealings with. Most generous of him, I think."

"Yes, yes," Aunt Jenny responded. "Sir Edward is certainly doing a fine job in helping to bring civilization to the poor wretches of the world. But—"

"I think what Edward is doing is wonderful," Lady Alison spoke up. "It's the most exciting thing that has ever occurred in these parts."

She breathed a hearty sigh, then looked directly at Cleo. "I've often wondered what it would be like to have adventures."

Oh, dear. With a sinking feeling, Cleo realized that Sir Edward must have mentioned her travels to Lady Alison, and Lady Alison wanted tales of derring-do and hardship in exotic, faraway settings. Aunt Jenny was not going to be pleased. But if regaling an audience with selected tales was the price of Annie's entrée into local society, then she'd tell Lady Alison what she wanted to know and Aunt Jenny's sensibilities could go hang.

Cleo smiled back at her hostess.

"I'm sure you can tell us what life is like in Egypt and Greece, my dear," Lady Alison prodded.

"Hot," Cleo answered. Annie, seated close beside her on the sofa, emitted the smallest of sighs, so Cleo hastened to add, "I've certainly missed the green hills and soft rain of home."

It was a blatant lie. Cleo could hardly wait to return to sun-washed lands, to the villages with their whitewashed walls and blue roofs bathed in heady gold sunlight, to the silver-green of olive groves, the orange-red of poppies blooming along a dusty roadside, the sweet taste of ripe melon, and the flap and creak of windmills of Greece. And Egypt! She missed Egypt a hundred times more than the lovely isles of Greece. There was nowhere in the world like it. Even if she had buried her heart and all her hope there, she held her memories of Egypt dear, the bitter and the sweet.

These highland ladies didn't want the reality, though, with its flies and fevers and hardships and heartbreak. They had enough reality at home.

But the joy . . . She could give them the joy.

"When I was a little girl, my father and uncle became part of a team from Oxford that excavated tombs in the Valley of the Kings in Egypt. Father took my mother and myself with him. Some of my first memories are of the narrow streets of Cairo, the sound of Muslims being called to prayer. Of donkeys and camels laden with all sorts of mysterious wares. And women out in the streets in heavy veils and dark robes—but wearing beautiful bright colors indoors. And the ruins! Huge and imposing, with statues of mysterious gods and ancient kings as tall as buildings. Ancient temples were my playgrounds. We would go to Alexandria on holidays so Father could pursue his search for Alexander's tomb. Alexandria is an ancient Mediterranean port city. The people there are from every part of the world, and the bazaars sound like the Tower of Babel. They smell of exotic spices and Turkish coffee and the sweet aroma of burning hemp."

"Why do they burn ropes?" Mrs. McDyess, the vicar's wife, asked.

Cleo looked into Mrs. McDyess's innocent stare for a moment and decided that it wouldn't be good for her sister's social future to discuss hashish. "It's used as a medicinal drug," she explained.

"Burned rope as medicine?" Mrs. McDyess laughed. "What queer folk."

"Aye," Lady Alison agreed with a sage nod.

Cleo strove to change the subject. "We kept searching for Alexander. Once we traveled through the desert on camels to the oasis of Siwah and were chased by Bedouin brigands out to rob us."

Lady Alison's hands flew to her cheeks. "Brigands! How exciting! Did they catch your caravan?"

"We were chased into some ruins."

"Then what happened?"

She dragged the wounded caravan guard behind the shelter of a broken column, quickly saw that the wound was not mortal, and snatched his rifle from his hands to defend their party. If the raiders got a chance to take up a circular position around the ruins, their caravan would be done for. The brigands could catch them in crossfire, or besiege them and wait for the harsh desert to do the work of finishing off the travelers.

The gunfire all around her was rapid and loud. It

took her a moment to realize that there was more of it than there should be. She ducked behind a statue of jackal-headed Anubis and took a look around. The place they'd run to for shelter held a campsite, and the people already there had joined them in fighting off the raiders. Thank God, they were saved! But they weren't out of trouble yet. She shouldered the rifle and took aim, but she was too far into the shelter of the ruins. Her shots might hit a defender. So she kept low and headed for the perimeter.

At the edge of the camp was a line of columns standing like bleached and broken ribs in the sand. Coming around one column she spotted a man in Western clothing and a wide-brimmed hat, a rifle held at ready in his hands. He turned slowly to face her just as she saw a shadow emerge from behind one of columns.

"Look out!" she called.

"Behind you!" he shouted.

She whirled around and fired. Her attacker dropped. She heard shots behind her and turned back to see that the man who'd warned her had dispatched his adversary as well. He turned back to her. "You!" he shouted.

He was tall, broad shouldered, his eyes dark as night. She moved toward him. As he took a step toward her, the fierce desert wind snatched off his wide-brimmed hat, revealing thick black hair.

"You!" She stood rooted in place. Two years fell

apart like a broken mirror. If someone had shot her in the back she wouldn't have noticed. "You're in America!"

"You're in Scotland."

"I'm here," *both said.*

"Cleo!" *Her father was suddenly between them, hustling her toward the horses.*

"But—" *She gestured behind her.* "Angel . . ."

He gave the man behind them a swift, contemptuous glare. "Forget him, girl! Can't you see what he's become?"

"What happened? Were you robbed?"

"Actually," Cleo answered, airily dismissive despite the shards of glass in her heart, "we were rescued by tomb robbers."

"Lady Alison has her own tale of robbery to tell," Aunt Jenny interrupted. "If someone broke into my home and stole a valuable necklace, I'd consider it quite adventurous enough."

Everyone's attention eagerly turned back to Lady Alison, more interested in local news than travel tales. Lady Alison had already said that she didn't wish to discuss the rumors flying around the countryside, and everyone had grudgingly obeyed her wishes until now, but there'd been an undercurrent of titillated curiosity in the room throughout the gathering. Aunt Jenny's words opened a floodgate for the opportunity they'd been waiting for.

"I'd heard the magistrate had been here," the vicar's wife said. "A robbery in Muirford! How shocking."

"I'm not even sure it was a robbery," Lady Alison said.

"Were you terribly frightened, my dear?" Mrs. Douglas asked.

"I wasn't even home."

"A window broken." The Honorable Davida MacLean shuddered. "And your jewelry stolen."

"One necklace," Lady Alison corrected. "Which I might simply have misplaced."

"But a window was broken," Aunt Jenny said. "Vandals, at the very least."

"Or a clumsy servant who hasn't admitted to the accident," Lady Alison countered.

"With so many strangers about, you can't be too careful," the vicar's wife said. She cast a dark look at Mrs. Jackson. "There are many reasons to be concerned about all the changes in our quiet little Muirford. We won't be safe in our beds with all these students and *sassenachs* about."

Before anyone could comment on this, the butler entered carrying an envelope on a silver tray. Lady Alison accepted the note with a decided air of relief. She seemed even more relieved when she looked back at her watching guests. "Sir Edward has sent carriages. He's invited us to move our entertainment elsewhere."

"Elsewhere?" Mrs. Douglas questioned. "Whatever does that mean?"

"This is a bit irregular, but I did mention this gathering to Edward. He told me that he was having a gathering himself today."

"Father was invited to Sir Edward's this afternoon," Annie spoke up for the first time. "Wasn't he, Cleo?"

"He sent his regrets, Annie. All the staff and all the guest speakers who have arrived are at Sir Edward's this afternoon," Cleo said. "A brandy-and-cigars sort of thing, I was given to believe."

"And we have been asked to join them," Lady Alison said. "Turn two parties into one. Edward has changed the gathering into a buffet dinner. He regrets the informality of the event, but we can hardly scorn his gallantry in sending carriages for us." Lady Alison smiled fondly and rose to her feet. Mrs. Jackson rose as well. One by one, the slightly scandalized ladies joined them, and shawls and bonnets were called for.

Cleo thought Lady Alison was happy to have a diversion from discussing her missing necklace. She was certainly happy to escape being the center of attention herself. In fact, she was rather eager to run to the familiar, dry, bland, emotionally safe company of scholarly males.

Chapter 3

⁂

"I didn't shoot the blasted thing," Sir Edward replied to Chancellor Jackson's compliment. "I think it's hundreds of years old. I'm told it's one of the largest racks of antlers ever seen in the Highlands. It came with the house." He smiled, looking almost fondly at the stuffed stag head over the mantel. "Some ancestors of mine probably had to gut and clean the poor beast, and got no reward for their trouble. Except for the reward of serving the laird, of course."

"You're the laird now, Sir Edward," Dean Smith spoke up.

"A laird protects the land and the people." Sir Edward rubbed his jaw thoughtfully. "I do want the best for Muirford. Aye. The rail line, the university, the museum, the hotel and all that. I'm proud to have brought them all here.

Despite my beginnings, I suppose I can reckon myself the laird now that the last of the McKays has gone to his reward."

Sir Edward Muir was not a man who tried to hide where he came from behind the protection of his huge wealth and new title. He was quite proud of his past, and Evans liked the man for it. He could tell that Sir Edward's bluff honesty set most of the other guests' teeth on edge, but then, most of those guests were British. Dr. A. David Evans was an American from iron-hard Maine. Where he came from, it was no shame to earn your fortune rather than inherit it. Evans smiled at the thought, but with irony rather than the old accustomed venom. Once, and not so long ago, he'd believed as firmly as any British lord that he deserved to have the world given to him on a gold platter, that everything he wanted was his by right of his simply—being. Sometimes he still did.

Pity he'd had to lose everything before he started learning a few lessons in humility. He didn't wear humility well.

Evans moved around the gathering in search of diversion. The great hall of the manor house had a beamed ceiling from which huge wheel-shaped chandeliers were suspended, a dark parquet floor polished to a reflective shine, and tall windows with stained-glass depictions of hunting scenes. Wall tapestries and stuffed trophy heads carried on the hunting theme. There was a suit of armor or two tucked into shadowy corners, and a feast was laid on tables along the walls. The long room was peppered with knots of academic gentlemen wearing dark suits and grave faces, each group engaged in intense conversation. Chancellor Jackson, Dean Smith, Professor Robinson, the retired admiral who was heading the mathematics department, and other dignitaries Evans didn't know were gathered around Sir Edward. Evans snagged a glass of wine from a footman and moved toward the nearest knot of scholars.

"Schliemann, of course, is a fraud," were the first words he heard as he approached the group.

"Fraud?" an aghast Professor Carter, who'd arrived from Canada, asked Professor Divac, from Budapest. "How can you call the greatest man in our profession a fraud?"

"Ha!" Divac gestured scornfully. "But he's not in 'our' profession, is he, young man? What university is he associated with? None. He's a grocer and a fraud. His claims that he's found the site of ancient Troy by simply reading the *Iliad* and digging up a mound in Turkey are ridiculous. He'll be found out soon enough!"

"But," Duncan spoke up, "the gold! The treasures!"

"Fakes. Every last one. I stake my reputation on it." Divac gave an emphatic nod, then bent his head forward. The others leaned closer as he confided, "I have it on good authority that a goldsmith created the so-called Gold of Troy from gold Schliemann procured in California." Divac glanced at Evans as though all Americans were in on this conspiracy tale he was spinning. "Then Schliemann buried the gold in the ruins he was excavating and dug it up himself the next day. I will be presenting my proofs at the conference," he concluded. "I will say no more for now. Be sure to attend when I read my paper, gentlemen."

"I wouldn't miss it for the world," Evans said, and received a blistering look from Divac.

Hiding a smile, Evans moved on toward Mitchell and Hill, over by the buffet table. Evans knew full well that Divac and his listeners had never done any fieldwork. There was many a fine historian in this room today, but he was the only one who had any archaeological experience. He was the outsider here, the rebel, a target for the bickering and backbiting and bloodless warfare these brilliant men indulged in with all their hearts and souls. Most never set foot outside classrooms, museums, and libraries. They were masters of dead languages and deep thoughts. He acted while they pondered, and many distrusted him for it. Some outright hated him. But he'd been invited, and he'd come. He'd put himself in the lion's den, and relished it. In fact, he felt right at home.

"Get a plateful while you can," Mitchell advised as Evans came up. "The ladies will be arriving any moment." He pointed toward a nearby window. "Just heard the carriages pull up."

"So Lady Alison decided to hell with propriety and accepted the invitation," Evans said. "Good for her."

"There shall be scandal," Mitchell said, his eyes twinkling behind his spectacles. "Mark my words."

Hill put a hand to his ear. "I hear tittering. We shall be inundated momentarily, I fear." He looked quite pleased by the prospect.

Evans liked these two. Neither of them was a digger, but at least they got out of school occasionally. He'd met Mitchell in Cairo, Hill in Aleppo. Both were first-rate scholars. Mitchell was happily married and a father many times over; Hill claimed to be ready to put himself on the marriage market.

Evans clapped him on the shoulder. "Perhaps the future Mrs. Hill is on her way to the great hall as we speak."

"I can but hope."

Hill turned to face the door, while Evans looked over the laden table. He heard doors open. A butler announced Lady Alison and guests, and there followed the swish of many skirts on the parquet floor. He paid the women's arrival no mind. Tension, anticipation, and a certain amount of peevish annoyance swept through the men in the room. Evans put down his wineglass and reached for a plate. Professor Carter stepped up and put a hand on his arm to get his attention.

So much for the roast beef, Evans thought. "Yes?" he asked Carter.

"You're Evans, yes? *Doctor* A. David Evans?"

"We were introduced not an hour ago," Evans reminded the Canadian.

"I've heard of you." Evans wasn't sure if the gangly young man was being belligerent or not. He didn't think Carter was sure either. "You're an excavator, right? A digger? Like Schliemann? I have a question for you."

"I'm a digger. And my doctorate's in history—from Bowdoin, if that's what you were going to ask next."

"A fine institution," Mitchell said. "For America," he added, the amused twinkle never leaving his eyes.

Carter looked abashed. He cleared his throat. He scratched his chin. "I . . . well . . . I've heard that you . . ."

"Yes?" Evans urged, aware that his tainted reputation was about to be called into question once again. Anger tightened in his gut, but he fought to keep his expression bland.

He must not have been successful, since Carter suddenly changed his question. "I was wondering, Doctor, what does the *A.* in A. David Evans stand for?"

"Azrael," a woman spoke behind him. "His first name is Azrael. Dr. Evans was named for the Angel of Death."

He had expected her. He was prepared for this moment. He had recognized her step. She did not wear perfume, but he could imagine exactly the scent of desert rose and sandalwood that would define her if she did. Yet Evans found it difficult to turn and face Cleo Fraser in such a civilized setting. Their meetings were never meant to be civilized. Nonetheless, he turned; he smiled. At least, he forced his lips into a semblance of a smile—which became real and revealing the instant he saw her.

It was not as if he'd never seen her wear a dress before, it was just that he'd never seen her dressed quite like this. The contours of her breasts and slender waist were emphasized by a form-fitting dark blue bodice. It was odd and somehow exotic to see her in a bustled skirt, with a hint of modest lace at her neck and wrists. This was the first time he'd ever seen her so fashionably attired, with her gold hair neatly pinned up in a swirling confection of a hairdo. The effect emphasized her heart-shaped face and high cheekbones, made her seem aloof and unapproachable. He was used to seeing her in a practical bun bent over a pile of books, or with braids tucked under a floppy hat with sweat and dust on her face, or with her breasts unbound and free beneath a thin cotton caftan, her hair flowing down her back in a shimmering invitation for a man to take it in his hands. The Cleo dancing in a garden with a scarf around her hips he understood, but this proper young lady in her corsets and stylish clothing was almost a stranger, and strangely alluring. Leave it to Cleo to surprise him. The sight of her like this both put him off guard and made him even more wary. Leave it to Cleo to confuse him.

He'd thought himself fully prepared. Then she was there, she spoke—and every bit of sense he'd worked so hard to achieve flew out the window. The irritating creature made him crazy. She made him—

His voice was cool when he replied, "Azrael is an apocryphal archangel, as you well know, Miss Fraser."

"I know full well that you are no angel." Her voice was as cool as his, an ice dagger aimed at his heart, her smile equally dangerous.

Perhaps he imagined the fire in her light brown eyes. Fire of battle. Fire of—

"That's why I wouldn't presume to use the name. It would be flying under false colors."

"Oh, no," she answered. Sarcasm laced her tone, and she arched an elegant eyebrow. She looked almost a stranger in her party clothes, but her tart words were deliciously familiar. "Using Azrael would be a warning. But, then, why would you want to warn anyone who crosses your path about how deadly you can be?"

He shrugged. "In the interest of fair play?"

"Do you understand the concept of fair, *Doctor* Evans?"

"I understand the concept of play." He smiled, and she blushed, and he could have sworn he felt the heat of her skin warming the air around them.

Or perhaps this always happened when they met, but he only noticed now because they were standing on cold, alien ground. He was tempted to stroke her fine, fair skin and let her reaction warm them both. But then, touching her was always the temptation, wasn't it? Especially when she goaded him as she was doing now.

Cleo Fraser was far from the innocent, scholar-spinster she appeared to be, but she thought her hatred made her safe from him. She wore contempt like armor. Unfortunately, he knew the chinks in the armor, the soft spots. And he could give as good as he got.

Calm down, you idiot! Evans warned himself. He meant to take a step back, but his feet moved forward of their own volition. Damn, but Cleopatra made him insane! She was as bad as the queen for whom she was named in her ability to drive a rational man to his destruction. Caesar and Marc Antony could have conquered the world but for desiring a woman named Cleopatra.

Cleo froze as Angel took a step toward her. She fought the urge to put her hands up to push him away, for she'd trained herself never to show any weakness before this man. Yet approaching him at all was the truest sign of the weakness she constantly battled over her *bête noire*, Azrael David Evans.

She'd seen him the instant she entered the room, a flash of movement and color to one side, one man among a group standing beneath a stained-glass window, taller than the others, tan and fit, with wide, wide shoulders shaping his finely tailored black suit. Then sun came out from behind a cloud for an instant, hitting him just so, revealing shining black hair and a fallen angel face. And the sight of him in the last place where he ought to be drove her mad. No, he'd driven her mad years before— proximity to the man simply made the condition worse. Blast it all, why *did* Angel Evans have to look at her like that—with all the arrogance in the world shining out of eyes so dark they might as well be black?

Black as his heart, she reminded herself. "What are you doing here?" she demanded. *Every time I think I've found a measure of peace, why do you always—*

"Perhaps I came to see you."

His words were husky, almost whispered. They stroked her senses like a caress—or a slap. Her mouth tightened in a hard line and tears stung at the back of her throat, but she did not let him see how the lie hurt.

"Dr. Evans came to present a paper on stratigraphy, I'm told," said a round-cheeked young man with an American accent standing beside Angel. "That's a way of measuring the amount of time a historical site has been buried, miss," he explained to her.

She pretended not to notice Angel's smirk, and remembered her promise to Annie. "Thank you," she said to the young scholar. She took a step back and bumped shoulders with one of the other members of the group around Angel Evans.

When she turned to apologize she found a familiar face. "Professor Mitchell."

"How nice to see you again, Miss Fraser," Professor Mitchell said. "May I introduce my colleagues?" He indicated the one who'd spoken. "Professor Vincent Carter from Toronto, who is probably unaware of the American saying about teaching your granny to suck eggs."

"What?" Carter asked.

"And this eager-to-meet-you fellow is Professor Hill, up from Edinburgh," Samuel Mitchell went on. "Dr. Evans you already know. They've worked together in the Middle East," he explained to Carter.

"Worked together?"

"My father and Dr. Evans were once associates," Cleo explained.

Her father had firm ideas about her presenting herself as any sort of historian, linguist, or archaeologist, especially to his colleagues in the field. He was certain that any hint of his having allowed a woman to participate in fieldwork would tarnish his reputation and hold her up to ridicule. She had promises to her father to keep, as well as promises to Annie. In fact the best thing for her to do was keep her mouth shut altogether. She must remember to practice a rapt look and vapid smile while the learned gentlemen talked. Problem was, she'd already made a fool of herself by approaching Angel—David—Evans.

Well, she would mind her manners from this point on.

"Her father and I are now bitter enemies and rivals," Angel explained, and she saw how his bluntness took Carter by surprise. Mitchell and Hill merely nodded. "Professor Fraser will be incensed at my accepting an invitation to present a paper at a conference where he plans to be the premier attraction. He will assume that I am here for no other purpose than to somehow ruin his presentation. It will never occur to him that he is not the center of my world and that I have an agenda of my own to pursue."

Angel's gaze was on her the whole time he spoke. Cleo fairly quivered with fury and the urge to refute what he said about her father, except he was right. The man ought to be ashamed for bringing the acrimony out in the open like this. But, of course, he was an American, and a more odd, outspoken people she had never encountered.

"Some people find Yankee brashness refreshing." Oh, Lord, why couldn't her vow to keep silent translate into actually doing so?

"You did once," Angel reminded her.

She ignored him. She was actually able to ignore him. She looked at Mitchell instead. "How is your wife? Your children?" There. A

51

nice, bland, *womanly* topic that was proper for her to discuss.

"I'm still interested in the subject of your name, Azrael," Hill said. Cleo tried not to sigh when she turned her attention to him.

He was smiling. At her. He had nice eyes; in fact, he was an altogether attractive man. Not in the vivid way of Angel Evans, but handsome in his own way. And his eyes held a twinkling mischief that was rather charming, if incomprehensible. Whatever did he find amusing? Since the polite thing to do was smile back, she did.

"What about my name?" Evans practically growled the words. He didn't know what Hill was getting at, he didn't like the way Hill was looking at Cleo, and he didn't like the way this whole day was going. Perhaps he should simply chuck it all and go see if Apolodoru had arrived on the afternoon train. If not, the man would surely arrive from Greece tonight.

"Well, if you were named for an angel," Hill said, "I was wondering if anyone ever called you that? Angel Evans?" He snickered. "Fallen Angel Evans, perhaps."

Evans didn't like the way Hill was talking to him but looking at Cleo. "Why would you want to know that?"

"Simple curiosity." Hill shrugged. "Considering your adventures, your reputation. I'd think it's something the ladies might decide to call you. Have you ever been known as Angel to a lady?"

Hill was trying to get some sort of reaction out of Cleo, wasn't he? Trying to goad a woman who'd gone from hellcat to kitten back into a temper. But why? Because she was beautiful when she was angry? That's why Evans would have done it. He smiled. And why he was *going* to do it. He was better at this game than Hill, and far more practiced.

"Known as Angel to a lady? No, never to a lady." He tilted his head to one side and rubbed a finger down the length of his jaw, letting a reminiscing smile lift his lips. "But there was a dancing girl once who called me Angel. Sometimes I wonder what happened to her."

Cleo merely looked at Mitchell and gave an imperious nod. "We seem to be blocking the buffet table," she said. "Besides, it's time I paid my respects to our host. Good day." And with that, she turned and walked away. They all watched her go.

Evans didn't believe it. She'd walked away from an argument with him. No anger, no outrage—she *never* missed a chance to argue with him. What was the matter with her? What was she up to?

"What an odd young woman," Carter said.

Evans glared at Carter.

Hill turned a wide smile on the Canadian. "You mean lovely, I think."

"Attractive, yes, but . . ."

Hill held up a hand. "It's quite all right with me if you don't see the beauteous Miss Fraser's charms." He looked around the room. "That narrows the playing field for me."

"What are you talking about?" Evans asked sharply. He had to ball his hands into fists to keep from grabbing the man and shaking him like a terrier.

Hill clasped his hands behind his back. "You suggested before that the future Mrs. Hill might be coming to the party." His gaze went inexorably again to Cleo. "And there she is: the future Mrs. Hill."

Blood pounded furiously in Evans's temples. "Cleopatra . . . Hill?"

Hill's nod was emphatic.

Evans smiled grimly. "Over my dead body."

Chapter 4

❦❦❦

"**E**vans? Evans! Here? What could Sir Edward have been thinking?" Everett Fraser's fist landed resoundingly on the table-top in his workroom at the back of the small museum building, rattling ancient pottery cups and a box of gold and blue faience beads. He tugged on the fringe of graying blond hair that circled his balding head. "To invite that—that—charlatan—that mercenary—to a gathering of serious, sincere, legitimate scholars! What could he have been thinking?"

Cleo faced her father's agitation with a certain grim acceptance. "Yes."

No lady ever called you Angel. No lady? She remembered how surprised he'd been to discover she was a virgin. *Had been* a virgin. What else would she have been? It still pained her to remember.

He undressed quickly, while she managed to unfasten her bodice with shaking fingers. He came to her, bare-chested, dressed only in his drawers, and helped her take off her bodice and skirt. She undid the ribbon holding together the top of her shift, but when he bent his head and brushed his lips across the tops of her breasts, she stood rooted to the earth, unable to do anything but accept the touch of his mouth and hands as they skimmed her body. She held on to him, too shaken by fear and desire to do more. She gasped when he touched her breasts, moaned when he guided her down onto his camp bed. His beautiful body covered hers, his mouth covered hers, hot and demanding, commanding and receiving a frantic response. She had no idea what to do, but need drove her. Her senses swam with heady awareness of her own body, and his. She touched his bare back and the naked skin of his chest. She felt hardness pressing against her belly and her hand groped toward—

"What do you mean 'yes'? What are you talking about? Are you listening to me, Cleo?"

She took a deep breath and made herself focus on her agitated father. "I am as upset by this development as you are, Father." More so. Far more so.

"And well you should be."

She ignored the accusation in his manner. Father had a tendency to be petulant when he was upset. She almost wished she hadn't brought him the news as soon as she'd been able to politely leave Sir Edward's manor house. Perhaps she should have put this off until morning, let her father get a good night's sleep after a hard day's work. She was glad that Father hadn't shown up at the gathering, and knew she would find him all by himself at the small museum in the center of the campus. The workmen were behind schedule, most of the display cabinets had not been delivered, and many of the artifacts to be displayed had yet to arrive from Greece and Egypt. She and Father had transported the treasures from Amorgis themselves. These treasures were Father's life, the reason for his becoming chair of the history department and curator of the Muirford Museum. They were the culmination of years of hard, often dangerous, work. And not just for Everett Fraser.

"I deserve this." His fist struck the table again. "I will not allow that tomb robber—"

"Evans styles himself an antiquities procurer these days," she interrupted. "And freelance archaeologist."

"It's the same thing." He turned a narrow-eyed glare on her. "I won't have you defending the man who dishonored you, girl."

It was at times like these that she regretted

having Confessed All to her father when she and Pia returned from Scotland over a year after her tryst with Angel. She spread her hands out before her in a placating gesture. "I'm not defending him. There is no defense for some of the things he's done."

"Some?"

She hated A. David Evans for many reasons, but her loathing of the man was more selective than her father's all-consuming distaste for everything Evans was and what he stood for. What little he stood for.

"There are reputable antiquities dealers," she reminded her father. "You've used them yourself. Evans has worked for them. His association with them gives him credibility."

"Ha!"

"And he has published several papers in the last few years. His name is in the journals. You know that."

"Papers you've no doubt read with breathless attention to every word."

She'd had plenty of practice in not rising to the bait this evening, and she refrained from doing so now. "I keep up with the literature."

Father ignored her answer. "What is Evans up to? He's up to something. I know it."

Cleo agreed. She would ferret out what the slippery, arrogant, ambitious, and unscrupulous Dr. Evans was up to, and she'd put a stop to it. But all she said was, "He has met Sir Edward. The day the tomb collapsed."

"Don't remind me! That was the worst day of my life!"

"And mine," she said softly.

"Sir Edward could have been killed. Then where would I be?"

Angel could have been killed. Then where would I be? The same place I am now, she reminded herself. *Limbo, with no way out.* But light and fire would have gone out of the world. She hated him, but . . .

"He's come for the Alexandrian treasure," Father declared, and banged the table again. "He's here to steal my treasure."

The Alexandrian treasure he spoke of was treasure indeed. The funerary items included a wreathlike crown of gold oak leaves; several small gold, ivory, and marble statues; a gold chest embossed with the sun symbol of the Macedonian royal family; and a gold wine goblet decorated with a magnificently detailed battle scene. This treasure had not been found in a tomb but buried in a haphazard heap in the ruins of an ancient house on the island of Amorgis, evidence of long-ago grave robbery. They'd explored the ruin almost as an afterthought a few days after the tomb they'd been excavating collapsed. Although they had no documentary proof, Father was staking his reputation that these looted grave goods could have belonged to no other person than Alexander the Great.

He also believed Angel would steal the treasure if he could. Lord knew, the two men had been chasing each other all over the Levant looking for the same thing for years.

A part of her, the very young, naive part of her, wanted to declare that Angel would never do such a vile thing as try to steal the precious artifacts now that Father had won. Cleo firmly pushed her innocent self back into the past where she belonged. A. David Evans—the black-eyed devil with the sinner's smile—was quite comfortable with vile behavior. "The treasure is safely hidden," she reminded her father. "And Sir Edward has made arrangements for it to be guarded once it is on display."

"Evans is trying to steal the treasure from me—and steal away Sir Edward's patronage while he's at it. I struggled along on practically nothing for years until Sir Edward Muir turned up to finance the dig on Amorgis. I *have* to return there next season. I can't do that without Sir Edward's financing."

"I know that, Father." She sighed. "Sir Edward is a nice man. A reasonable man. He won't—"

"You must be nice to him. You know that, don't you, Cleo?" She did not like the look of calculation that came into her father's eyes. "You have to be much nicer to Sir Edward," he told her. "Flatter him more. He likes you. I can tell."

She ignored this sudden change of subject. Angel was the problem, not Sir Edward—not unless Angel did somehow manage to find a way to influence Father's wealthy patron. "Evans will be gone soon enough. The conference is only for a few days," she said, reassuring herself as much as her father. But the thought of the cold winter ahead after the blazing sun of A. David Evans's personality passed through Muirford was not reassuring. It left her feeling bleak and chill, though it was the height of summer. "His reputation precedes him. I'm sure no one will pay him much mind, including Sir Edward."

"You think not?" Her father brightened and gave an emphatic nod. "Evans is a fool if he thinks he can succeed among *true* scholars." He waved dismissively. "He'll embarrass himself. And I'll be delighted to be there to see it."

"Especially when you present your monograph on the Alexandrian artifacts."

He looked puzzled for a moment. "Yes, yes. Monograph. Where is the monograph?"

"On the desk in the library at home," she answered patiently. "You will give it careful study before you present it, won't you?" she asked with careful delicacy for his feelings. "It's not just presenting the artifacts that is important."

"I know that, girl," he snapped. His expression became distant. He looked down, sifting the beads in the small box. They made a dry sound that reminded her of cicadas in a Greek summer night. After a few moments she didn't think he remembered that she was in the same room with him. This was not an unfamiliar experience. But he did remember her, because after a few more seconds passed, he said, "Go home, girl."

Cleo left for the small house on the edge of the Muirford campus. As for going home . . . she hadn't the faintest notion of where that would be.

It was the height of summer yet she had to wear a shawl to fight off the evening chill. Cleo drew it tightly around her as she nodded to the guard who stood in the shadows near the door. She walked from the columned portico down the shallow marble stairs fronting the museum entrance. Once she reached the bottom, she turned around and took a few steps back to observe the building in the silvered brightness of the moonlight. It was a clear night and the moon was still nearly full. The front of the building looked like a Greek temple transported to a harsh northern clime. The marble facade would never know the kiss of the hot Mediterranean sun, nor would the dust of hot sirocco winds ever grate against the smooth, polished stones. She sighed and wondered if she would know sun and sirocco herself ever again. Though she'd been born in Scotland, she felt as false and out of place here as the pseudo-Greek temple they'd designed to hold the relics of the past.

Well, being melancholy never did anybody any good. And she wasn't really feeling melancholy, she was feeling restless, which was worse. When she was restless, she was reckless. Add Angel—A. David Evans—to the mix, and she tended to lose her head. She couldn't afford any wild, outrageous behavior now. Father's position depended on it; her sisters' futures depended on it.

She knew the true name of the hot emotion that curled deep within her, and it wasn't restlessness. She still couldn't let it matter. Yet she couldn't help but remember the wide, sensual slash of his mouth, and the way his lips felt, hard and demanding, on hers. She touched her lips now, and they ached with a memory that was a decade old and yet as fresh as—

"This goes too fast," he said. *"I'm too eager."* He

lifted his head to smile down on her. Then he kissed her again. His lips were so, so sweet, and his tongue so very wicked, teasing and teaching her how a woman and man should kiss.

The first time she'd seen him, standing on a sandy rise of ground with the sun at his back and his black hair long and shining, something inside her fluttered and bloomed, and she murmured, "He looks just like an angel." That was before she even knew his name.

He was a scholar with large, elegant hands that were hardened after a season of sharing the work with the diggers. They touched her gently, urgently, skillfully. There was nothing soft about him, not anywhere. Cleopatra was amazed, fascinated, thrilled by all the differences between man and woman as he took her hands in his and showed her where to touch him in turn, and how. Her breathing grew sharp and ragged; the worries and fears of the last days burned away. The world circled down to the two of them, to the sense of touch. Cleopatra discovered to her awed delight that it was as pleasurable to touch as it was to be touched. And the sense of taste. There was a tang of salt to his skin, a lingering trace of the delta water in which they bathed.

Her hands were no smoother than his since she had dug in the hard dirt and stones as much as he had over the summer, but he made her feel beautiful all over when he kissed her palms and stroked his tongue languorously up her fingers. She melted *against him, barely able to breathe for the rush of desire his touch sent through her.*

And sight. She wanted to see all of him in the warm glow of lamplight, to see shadow and light play over his skin and to trace those patterns with her lips and fingertips. She would be bold, daring . . . wanton. After all, she was no stranger to the male form. She had learned a lot from statues and pottery. She had seen naked gods and men in stone, but never touched the hot flesh of a living man. They had only this one night. Only a few stolen hours. Only—

"Oh, do calm down, Cleopatra," she muttered. The man was *such* an irritant to her peace of mind.

Cleo resolutely turned her back on her mood and looked down the length of the university commons. The scents of dew-damp grass and fresh-turned earth were pleasant, as was the breeze, though she was glad of the shawl wrapped around her shoulders. Not all the buildings were finished and many of the trees were newly planted, but darkness covered most of the rough edges of the new campus, and moonlight softened what was left.

However, darkness did not cover the sight of a familiar figure moving toward the museum. "Pia?" she said, and went to meet her youngest sister. They met beside a hole in the ground and the piles of pipes that marked where a fountain would soon be installed. "What are you doing out so late?" Cleo asked her sister. "Have you come to see Father?"

"It's not so late." Pia gestured toward the museum and laughed. "And disturb Father? You're the only one who dares."

Pia and Father were not on the best of terms at the moment. Pia was going through a rebellious phase, which Father hadn't actually noticed. Considering the tantrum his youngest and favorite daughter had thrown over returning to Scotland, Cleo didn't know how he could remain oblivious. "I'm sure Father would be happy to see you," Cleo said, not certain of this at all.

"I'm not here to see him," Pia said. "I felt restless after coming home from Lady Alison's stables, so Aunt Saida said I could bring you a message." She looked around dramatically. "Are we alone?"

Cleo's laugh was as clear and clean as a crystal bell. Evans hadn't heard her laugh like that for a long time—genuine, unguarded, truly amused. He smiled in response to it as she said, "Of course we're alone."

Concealed in the shadows of a huge oak tree on one side of the museum lawn, he'd watched her come down the shallow marble steps. Spotting her distracted him from his examination of the building's security measures. What he'd seen of the building so far had impressed him, but her gold hair silvered by moonlight impressed him more. There was nothing conscious about Cleo's seductiveness. All she'd ever had to do to catch and hold his attention was simply *be*. The hold she had on him after all these years was infuriating, but fury only added zest and zing.

Pia looked around conspiratorially. "Good. Aunt Saida said I should tell you that Walter Raschid told her he'd seen *someone* at the hotel today. *Someone* Father hates. Who shouldn't be here. She said you'd know *who*."

"Angel Evans," Cleo said. "I've just come from Sir Edward's house. Evans was there. Good thing Father wasn't; there are suits of armor with real swords and axes in the great hall."

Pia giggled. "You saw him? Did you say hello from me? Did you yell at him?"

"Perhaps a little. We're never very nice to each other, he and I," she confessed.

"You should be. I like him. Especially after he saved us from Sheik Haroun."

"He didn't save us; we'd already escaped when he arrived."

"But he brought the horses, and it was easier to escape on horses. He let me keep Saladin."

"Yes, but he stole the Alexandrian papyrus from us, didn't he?"

"You got it back."

The deal had been for Haroun's men to steal into the Frasers' camp and take the Alexandrian papyrus. That's all Evans had agreed on. It wasn't *his* fault Haroun's son decided to take a couple of European females as harem prizes. Evans certainly hadn't wanted Pia, who was all of twelve at the time, in any danger.

"It was Evans's fault we were abducted in the first place. The blasted papyrus has been nothing but trouble for all of us for years."

Evans nodded his agreement. Cleo had won the previous round, but this would be the final round. And it would be his. *Forget the papyrus. This time, Cleopatra, I take the treasure.* It was desperately important. He was not going to fail. He closed his eyes at the sudden stab of pain—in his heart, in his guts, and in that withered thing that used to be his conscience. "Not again," he whispered, so low that not even the passing breeze heard the words. "This time I'll make it right."

"And a good thing Father never found out about the Haroun incident," Cleo said to Pia. "Let's not discuss adventures, shall we?" Cleo looked around. "Aunt Jenny might have spies out."

"What?" Pia asked. She gestured toward the tree. "Owls?"

Evans pressed himself close to the rough bark of the ancient tree trunk. He was confident he was hidden, but with Cleo it was wise to be cautious.

After a pause Pia asked eagerly, "Did you kiss him?"

Even in the moonlight, Evans could tell that Cleo went pale. He saw her spine stiffen, and almost saw fire in her eyes. "Kiss him?" Her outrage singed him. "Why would I kiss him?"

Good question. And why would he want to kiss Cleo Fraser? Because she tasted of honey and fire, and the taste of her lips was as heady as date wine? That was reason enough. And she'd enjoy it. It would also outrage her, which he would enjoy. *And* it would outrage Everett Fraser. There was almost nothing Evans liked better than that.

"Because Father wouldn't like it?" Pia asked Cleo.

That wasn't a good enough reason for *her* to want to kiss *him*. Not good at all, he thought, nearly poisoned by his own bitterness.

"That's not a reason for kissing anyone," Cleo answered her sister. "That isn't love, it's *exploiting vulnerability.*"

She sounded very, very sad, and it twisted

like a hot knife in his gut. *She likes being a spinster*, he reminded himself sternly. *How many times has she told you she wants her books and not a man?*

"But what if you *wanted* to kiss him?"

"You're too young to know about kissing."

"I'm not. I don't *care* about kissing, but I know. Annie can hardly wait for her first kiss."

"She can wait."

Evans didn't know whether to smile or wince at Cleo's grim tone.

"Father doesn't like for her to think about having beaus, you know. He never wants us to grow up. We're supposed to exist to help him find Alexander. That's all he cares about."

You tell her, girl. Evans was half-tempted to cheer Pia on. There were a great many things that needed to be said about Everett Fraser, but Cleo wasn't interested in hearing them. And she certainly wouldn't listen to them from him—not that it was his business to tell her.

"You do all the work," Pia went on. "I know you wrote the paper he's going to present, but you won't get any credit. I hate that."

"I help Father." Cleo looked around nervously. She put a hand on her sister's shoulder. "What has gotten into you this evening?"

"I hate it here! I want to go back to Cairo or to Amorgis. Anywhere but here."

"I know how you feel, darling."

Pia tugged on Cleo's arm. "Then why don't we? Why don't we run away?"

Evans backed away swiftly, not waiting to hear an answer, almost too tempted to join in the conversation. The Frasers—Cleo—had complicated his life too much already. He'd followed them to Scotland to accomplish one thing; he would get what he came for and go back to Cairo. Back to where he belonged. If Cleo was not there—his beautiful, irritating, seductive, challenging *bête noire*—well, let her have a safe, solitary life. It was for the best. For both of them.

But Cairo would be a cold place without her.

And it was foolish of him to stand there eavesdropping. He needed to have security information for Apolodoru when he arrived on the ten o'clock train that evening. It was time for him to check out the back entrance to the museum.

Chapter 5

This day was too full of difficulties, Cleo thought. Difficult promises, difficult social situations, and difficult men. And now Pia. Father had dragged them around the Levant almost all their lives, and that had been just fine with both of them. But the land of their birth was as circumscribed as any harem society in the East, and it was a bitter pill for his two adventurous daughters to swallow. Cleo was old enough to accept the necessity, and hoped her youngest sister would adjust.

"We will return to Amorgis—in a year or so." Cleo patted Pia's shoulder sympathetically. "I'm sure we will." It was the only reassurance she could give.

"If you're nice to Sir Edward."

She didn't like what Pia seemed to imply.

But, then Pia was fourteen and sometimes pretended to a worldliness she hadn't a clue about. "You have Saladin," Cleo said. "And Annie. Aren't you grateful to have the family together again?"

Pia nodded. "I'd rather have us together in Cairo."

"Well, we can't always have what we want." She put her arm around Pia's shoulder. "Let's go home now."

It wasn't a long walk to their house. Cleo made it a brisk one, and stopped at the front gate. She kissed Pia on the forehead. "Go on in," she said. *Be safe and well.*

"Aren't you coming?" Pia asked as Cleo turned back to the gate.

"I forgot something," Cleo answered. "I have to go back to the museum."

"But—"

"Go."

She waited only long enough to see the door shut behind Pia, then turned and briskly followed her instincts back to the center of the campus.

She'd seen very little of the campus, the village, or the countryside since arriving, which wasn't like her at all. Just because she'd been busy with unpacking the house, settling the girls into their new home, and working with Father's papers was no excuse for her not to be out and exploring. Yes, yes, she'd promised not to do anything "adventurous" that would embarrass or discredit the Fraser name, but she was alone on a dark and lovely night. If this was going to be her home, it was time for her to learn the lay of the land. Not to mention protect what was hers.

Besides, it would do her good to work off the agitation that coursed through her, sensitizing her skin, boiling in her blood and bones and brain. Passion wasn't everything. She'd convinced herself of that years ago. But whenever she saw Angel Evans again she had a great deal of trouble remembering just what was important—or thinking at all, for that matter.

There was a newly planted rose garden behind the museum that reminded her of the one thing she'd enjoyed most about the months she'd spent at Oxford—the lovely gardens. She headed toward it now. She'd always delighted in the seductive sight and scent of roses.

She took a seat on a bench in the garden and turned her face toward the dark bulk of the building. A light shone in the room where her father worked. The rest of the windows of the building were dark, as they should be. With her shawl wrapped around her like a veil, Cleo folded her hands in her lap and waited. And remembered back to eight years before.

"If I'd known it was you I'd have shot you

myself!" Those were the words that Angel shouted to her father—or possibly to her—as they rode away from the ruins. She couldn't get those words out of her head as she walked through Cairo's noisy, crowded bazaar. Even the sights and sounds of this place could not distract her from the memories of the poisonous hatred her father held for Angel Evans. Hatred that was apparently returned.

When she'd asked why she hadn't heard that Angel was in Egypt, Father's answer had been, "The man dishonored you. I'm lucky he doesn't brag about it. Or perhaps he does to his thieving friends."

She'd pointed out, without resorting to humiliating tears, that that was no answer. How long had he been back? Was Father sure he dealt in stolen antiquities? And why hadn't Angel contacted her? She didn't ask that last question, because she knew it was a foolish one.

Clearly, one night with her had not been important to him. In fact, she knew he'd been disappointed at her inexperience. What had been heaven for her must have been tedious for him. But she knew full well it was wrong to think of those stolen hours as heavenly. As a matter of fact, it was useless to think of them at all.

So she concentrated on finding out what Father had kept from her for nearly two years.

"Evans and I argued over the interpretation of what was found at the delta site," Father told her. "You know that. We'd been arguing the day Pia's *fever broke. I told him to clear out and he stormed off before you even left the next day. But instead of going back to America, he went to Aleppo to explore the Irbidi ruins with DeClercq. You know how that ended up."*

"Almost everyone was killed."

"Evans survived. It's said he threw his lot in with the bandits that attacked DeClercq's camp. When he turned up in Egypt again, he was working for Osmani."

She was shocked, but Osmani had a reputation for dealing in legitimately acquired antiquities. Mostly. It was said he hardly ever dealt in the fake treasures that were so often peddled to inexperienced collectors.

Then Father added a more damning fact. *"Evans is involved with the Haroun tribe."*

She knew about Sheik Haroun. His whole family had been professional tomb robbers for a hundred generations, possibly longer. They liked to claim they were descendants of the artisans who built the tombs of the pharaohs, so they had a better right to despoil them than Western scientists.

"The man's gone from being a scientist to a treasure hunter. He's only interested in using history to make a quick profit. He's a thief and a wastrel. He lies and cheats, and consorts with the lowest scum in the Middle East. He likely had a hand in the attack on DeClercq's expedition. And I don't want you to have anything to do with him."

The words devastated her. But Angel had also saved them from desert marauders. She had to find out the truth for herself.

Which was why she now followed Angel Evans through the ancient market of Cairo. She'd crossed the river from the small British enclave on Geziria Island on a simple shopping expedition. She'd been on her way to a bookseller's shop near the north entrance of the Khan el-Kalili marketplace when she looked up and spotted broad shoulders and a flash of silky dark hair ahead of her in the crowd. There were quite a few Europeans in Egypt: scholars studying the ruins, merchants, engineers working on the many building projects the Khedive Ismail government hoped would bring the country into the modern world. Many European men came to the Khan el-Kalili, and many of those men were tall and dark haired. She could have been mistaken—except that she would know the long, lean, graceful form of Angel Evans if the two of them were at the bottom of a well during a total eclipse.

He headed north, past the bookseller's stall and into the streets where coppersmiths made and sold their wares. She knew very well that more than copper pots were sold in some of the shops in this part of the city. She suspected where Angel was headed, and Cleo's heart cracked a bit more. She would have liked to turn back, but she had to know if what Father claimed was really true.

She wore robes and veils rather than the corsets

and bustles and skirts that would mark her as an outsider in the streets of Cairo. She felt safer this way, anonymous, free. It would cause a scandal, of course, if anyone ever discovered she moved about the city dressed as a native woman, but it was also a godsend for her to be able to observe Angel without any fear of being recognized. Father had forbidden her to speak of him or to him, and Angel had certainly made no effort to contact her. But he thought I was in Scotland, *a forlorn voice in her head pointed out.* And the post is delivered in Scotland, *she reminded herself.* Besides, she had thought she'd resigned herself to never seeing him again before *she went to his tent.* Afterwards, of course, she had felt completely different—but the damage had been done.

She put that out of her mind. She tried not to think at all, merely to observe. She followed Angel to the shop of Osmani the coppersmith, who was better known for his second occupation as a dealer in dubiously acquired antiquities. She moved to finger shining rows of copper pots and coffee urns while Osmani ignored her to effusively greet and deal with the foreigner who had arrived a few steps ahead of her. The men made no effort to hide their dealings from her.

She watched, forgotten in a corner, her face hidden behind a veil, while Angel took a seat opposite Osmani. A servant brought small cups of strong, fragrant coffee, and the men dickered. Angel slouched with a graceful ease, his wide shoulders and elegant back betraying not a line of tension. His wide mouth curled into a careless, devastating smile as he took small, precious, ancient objects one by one from a leather saddlebag, unwrapped them, and placed them on a table before the black market antiquities dealer. Osmani fingered the objects while the servant brought more coffee and cakes.

Eventually the men agreed on a price. Angel took his money and left, brushing against her as he passed her on the way from the shop.

It was true. Angel Evans had fallen from man of science to common thief. She had never been so hurt in her life.

Something in her died, and anger as hot as the fire of hell took its place.

She'd bought a copper tray she didn't want and left.

Several years later, she would smash the same tray over Angel's head.

What she hadn't known at the time was that he had somehow recognized her and followed her back to the bookseller. It turned out he was looking for the ancient documents written on papyrus she bought almost on a whim from the bookseller that day.

That day was the start of everything that led to this night, this garden, and her waiting to see if Angel Evans would come sneaking around the back side of the museum specifically built to house the treasure he and she had been vying for for nearly a decade.

For a while she had only the scent of roses and the silvery moonlight for company. Then she heard the faint swish of cloth, the lightest tread of footsteps—but the sound came from behind her rather than the direction she watched.

Her heart tightened, but she did not let her breath catch. She smiled. "I'm glad you decided not to take me by surprise," she said to the man who came up behind her. If A. David Evans wanted to move silently, he would have.

Angel took a seat on the bench beside her. "You should have brought a chaperone," he said. "What will people say if we are seen together?"

She pointed toward the lit window. "Father is only a few feet away. I'll scream for him if you like."

"Don't bother. What made you come back?"

"Protecting what's mine, of course."

"Of course."

She firmly kept her gaze on the building before her, kept her hands folded decorously in her lap. She couldn't help but be aware of his size, of the warmth of his body. It was not a large bench. The hard, hot muscles of his thigh brushed against her skirts. She ignored her response to his nearness, and answered, "I thought I saw someone lurking in the shadows when Pia and I started for home. I see I wasn't imagining things."

"You are a perceptive and clever woman, Cleopatra."

She was not fooled by this compliment, even if he spoke with less sarcasm than usual. "Magnificent building, isn't it?" she asked. "I trust you've had a good look at it."

From the corner of her eye she saw him run his hand down the length of his jaw. It was a gesture she'd seen many times, which didn't stop her from still wanting to trace the same path with her own fingers. It was a gesture she'd allowed herself only once, and that would have to do.

"Been out for a stroll," he said in his laconic American drawl. "Stretching my legs, having a look at the whole campus." He chuckled. "Who knows? Maybe I'll be offered a teaching post here. Have to see if I like the look of the place, don't I?"

At another time Cleo might have pointed out hotly that no one in his right mind would offer him a position, but she didn't rise to the bait. "The papyrus won't do you any good now, Evans. Why don't you let it go?"

He stretched his long legs out in front of him. The movement stirred a branch on the nearest rosebush, sending a wisp of heady, sweet aroma into the air around them. Cleo had a great deal of trouble not closing her eyes and breathing in the mingled dark scents of the night and the man beside her.

"I'm not looking for the papyrus anymore," he told her. "It's stopped being important to me." He sounded brisk and confident. "I've accepted an invitation to present a paper at the conference. That's the only reason I'm here."

She laughed softly. "Tell me another one, Dr. Evans."

"I've changed, Cleo. Reordered my priorities. I almost died a few months back," he said. "You might recall the incident."

Her insides clenched with terror even at the memory of it—which was ridiculous. The man was here beside her, huge and healthy and out to make trouble, as always. "I recall some minor accident," she answered.

"You didn't visit me while I recovered."

"I did. I brought you flowers while you were unconscious. I liked you when you were unconscious," she added.

"I make much less trouble that way," he agreed. "By the time the headaches subsided and the bones knit, you'd left Amorgis. I heard you returned to Cairo to put together a museum collection for Muir's university."

"I—Father did."

"It was so pleasant on Amorgis that I stayed on and wrote a few papers."

"So I heard."

"I have decided to revive my academic career. Which is why I am here."

She laughed. "Please. We both know that you have followed my father to Scotland."

"Who said I followed him? That's a lovely building, by the way," he added before she could protest. "I've spent quite some time admiring it this evening."

"I'm sure you have."

"You're sounding particularly smug, Miss Fraser."

"I? When do I ever sound smug? Why?"

"When? Why?" He laughed, and the sound was so caressingly soft and wicked it sent a shiver through her. "Whenever you think you've gotten the better of me, that is why and when. Not that you ever have—at least not for very long," he added.

"And you call me smug. You're the most arrogant, self-deluded creature I have ever met. But I am glad to see you looking healthy again," she added before she could stop the words.

"Thank you," he answered, with more meaning in the two words than either of them were comfortable with. "I suffer from Yankee self-assurance and faith in my own talent," he went on. "I won't hide my light under a bushel—like some people I could name. Pia's right, you know."

Cleo shot to her feet. "You were eavesdropping!"

"Yes." He tugged on her shawl, pulling her back down to the bench. "Hush. There are guards at the doors."

"I know that! Who do you think's responsible for their being there?"

"Me," he said. "You did it for me."

The smile in his voice was infuriating. "The security arrangements are to keep out thieves—like you," she agreed.

Of course, she wasn't officially responsible for the building's security, but she had made suggestions, and Sir Edward had listened. It seemed like she spent her life making suggestions rather than decisions, and she hated it when Angel Evans pointed this out to her. He hadn't this time, she recalled. There was no need for her to be angry with him for a sin he hadn't committed—yet. Being angry at him was habitual; it was necessary. It was—

"If we get into a shouting match we'll be overheard, interrupted, and you'll be the one embarrassed. I know all about your Aunt Jenny," he pointed out. "And, of course, we don't want to do anything to besmirch Daddy's reputation. Let's walk," he suggested. "Neither of us likes being in one place for too long."

Cleo considered for a moment, then reluctantly replied, "There are some things I can't argue with you about."

"I know. It's a shame."

"But not many." She tried not to smile when she said it, but didn't succeed. Well, it was dark, he wouldn't see her humor. She turned and marched stiffly from the fragrant shelter of the little garden to the front of the museum building. He followed, his large shadow running ahead of her in the bright moonlight, back to the cobbled walkway that ran down the green center of the university commons. Well, what would eventually be a long, manicured swath of lawn. Someday soon the fountain at one end would be finished, gardeners would be done with the landscaping, the buildings would all be up, and the grounds would be bustling with students, faculty, and staff—none of them women. None of them her. Still, it would be a proud achievement and a beautiful place.

Evans enjoyed walking behind Cleo; he always did. It didn't matter what she wore or where they were, he'd appreciate the unconsciously seductive sway of her hips and the decisiveness of her stride anywhere. He'd spent a lot of time trying to forget about her, or at least ignore her, but his body wouldn't let him. Ten years had passed, and a lot of poisoned water had flowed under the bridge, but he'd never stopped wanting her.

"I've got a soft spot for you," he said, though he hadn't meant to speak at all. She glanced briefly back at him. "Really. I mean it, Cleopatra."

This time she swung all the way around, hands on her hips, chin defiantly raised. Her look sizzled along his nerve endings. He fought the urge to reach out and put his hands on her shoulders, pull her to him, and kiss the skepticism clean out of her. He held up his hand in a placating gesture rather than let it do what it wanted and touch her.

"Soft spot, indeed," she declared indignantly.

"It's true." He looked her up and down, and a slow grin spread over his face. His body reacted as it usually did. "Well, maybe it's more hard than soft," he admitted.

"Disgusting." She strode off in front of him again. "As usual."

"You like me this way," he called after her.

"Yes," she called back. "It constantly reminds me how despicable you are."

He was, indeed, despicable. There was no denying it.

He glanced back once at the museum. Getting inside was going to be harder than he'd hoped; the windows were set up high and were rather small. There were only two entrances he'd been able to detect, both guarded. Now that Fraser knew he was in Muirford, security would no doubt be stepped up. Of course, breaking in wasn't the only answer, it was just the easiest.

When the path widened a bit, Evans moved up to walk beside Cleo. Being next to her reminded him that she was small and slender; made her seem fragile and in need of protecting. He told himself any fragility was a trick of light and shadows. She was tough as nails, resilient, and capable. Cleo Fraser could stand her ground against tigers, or at least a herd of stampeding camels . . . which had not really been his fault . . . and hold her own. She didn't need anyone, and didn't want anyone, least of all him.

Especially not him.

And if what he was going to do hurt her . . . it would hurt her. He had to retrieve the treasure. That was how it had to be. She'd survive. It was important to him that she survive. How important, he couldn't tell her. Hell, he couldn't tell himself, because he didn't want to know.

"You're being too quiet," she said suddenly.

He almost jumped at the sound of her voice.

"Which leads you to suspect that I'm up to something."

"I'm not in the least suspicious; I'm perfectly sure."

"Are you claiming to be per—" Evans came to an abrupt halt in front of the half-finished brick wall of one of the buildings. He automatically took a protective step closer to Cleo. "What's that?"

The moon was so bright that the stark slashes of white paint defacing the wall were almost luminescent. He made out angular lettering and crudely drawn designs.

"Greek," Cleo said after staring at the graffiti for a few moments. "And very bad Greek, at that."

He looked from the vandalized wall to Cleo. If she didn't notice that they were somehow holding hands now, he wasn't going to bring it up. "Looks like we're not the only ones out tonight."

Chapter 6

"Foreigners," Aunt Jenny said decisively, harping on the subject as she had the day before. "That's who it was. Who else would deface property like that?"

"Students," Cleo answered promptly. "A professor's widow ought to know how rowdy the beginning of term can be."

"But it isn't the beginning of term yet," Aunt Jenny pointed out. "The students have barely begun to arrive. But the town *is* crowded with all sorts of unsavory types." She put down her teacup and looked around the hotel dining room suspiciously, her gaze pausing at a nearby table.

Cleo deliberately did not follow her aunt's gaze. She knew very well that Aunt Jenny concentrated her attention on where Angel Evans sat with a pair of distinctly foreign companions, one man eagle-beaked, graying, and distinguished. The second man was young, with curling dark hair and large, bright eyes under high arched brows. He was wildly, exotically handsome. Jenny was upset because the trio commanded one of the best tables in the room, overlooking the view of the terrace, the woods, and the deep loch beyond.

Aunt Jenny was unaware that Angel had been with Cleo when Cleo first saw the graffiti. Cleo ran the thumb of her left hand over the back of the right, the memory of his lifting it to his lips and saying "I think this is where we part ways" fresh in her mind and on her skin. It had shaken her down to her shoes. Then he was gone into the night. Blast the man!

"Americans," Jenny sneered. "The worst foreigners of all, if you ask me."

Cleo put her hands in her lap. At least Aunt Jenny had the decency to speak quietly. The room was full of people having breakfast, many of them fitting her aunt's rather broad definition of *foreigner*, but the chances of Jenny's rudeness being overheard were minimal. The clink of silver and china and the murmur of conversation ensured a degree of privacy for everyone in the large room.

She did smile and say, "Don't tell me you're

still angry at the Americans for winning their Revolutionary War?"

Aunt Jenny blinked at her, then said, quite seriously, "I cannot imagine why anyone would not want to be part of the British Empire."

"Nor I," Annie spoke up stoutly from her seat opposite Cleo.

There was a vase of flowers at the center of the table, and Cleo had to look around it to get a good look at her sister. Annie looked fresh and bright and pretty this morning, dressed in a simple white frock. Cleo felt grumpy and underslept, and knew she would blush if she let herself remember the dreams that had haunted what little restless sleep she'd had. It was all Angel's fault, of course. Her gaze went to him without her volition, but she managed to look past him, out the window, to watch mist swirl through the blue-green pines at the edge of the water. The setting really was lovely—and peaceful but for the tension she'd brought with her that centered on the raven-haired man seated nearby. As far as she could tell, he was completely unaware of her presence. She should be glad of that, but, perversely, she was not.

Cleo and her sister had met their aunt at the hotel for breakfast at Aunt Jenny's invitation, and Annie was quite pleased at being able to see and be seen by the younger men staying there. Cleo had noticed Annie exchange a shy look and smile with the Canadian, Carter, who was sharing a table with Professor Hill.

Cleo would like to attend the day's conference proceedings. She believed Carter was on the schedule to read a paper. She thought Annie might like to be in the young historian's audience, too, but most of the day was to be spent in Aunt Jenny's room with a local dressmaker, doing the final fitting of the gowns that had been ordered for the upcoming Highland Ball. Cleo didn't have much interest in her own ball gown, but she knew Annie was going to look lovely in the dress that had been ordered from a pattern book of an exclusive London shop especially for the occasion. She was glad that Father had not balked at the expense. In fact, he'd been insistent that she and Annie look their best, that they make a good impression on Sir Edward.

"Foreign lands have their appeal," Aunt Jenny conceded. She sipped tea, then took a bite of a saffron cake. "They provide the Empire with any number of pleasant commodities. But I think it's best that all people stay where they belong."

Cleo wanted to say that the world was a large and lovely place, but she had seen first-hand that the majority of her countrymen simply brought their culture with them wherever they went. She was the odd one at the table, and she wasn't going to try to argue for a different point of view.

"But I do think the Americans made a terrible mistake in insisting on leaving the Empire," Aunt Jenny stated. "I see no reason we have to deal with them after their being so rude."

"Some Americans can indeed be . . . difficult to deal with," Cleo said to sound agreeable. It really was annoying to be so *aware* of Angel. The dining room was large, but it seemed small and enclosed and intimate compared to the open spaces where she was used to encountering the American treasure hunter. He didn't belong in a civilized setting; he filled it up with his size and vital energy. The tame indoors made him seem larger, somehow concentrated his—

"Oh, bother," she muttered, and picked up a currant scone from the basket in front of her. She concentrated on buttering the roll, then taking a few bites.

"Just what did the vandals write?" Annie asked.

Aunt Jenny shot Cleo a warning look. "Something rude and unfit for your delicate ears, I'm sure. Of course, it was in some incomprehensible foreign tongue—"

"Greek," Cleo broke in. Her gesture took in the tables crowded with historians. "The words were in Greek. Most of the people in this room can read Greek."

"Even I can read Greek," Annie said. "With a name like Ariadne and a Greek historian father, I think I better know at least a bit. What did the graffiti say, Cleo?" She leaned closer and whispered, "Something wicked?"

"Annie!" Aunt Jenny declared. She wagged a finger sternly at Cleo. "Don't say a word, young woman."

"Put the candle back," Cleo answered, ignoring her aunt.

Annie tilted her head to the side and mouthed the words Cleo had spoken. Her brows drew down over her pretty brown eyes. "Are you sure that's what it said?"

"As near as I could make out. *Put the* something *back*, at any rate."

Annie sat back in her chair, losing interest. "How strange." Her gaze wandered to Hill and Carter. She smiled and touched her hair. "Be good, Cleo. They're coming over."

What the devil is the woman doing here? Distracting me, Evans thought resentfully. *As usual. Can't even have a meal and conspire in peace.*

He had serious, dangerous business to discuss this morning with serious, dangerous men. His coffee and eggs were cold, and British toast was always cold, and the weather was cold, and the sense of burning up with fever was only heightened every time he looked her way. She looked as cool as ice herself amid the china, silver, and linens, remote as a marble statue of a goddess—only he couldn't make up his mind whether she was a goddess of desire or remote, virginal Artemis, the man-hating goddess of the hunt. He'd rather think of her as Artemis instead of Aphrodite. He'd touched Cleo last night, had the briefest taste of her soft skin for the first time in years.

Why had he done that? He certainly hadn't meant to—but the moon was bright and she'd been so vibrant and beautiful in the pale, silvery light. For a few minutes it had all seemed like a dream, and he knew what he did with Cleopatra in his dreams. He'd managed to do no more than brush his lips across the back of her hand last night. No harm done.

Except it left him aching for more than a taste. He was a fool, and Cleo was no idol of a dead religion but a living, breathing, sensual—

What the devil did Hill think he was doing? Smiling at her like that when he didn't think she was looking. Who did he think—

"Evans!" Apolodoru's voice was low and sharp. "Are you awake, man?" the Greek demanded, speaking in his own language.

Evans did not show any startlement, but turned a hard look on the older of the two men seated with him. He ignored the expression of intense dislike Spiros, the younger man, turned on him. Spiros wasn't a bad kid, but he was so *sincere* he set Evans's teeth on edge. Evans wondered if he'd ever been as young as Spiros. He certainly had never been even half as idealistic. Dangerously idealistic, he reminded himself.

"Have you found the treasure yet?" Apolodoru asked. "Has the woman told you? You said she was the one to concentrate on."

"I arrived in Muirford yesterday morning." He jerked a thumb at Spiros. "Your boy here arrived before I did."

"My duty is to keep watch on the Frasers," Spiros pointed out. "But they were two days ahead of me. I have not been able to get inside their precious museum."

"You won't," Evans told him.

Apolodoru put a hand on his associate's arm. "This way is best for our purposes. Dr. Evans is necessary."

"Dr. Evans is your fall guy," Evans said. He knew that neither man understood what he meant, but didn't bother to explain. He would only be the fall guy if he got caught, and he had no intention of getting caught. "I don't need any help with distractions and diversions." He looked at Apolodoru, but his words were meant for Spiros. "The vandalism was a stupid move. Why call attention to yourselves after hiding out for twenty-one hundred years?"

"It was not I!" Spiros banged a hand on the table, and got a warning look from Apolodoru for it. "I did nothing!" He spoke with quiet fierceness.

"We will discuss this in private," Apolodoru said to Spiros.

Evans nodded. He had made his point; he didn't need to push it. It was up to Apolodoru to keep his people in line. "I've only had time to have a look at the outside of the museum," he told the others. "No one's allowed inside yet. They're planning a grand opening ceremony on the last evening of the conference."

"That cannot be allowed," Apolodoru stated flatly. "It will not happen."

Evans ran a finger down his freshly shaved jaw. "No one but the Frasers know what the museum will contain. There's a great deal of buzz and rumor about Fraser's artifacts, but it's all conjecture. Fraser has made no announcement about having found anything from the time of Alexander the Great. He's scheduled to read his monograph last, and there's no description of what it's to be about in the conference catalog. Most people assume that the museum will house Egyptian antiquities, with maybe a few pieces from the Hellenistic era. Fraser's playing his hand very close to his vest. Wants to upstage Schliemann, is my guess, especially with people like Divac and DeClercq here to impress. Sir Edward has given Fraser carte blanche in the design of the collection."

Apolodoru nodded, and his full lips actually curved in a slight smile. It was a grave, serious smile, but it made Evans feel as if he'd earned this faint expression of approval. "I think you have learned quite a lot for having been in Muirford for only a day."

"I'll keep up the good work," Evans answered as his gaze drifted back toward Cleo. "I'll get the Alexandrian treasure for you."

"You had better," Apolodoru said, then leaned close to whisper in Evans's ear. "Or your woman's life is forfeit."

"She's not *my* woman," Evans answered, in no way showing that Apolodoru's threat chilled him to the bone. Nor did he show that he was annoyed with Cleo for getting him into this. "But she's certainly not Hill's woman," he added under his breath. He rose in a swift, fluid movement, threw his heavy linen napkin on the table, and strode across the room to intercept Hill and Carter on their way to

Cleo's table. Spiros and Apolodoru followed after him.

Cleo had no idea where the crowd had come from, but all of a sudden there were men all around the table. In other circumstances she would be reaching for a weapon in case of impending attack, but such a response might be a slight overreaction in the dining room of a Scottish resort hotel. Aunt Jenny certainly would have something stern to say if Cleo was responsible for getting bloodstains on the tablecloth. She smiled at the thought. Still, she noticed that a heavy silver butter knife was clutched in her right hand, and made no attempt to put it down. Especially since Angel Evans was among the men surrounding the table.

Counting heads, Cleo saw that the crowd wasn't all that large: five gentlemen. Well . . . four gentlemen and Angel. Cleo rose slowly and said, "Professor Hill, Professor Carter. Dr. Evans." She supposed she was usurping Aunt Jenny's place when she spoke first, but Cleo was used to performing the duties of the head of a household.

"Good morning, Miss Fraser," Hill answered.

"How do you do?" Aunt Jenny pronounced gravely.

"Very well, ma'am." Hill smiled broadly at Cleo. "Carter and I," he said, gesturing toward the young man at his side, "were wondering if you, and your aunt and sister, would like an escort to the lecture hall this morning."

"There is seating available in the upper gallery," Professor Carter spoke up. "You ladies might find the opening ceremonies interesting."

"We are not attending *any* academic ceremonies," Aunt Jenny told the men. "Therefore, we do not require an escort." Her tone was frosty, her disapproval at the young men's approach evident. People at other tables were watching them, and this was a most inappropriate setting for single women to hold a conversation with single men with whom they had such short acquaintance.

Cleo liked Hill's direct approach. "When does the ceremony begin?" She knew very well when the conference started, since she had helped draw up the schedule, but she'd promised to remain discreetly in the background.

"At ten o'clock, Miss Fraser," Carter replied. His gaze was on Annie; his eyes were filled with puppylike longing. Cleo noted that Annie was gazing back—past Carter, to where Angel and his friends stood.

She consulted her pocket watch. "We have plenty of time before the dressmaker arrives. I, for one, would like to see the opening of the conference."

Good Lord, she still has my watch! Evans saw it clearly from the back of the group, since he was half a head taller than all the others. He wanted to grab her and shake her and demand why she'd kept it, why she tortured him with the memory. Then he noticed the way her thumb slid caressingly over the gold case before she tucked the watch back into her skirt pocket, and the urge shifted from wanting to shake her to wanting to kiss her first and ask questions later. God, how he wanted her fingers to touch him the same knowing way they touched cold, lifeless metal. It was torture indeed to say nothing, do nothing.

The worst of it was that he didn't think she noticed what she did, or even that he was there. He'd worked so hard that season to seduce her, and that lone night with her had not been enough to dissipate the desire that months of longing had built in him. Sometimes he'd had dreams of going back and starting over, showing her how much better lovemaking could be. He lived with unrequited passion every minute of every day of his life. She'd locked what had happened between them in some tomb in her mind and locked her emotions in there with the memories. He'd ruined her in more than one way.

But she'd kept the watch.

Not that he'd given it to her as a gift or memento—or payment—for a night of love-making. No, he'd tossed it to her almost casually four years later, in the prison courtyard in the rebel fortress of that old scoundrel Sheik Khamir.

"Does your father know you led the assault on the fort?" The sun beat down hot and bright. He turned his face up to the fierce blue sky, then lowered his gaze slowly, taking in the sight of Cleo, her beautiful breasts and hips outlined and emphasized by the cut of the men's clothing she wore. Cleo's gold hair was covered by a wide-brimmed hat, and her favorite rifle was in her hands. Grime smudged her cheeks and disapproval filled her eyes. He didn't dare tell her how beautiful she was. Or thank her. Because she wouldn't believe either.

She hadn't believed anything he had said or done since that day in Cairo a couple of years ago, the day he'd found her spying on him and had done a little spying of his own. They'd both discovered a clue to finding Alexander's tomb that day. And the chase had been on.

"Does your father know you were about to be beheaded?"

"My father and I don't speak."

"With good reason. You should have returned to America when he wanted you to."

"Fathers' wishes aren't always that important. You should learn that."

"I help my father. He's been in London, presenting a paper," she added. "Actually, he should be arriving on the Al Fayyum mail packet today."

Of course, Everett Fraser didn't know about this excursion. Everett Fraser was either the stupidest man in the world, or he turned a conveniently blind eye to whatever Cleo had to do to keep him working on his scheme to find the tomb of Alexander. Fraser didn't love his children; he loved Alexander the Great.

"And what are you doing here?" He gestured around the courtyard. It was not a quiet place. It was full of gunsmoke, dead rebels, a swarm of victors, and released prisoners. The looting was already well under way.

"Sheik Khamir's followers raided one caravan too many. The local villagers, tribesmen, and regular brigands had enough. They formed a coalition and asked if the English and their guards digging at the tomb outside the Sakara oasis would help them get rid of Khamir since they certainly couldn't trust the Khedive government to help them. Since some of our diggers coming from Cairo were hurt when the last caravan was attacked, I decided to help the locals get rid of Khamir. I heard Khamir was holding a Yankee ferengi, and assumed it was you," she added casually.

105

He grinned with delight. "Did you come to save me, Cleo?"

"Don't be ridiculous. How did you end up in Khamir's prison?"

"He offered to sell Osmani some Eighteenth Dynasty artifacts. I came to authenticate them." Her lips thinned with disapproval as he spoke; her nostrils flared. She really was beautiful when she was angry. He shrugged. "When Kamir wanted guns in exchange for the treasure I balked. He decided to lock me up while I thought about it." After three days of working on the lock Evans had broken out of his cell about the same time the attack began. He'd managed to make the assault short and successful by opening the gates of the fortress for the attackers. He'd left the small box of tiny, ancient gold statues he'd appropriated concealed near the fortress entrance, and he needed to get back to it before a looter got there first.

"Now I suppose you'll take the artifacts and go back to that thief Osmani."

"That's what he pays me for," Evans agreed.

"Scum." The word was so vehement she might as well have spat on him. Her assumptions didn't make him anxious to explain why he had to work with Osmani from time to time.

"I do real research as well," he said, defending himself despite his annoyance at her and the fact that they were standing in the midst of chaos. Several frightened, riderless horses were wheeling *about the courtyard. Evans eyed a fine white geld-ing as a possible future mount. Occasional rifle fire sounded in the distance. Cleo said nothing, only looked more disapproving. Frustration destroyed his pleasure at seeing her. "You better get home before Daddy shows up. Wouldn't want him to discover you have a life of your own."*

"Home? Father?" She touched her forehead, then looked distractedly around the riotous scene. "Yes. I'm supposed to meet his riverboat in Al Fayyum at three. Do you know what the time is?"

Evans laughed, then dug into a deep secret pocket of his vest, one Khamir's men hadn't discovered when they searched him. He brought out his gold pocket watch, the one his father had given him when he graduated. He tossed the watch to her. "Keep it," he said, rather than thanking her for the rescue. He turned and ran, and bounded upon the back of the white horse he'd chosen. She called after him as he rode from the courtyard, but shouting and distant gunfire covered her words.

And she still had the watch. Amazing.

Chapter 7

❦

Evans was staring at her. Cleo struggled not to let her awareness of him show, but she found his nearness even more disconcerting than usual. *You're too big,* she thought. *Too blasted* alive *for the room to contain you.* How could she be aware of anyone else when Angel's presence swooped over her like the shadow of a great black Horus hawk? She forced herself to smile at Professor Hill.

But before she could say anything, Evans wedged himself forward and clapped his hand on Hill's shoulder. "Hill, Carter. Good to see you." He exerted pressure to turn Hill away from the table. "Have you met my good friend, Dr. Apolodoru, from the Bureau of Antiquities in Athens?" Hill, Carter, and Apolodoru dutifully shook hands.

"And your other friend?" Annie spoke up suddenly. She moved around the table and held out her hand toward Angel's younger companion. The one with the huge, soulful eyes, elegant cheekbones, and dramatic dark curls.

"Spiros," the young man said, his attention on no one but Annie. He took her offered hand in his. "Spiros Tskretsis."

"Ariadne," said Annie, who hated her mythologically inspired Greek name.

Oh, dear, Cleo thought as she glanced from her dazed-looking sister to the—*oh, dear*—equally dazed-looking young man. She found herself sharing a quick look with Angel. True love, they acknowledged to each other, had just come to Scotland from the sun-kissed shores of Greece. She looked to Aunt Jenny to see how her staunchly British relative was taking this development, only to discover that Aunt Jenny's attention was riveted on Dr. Apolodoru.

He was looking at her, a wry half-smile lighting his distinguished features. He moved around the table to help her rise, and kissed her hand with a devastating courtliness. He murmured a soft question in a deliciously accented deep voice, and there was a look of total concentration in his eyes when he looked into Aunt Jenny's.

"Aunt Jenny?" Cleo asked, and was ignored. She turned her attention back to her sister.

"Are you a student at the university?" Annie asked Spiros hopefully. "Will you be here for years?"

"Yes," he answered her, his huge eyes shining. "I have one of the scholarships doled out by Sir Edward Muir."

"Then we'll be seeing a great deal of each other."

"But not anymore today," Cleo said, putting herself between her younger sister and the incredibly handsome young man.

Young Spiros was almost as handsome as Angel Evans, and Cleo knew all too well how a young girl could get caught up in longing for such splendid male beauty. How it could turn innocence into reckless worship, and exactly where that could lead. She gave Spiros a stern look that said, *Not with my sister, you don't!*

Cleo backed Annie away from the table. "Excuse us, gentlemen, but our dressmaker will be here at any moment."

"But, you said—" Hill began.

"Of course, a dressmaker's appointment is far more important for you ladies than a day of dry speeches," Carter cut in graciously. He consulted his own pocket watch. "For myself, I dread the idea of being late."

"We won't keep you, then," Cleo said, and took her sister *and* her aunt by the arm, and shepherded them out of the dining room.

Evans looked after the departing Cleopatra in shock. *She let Carter live. He's insulted her intellect at least twice now, and she's let him live. Cleo, what's gotten into you?*

Carter looked somewhere between crestfallen at Annie's departure and relieved that the women hadn't taken up the invitation to invade the male precincts of the conference hall. He looked from Hill to Evans. "I suppose we should be going if we're going to find good seats for Divac's lecture."

Evans's glance moved to Apolodoru, and his mouth thinned to a grim, angry, line. He stepped close to the older man and said quietly. "A word with you? Excuse us for a moment." Spiros waited with the others while Evans and Apolodoru crossed from the dining room through the French windows onto the terrace overlooking the expanse of calm gray water.

"Your behavior in there was despicable," Evans informed the older man once they were out of earshot. "What did you think you were doing, approaching one of the Fraser women like that? There's no point in trying to use them when you've got me to do your job for you."

Apolodoru gave an unconcerned shrug. "Is the lady one of the Frasers?"

"An aunt. Fraser's sister. Widowed, I think."

Apolodoru stroked his jaw thoughtfully. "A Fraser *and* a widow? Interesting. Handsome woman . . . for a foreigner. Lord Alexander encouraged his men to take foreign wives to teach tolerance for all people in the empire. I'm a widower myself, you know."

"The Macedonian Empire died with your beloved Alexander."

"But not his dreams. We are his descendants, his protectors." Apolodoru smiled and shrugged. "Spiros is young and hotheaded. If he is attracted to the young woman, what can I do?"

"Discourage him." Evans clenched his fists, and his voice was deathly quiet when he spoke. "You will not harm them."

Apolodoru was unaffected. "I will get to know the Fraser woman."

"What do you plan to do? Worm your way into her confidence to get her to tell you where the treasure is? Fraser's sister wouldn't know. Neither would Annie, so you had better tell Spiros to back off. Annie hasn't been out of Britain since she was a child."

"Save your fury and protectiveness for the one you claim is responsible for the theft. It is she who is in danger. It is not the sister or her aunt that you need to be concerned about," Apolodoru told him. "Not at all."

The words were spoken calmly, even pleasantly, as the commander of the Order of Hoplites gazed out over the calm Scottish loch, but his tone left no doubt just what was in store for Cleopatra Fraser should Evans fail.

Evans bit out a curse, turned on his heel, and walked away. He was only one man, and the Order of Hoplites was an ancient, mysterious secret organization of fanatics. He would do everything he could to protect the woman he— owed—from them. And he would help them because he happened to agree with the order about the artifacts being returned.

And the most damnably annoying part of this was that the whole dangerous situation was Cleo's own fault.

"Damn your beautiful hide!"

"So you can see, gentlemen," Divac's voice droned on from the podium, "that the dilettante Schliemann's findings are ambiguous at best. Furthermore . . ."

It was a huge, high-ceilinged room where the paint was still fresh, on the walls and on the huge portrait of Sir Edward Muir behind the stage where the Romanian scholar held forth with his scathing diatribe. The rows of seats were upholstered in plush green velvet that matched the heavy curtains on the high, narrow windows. Almost all the seats in the auditorium were occupied by serious, attentive men in tweed or dark wool suits, mostly bearded, many with notebooks open in their laps. Evans should have been comfortable in this milieu, but all he really wanted was to be somewhere, anywhere, else. Not that he could escape his thoughts no matter where he was.

It's all my fault. Everything.

Azrael David Evans knew full well that his past was littered with burned bones and ruins, all of them of his own making. Opportunities had been stolen from him, but he'd walked away from a hundred more. He'd walked away from the one thing he should have fought for, and had been making excuses and putting the blame elsewhere for his actions ever since. But it was too late to go back. You could only study the past; you couldn't relive it.

While lying in bed recovering from the accident, he'd thought long and hard about the mistakes, the dead ends, the wasted opportunities. As he grew stronger, he got sick of self-examination and started to nurse dreams. For good or ill, he was nothing if not an opportunist. He'd had some hope of picking a few shards of honor, respectability—something good—from his own ruins when Sir Edward offered him the chance to mingle here with respected historians in a civilized setting. It had been a parting gift to an injured man from someone who'd shared danger with him. He'd grabbed it like a lifeline, fully intending to dazzle the academic world with his work.

And, besides, the conference was where Cleo would be.

He'd even nursed a daydream of her looking up from the audience, eyes shining with admiration for his erudition, of her leading the standing ovation when his speech was done. And—why not?—her throwing herself in his arms in an excess of fervor at his learned brilliance.

Right. Sure.

He'd pulled the learned brilliance scam on her when she was sixteen—*I swear to God, I didn't know!*—so she wasn't likely to fall for it again.

He stirred restlessly in his seat in the center of the crowded lecture hall. The last thing he gave a good goddamn about right now was whether or not the site of the Trojan War was in Turkey, Greece, or the back forty of Hell.

If only Apolodoru and his Hoplites hadn't put in an appearance just as Evans had been ready to leave the sickroom overlooking the blue sea of Amorgis.

If only Everett Fraser wasn't such a selfish,

foolish, preening, touchy, pretentious, pompous fool who thought it was his natural born right to live on his reputation and his daughter's hard work.

If only the Alexandrian papyrus hadn't come to light.

If only he and Cleo hadn't chased each other all over the Middle East fighting over the thing. Sometimes Evans wondered if maybe he wanted to be the one who found the tomb of Alexander because he wanted revenge against Everett Fraser for blackening his reputation. Revenge for the things Fraser said before summarily throwing Evans out of the delta encampment. Or if he pursued finding the tomb because of the thrill he received from the encounters with Cleo. It had gone back and forth for years, snatching clues from each other, especially that bit of papyrus that contained a long list of instructions, some of them in code, for finding the tomb.

If only Cleo hadn't won the last round.

The café in Cairo was small, dark, noisy, and full of smoke, only some of it from tobacco. A young man and a veiled woman played rigg and dumbec in a spot near the door. Their music accompanied the gyrations of a willowy, henna-haired belly dancer as she moved sensuously from table to table, pausing just long enough to excite the men at each stop. As if her daring dancing style wasn't enough, the girl wore a heavy, jingling belt of coins and belled bracelets on her slender wrists and ankles, sewed onto her swirling orange and pink skirts, and braided into her hip-long red hair. The noise was almost as distracting as what she was doing with her hips and jiggling breasts. The crowd loved her. She was slowly heading his way, but Evans didn't plan to stay long enough to witness her show.

He was more interested in the man opposite him than in the entertainment, though his gaze couldn't help but wander toward the dancing girl from time to time. Only a dead man would have been unaffected.

"Why are we meeting here, Haroun?" he asked, deliberately not looking toward the dancer. "Give it to me. I already paid you for the papyrus." Evans held out his hand across the width of the narrow table.

"And you took my favorite horse," the grizzled old sheik replied. "Now you must bid for the papyrus like everyone else."

Evans looked around the crowded room. "And the other bidders are?"

"You and Fraser are not the only ones who seek the secrets of the papyrus."

"We are, and you know it," Evans answered. "Just name your new price, all right?"

Haroun put the familiar leather case that contained the papyrus on the table. He took a sip of thick, sweet coffee and looked around as if he expected a huge crowd of bidders to materialize out of the grimy walls. What he got was the dancing girl stepping in front of him.

What the girl did with her body was enough to make any man sweat.

"She's worth a fortune," Haroun said after a few moments, wiping his upper lip. He held out his hands. The girl backed a step away, then moved closer, but stayed a hairsbreadth out of Haroun's reach.

Evans couldn't help but be affected by the girl's sinuous sexuality. Her teasing movements gave a sharp edge to her dance. All eyes were on her and she knew it. Her laughter rang out from behind the mask of a thin silk veil. Her face might be covered, but her long waist was bare and much of her firm, round breasts was revealed by the low-cut top of her costume. The hunger in the room was palpable, and despite his own growing interest, Evans smelled trouble.

He noticed that the musicians had edged closer to the door. He saw a pair of big men rise from a nearby table and begin to push each other in the effort to get a better look at the dancing girl. Someone shouted from behind him. He was barely able to duck when the bottle came flying toward his head.

As the fight really got going, the dancer disappeared. He did his best not to get involved. He ducked under the table as Haroun jumped up and drew a knife. When Evans came up again, he *grabbed the leather papyrus case and ran for the door.*

Once again, the Alexandrian papyrus was his.

Except it wasn't the right case, and it was empty.

"You could have left a note, sweetheart," he muttered now, and got a stringent look from Carter, who was seated beside him. Divac was still droning on about ancient Greece to a rapt, or possibly asleep, audience.

The dancer had somehow pulled a switch in the confusion. Cleo got the papyrus back and finally finished the translation. By this time Everett Fraser had found a rich patron to back his archaeological work, and an expedition set out for the island named in the ancient text. It took Evans several weeks to find even a hint of where the secret dig was taking place. He followed Fraser and his lovely, far-too-clever daughter, exploring several possible sites in Greece before he tracked his arch-rival to the isolated Aegean island of Amorgis.

Maybe he should have let it go, conceded victory and concentrated on one of the other projects that interested him, but his blood still boiled at the thought of the trick the dancing girl had played on him. His dreams were heated by more than anger at the memory of her swaying hips and rich, ripe breasts. He was haunted, driven. His mouth drew down in a hard line and his body now tightened again at the tantalizing memory. He took a deep breath and tried to pay attention to the lecture as a means of dulling his senses. Unfortunately, Divac stopped talking before Evans could get his mind off that night in the Cairo café.

He rose from his seat with the rest of the audience and clapped dutifully. Divac bowed gravely and left the stage. When Chancellor Jackson stepped to the podium to announce a short recess, with refreshments available in the entry hall, Evans sighed gratefully and filed out of the auditorium with the others. Carter tried to catch his attention to draw him into a conversation, but Evans kept going. He needed a walk. He needed to be alone.

He needed to see Cleo, but knew that was too much to hope for. Cleo was tangled up inside the frilly, feminine world of dressmakers and afternoon teas. It was the safe, sane, predictable life where a woman of her rank and social standing belonged, even if she did look vibrantly alive on horseback with the desert wind blowing through her hair. She was the daughter and granddaughter of respected academics. Even more important to the British class system, she was the great grand-daughter of an earl. The youngest son of the earl had come down from the Highlands to the University of Edinburgh, and shocked his family by marrying a professor's daughter and then staying on to become a professor himself. All his sons followed him into academia.

Evans had never heard Cleo mention the noble birth nonsense, but Everett Fraser had certainly brought it up to him on one painfully memorable occasion. It still stung him deeply to remember being told that Cleo's birth and breeding made her far too good a "catch" for the son of a Maine fisherman. It meant nothing to Fraser that the fisherman in question owned a fleet of ships, as well as factories and farms and interests in many growing companies. Yankee commerce, Yankee ingenuity, and Yankee hard work were less than nothing to a man with watered-down blue blood in his veins.

"Forget about Fraser," he muttered to himself as he stood on the steps of the lecture hall. "Let it go." Let her go? He'd been trying to do that for years, and every time he thought he'd succeeded . . . He shook his head, and as he did his attention was caught by the sight of two people across the commons, just outside the rose garden. He recognized the lean, dangerous figure of Spiros Tskretsis standing over the petite, dark-haired figure of Pia Fraser.

"Oh, no!" he said, his heart jolting with sudden panic at the sight of the Hoplite fanatic with the innocent girl. Evans didn't know what Spiros was doing, but he hurried forward, intending to put a stop to it with his fists if he had to.

Chapter 8

A fter the morning's trials and tribulations
with the dressmaker, Cleo was glad to be
out in the fresh air. Though her errand promised that she was in for an even more unpleasant afternoon, she was glad to be away from
domestic drama and heading for an arena of
conflict where she was at least sure of the rules
of engagement. Father was not going to be
happy, but he had not been happy about anything for so long, so what difference did it
make?

She was simply going to have to convince
him that Sir Edward's latest entertainment idea
would not cause a security breach in the
museum, and then she'd have to make sure
that it didn't.

She smiled, rather enjoying the notion of

outthinking Angel Evans. Of course, the way their luck alternated, Angel was about due to win one. That thought made her frown, and she told herself that there was no such thing as luck. Chance, yes, and quick recognition of opportunity—but luck? Well, if luck existed, it had certainly been her bad luck to meet Angel Evans in the first place.

Ah, but then there would be no spice in her life. *You are British*, she reminded herself, *and back in Britain whether you like it or not. Get used to everything being bland.*

She stepped around an oak tree that blocked the view of the museum from the commons, and the sun came out all of a sudden. There stood Angel Evans, large and vibrant, a conservative dark suit doing nothing to disguise his powerful, broad-shouldered body. Tension radiated from his taut muscles and there was a dangerous look in his dark, dark eyes.

Cleo was so taken by surprise that she halted in her tracks, her heart racing and the breath catching in her throat. Her brain shut down for a second, and a completely visceral reaction took her, washing heat over her with a force that nearly drove her to her knees.

The reaction passed. She'd trained herself for years to face this man, and face him down more often than not. This was the enemy! Never mind that he was more beautiful than

Lucifer and that the sixteen-year-old girl who'd loved him still lurked deep within her heart. The grown woman knew he was not to be trusted. She was armored against the attraction that would never go away. She pulled that worn, battered armor around her now and walked forward to find out what the Yankee fiend was doing in front of *her* museum.

It took her a moment to see that Angel was not alone. He had his hand on the arm of the handsome young Greek from the hotel, and Pia stood on the second of the museum's wide marble steps, putting her at eye level with Spiros.

"Pia," Cleo said, hurrying forward and turning a warm smile on her sister. "What are you doing here? Hello, Mr. Tskretsis."

"Spiros, please," the handsome young man answered.

Pia held up a basket. "Bringing Father his lunch. Aunt Saida didn't want to leave the house," she added significantly.

It had been Saida's habit to bring Father his meals whenever he got caught up in fieldwork and forgot to eat. Cleo was quite aware that Saida had not been out of the house since they'd arrived in Muirford. She might be the widow of Walter Wallace and a staunch Church of Scotland convert, but she was also the Egyptian-born daughter of Muslim scholars. She had adapted to the nomadic way her late husband's family lived in her own country, but wasn't adjusting to being transplanted to the Highlands any better than Pia was. Aunt Saida had put herself in seclusion since they arrived, and Aunt Jenny had made no secret about being relieved at Saida's keeping to the house instead of accepting social invitations.

"I'll talk to Aunt Saida," Cleo promised Pia. "Maybe we can get her to come to the Highland Ball." She touched the tip of her sister's chin. "Don't I take care of everything?"

"You shouldn't have to."

The words did not come from Pia but from Angel Evans, whom she had been conspicuously ignoring. She would deal with *him* once she got the two innocents out of the line of fire.

"Pia and I know each other from Amorgis," Spiros spoke up. "So please don't think that I was being rude and speaking to her without an introduction. I understand how things are done in your country, Miss Fraser."

"You know Pia?" Cleo and Angel asked together.

"His mother owns the inn," Pia said. "His aunt and uncle sell melons at the market." She smiled at the young man, who smiled back. "Spiros took me fishing with him one day. Remember when I brought the octopus home for dinner?" She looked at Angel. "That was the day before the ruin fell on you."

Spiros cut through a moment of awkward silence to ask eagerly, "And how is your sister Annie? And your aunt, of course," he added.

"Aunt Jenny is currently suffering from a fit of vapors."

The young man looked genuinely distressed. "I am so sorry to hear that."

Pia giggled.

"Another crisis," Cleo said, but she grinned at her sister. "Over a ball gown." She shooed Pia away. "Take Father his lunch, and tell him I'll be in to speak with him in a moment. Nice to see you again," she said to Spiros in a tone that clearly dismissed the young man. She softened the order with a genuine smile. "I am looking forward to seeing you at the chancellor's reception this evening. So is Annie."

Spiros exchanged a brief look with Evans, who growled "Go" at him. Then the young man walked away, smiling.

"Well, that was rude," Cleo said to Angel after Spiros was gone. "I thought he was your friend."

"I know him." He glowered at her. "I don't need friends."

Much to her surprise, Cleo found herself asking, "What, precisely, *do* you need?"

He took a step back, as though her words had hit him like a hard blow. His eyes suddenly glittered like black diamonds; his stormy look sent a seismic shock through her. "I want what you want," he told her, in a rough, unrecognizable voice.

It was her turn to take a step back. She shot a protective glance toward the museum door before looking at Angel again. She backed a few paces farther away. His hands were balled into tight fists. "The Alexandrian treasure?" she asked.

"For that night to never have happened."

He turned and walked away.

"I need one more year," her father said, pacing back and forth along the length of the main exhibition hall. "We were very close to finding the tomb. We must return, and soon." He swiped a hand though his fringe of thinning hair. "Finding the tomb of Alexander will be my crowning achievement!"

Cleo couldn't have agreed more, but she ignored her father's obsession for the moment and looked around from her seat on top of a rough wooden box. She tried to concentrate on the latest crisis to take her mind off Angel's callous, casually cruel words.

The floor of the central hall was of shining, black-veined, white marble, and the ceiling sported a mural allegorically depicting the epic grandeur of Scottish history. Sir Edward was quite the champion of all things Scottish. The walls sported gilded bas-reliefs of historical figures and mythological creatures, many of them associated with Scottish culture and folklore. This grand showpiece room was also stacked with packing crates of all shapes and sizes, its marble floor covered with a fair amount of sawdust and mud trailed in by workmen. The place was a mess—and Sir Edward wanted to show it off.

Tomorrow night.

A reception was already planned at the museum for the end of the conference, a week from today. But Sir Edward was a rich man. Rich men were allowed to have whims, and other people had to turn those whims into reality. He'd sent a note to the house announcing that he wanted to host a small reception in the museum building tomorrow night, to show it as "a work in progress, so to speak." Apparently the idea had been suggested to Chancellor Jackson by several conference attendees, and he had passed the notion along to Sir Edward, who passed the command on to Everett Fraser—which meant that Cleo Fraser had a great deal of work to do. And she blamed Angel Evans for every bit of it. "Several" to her translated as the devious American treasure hunter manipulating the natural curiosity of the ivory tower types about Fraser's secret project. It was a ploy to get inside the building and snoop before she was ready for him.

"Well, it won't do you any good," she murmured with her arms crossed tightly under her breasts. "None at all."

You shall not have your own way, she vowed, biting her lip to keep the pain inside. *Never again. Not after—*

Cleo took a long, deep breath and told herself she had more important things to think about than her personal relationship with Angel Evans. It was Angel the grave robber whose plots she had to foil. Normally the thought of matching wits with him was exhilarating, energizing, and gave an edge and purpose to life. Right now all it did was leave a hideous aching emptiness deep in her soul. Her head felt heavy, her wits slow. She stared at the martial scene depicted in the mural across from her and saw nothing. Time stretched out while she woolgathered and Father ranted. She sighed, the sound as wretched as any sound made by any miserable adolescent pining for some impossible dream. The coolheaded, sensible part of her mind found this manifestation of weakness quite ridiculous. *Never show weakness,* that part of her said. *Never show fear.*

"I'm tired," she said. She rubbed her temples. "My head hurts." If Father heard her he paid no mind. He continued pacing, weaving around the boxes and talking about next season's triumphant excavation. To be fair, she never paid much attention to him when he went off on such tangents. He had a right to his dreaming; she was the practical one. Most of the time.

For a few minutes Cleo let herself stare off into space and be overcome by misery, but it was not in her nature to stay self-absorbed for long. Feeling sorry for oneself was a nice indulgence, but hardly productive. She had responsibilities. Never show weakness, indeed—never allow yourself to be weak at *all*.

So, Cleo stood up, took a deep breath, squared her shoulders, and said, "Father!"

If any dogs had been in the room, they would immediately have sat down and paid attention. Her tone brought a similar reaction from Everett Fraser. He stopped in his tracks and turned to look at her, head tilted attentively sideways. "Yes, my dear? What is it?"

On the rare occasion when Everett Fraser focused his attention on anything but his work, he projected an endearing, absentminded charm. Cleo, as exasperated as she frequently was with him, couldn't help but smile as fondness washed over her now. Father was a difficult man to love, but she believed that when you loved someone you accepted them warts and all. *Angel Evans has no warts,* she told herself. *Which is possibly why I don't love him.* It was as good an excuse as any.

"Sir Edward—" She stopped herself from saying what she'd intended—that their patron was about to make their lives difficult. Instead, she rubbed her hands together and said, "Sir Edward has offered us an opportunity to give a preview of the collection tomorrow night."

"Tomorrow? But—"

"Hear me out, please." She made a sweeping gesture and firmly did not look at the chaos all around her. "It will take a bit of doing, but I'm sure I can get help from the workmen and Sir Edward's staff in making the hall presentable. And Walter Raschid and Aunt Saida can help with selecting and arranging the displays."

"But—the treasure! That devil Evans!"

"The treasure will be quite safe." She smiled. "None of the Amorgis artifacts will be on display tomorrow. Most of the conference attendees have never ventured farther afield than a university library and are anxious to see any tangible object from the ancient people they study. And the local people will be quite impressed with seeing items from exotic, foreign places. This is a party, Father, an entertainment, not a scientific meeting."

Fraser rubbed his jaw thoughtfully. "Jewelry," he said. "The ladies will like the necklaces and perfume jars from Princess Mutnefer's tomb. And the statues of Anubis and Thoth are interesting and easily unpacked."

"That is important," Cleo agreed. "And a mummy. We need a mummy in the very middle of the room. The princess is in excellent condition."

"You're sentimental about that mummy even though you know it's probably a fake."

"It's a party, Father. If someone spills punch on it, we won't be losing a valuable relic."

"Good point, my dear. The main thing is to keep Sir Edward happy. Everything depends on that." He stepped up to her and took her hands. Her father's hands were strong and warm, but not so callused as they'd been when she was younger. Father didn't do much of his own digging these days. There was a desperation lurking deep in his eyes when he said, "You are a treasure to me, Cleo." She felt a warm surge of pride until he added, "And you could be a treasure to Sir Edward if you made more of an effort."

She carefully withdrew her hands from her father's and clasped them tightly behind her back. "I will never be a *treasure* to any man, Father. Certainly not to Sir Edward."

"No. You've already given away what

should have been saved to bestow on the proper man."

"Father!"

He gave her no time to protest. "You had your innocence stolen from you, rather." He put his hands on her shoulders. "My poor dear!"

"I am *no one's* poor dear," Cleo snarled. She strode angrily down the length of the room, putting as much distance as possible between them. Then she unclenched her fists and firmly recaptured her equilibrium. "Shall we continue discussing tomorrow evening, Father?"

Everett Fraser had the sense to realize he'd pushed her too hard, and gave an acquiescing nod. "You'll do whatever is best. You know I trust you. But, about Sir Edward . . ."

The man couldn't seem to give up this subject. "You want me to be nicer to him. I know." She couldn't see how she could be any nicer than she already was, and she didn't think Sir Edward liked being flattered. She glanced around her, at the heroes painted on the walls, and thought of his whole purpose in building a university in the rough Highlands of his beloved homeland. "I'll talk more about Scotland with him. He'll like that."

Her father scratched his jaw. "I'm sure he will. Promise me you'll pay him particular attention. Talk him into more financing for my work."

Cleo winced at the thought of such begging. "I will make a bargain with you," she said. He frowned. "I will be effusive about Sir Edward's projects if you will do something about Aunt Saida. She listens to you."

"What's wrong with Saida?"

"She's homesick and unhappy here," she explained. "I think you should introduce her to the local ladies, take her to church. Even better, take her to the Highland Ball."

"Why can't you take her to church and all that?"

"Because Aunt Jenny couldn't say anything if you did it."

"Jenny's a fool. Saida's a wonderful, charming woman."

"Then you'll take her to the ball?" she urged. She was not going to allow a beloved family member to be shunned or to pine away. "Please, Father?"

He smiled. "You sound just like you did when you were twelve. Of course I'll see to Saida's welfare. She's seen to mine for years." He walked toward the plain door set inconspicuously behind a marble pillar. It led to the heart of the building where the real work of the museum was done. "Now I have work to do, girl," he announced, leaving her to the piles of boxes and crates and empty cases. "I'll see you and Annie at the chancellor's reception tonight," he added before disappearing behind the pillar.

She wasn't going to have time to attend any reception. But Annie couldn't go without her, and Father wanted her to "be nice" to his patron. Then she recalled that Angel Evans would also be at the reception.

"Well, at least I won't have to be nice to *him*," she sighed.

Chapter 9

"**W**here is she?"

Evans glared at the back of Hill's head, though his thoughts echoed Hill's words. They were both watching the door. It was all right for *him* to be impatient for Cleo to make an entrance, but for no logical reason at all, he found that it was distinctly *not* all right for Hill to. Who was Hill to talk about her? To think about her? To want to see her? Hill had barely made her acquaintance.

"She's beautiful, isn't she?" Hill asked, turning to him. "Miss Fraser, that is."

Evans peered through the crowd toward a group of young women gathered in the center of the room. Annie Fraser was certainly the prettiest among this group, though to him she seemed a pale, overcivilized version of her vibrant older sister. "Too young for me," he said to Hill. "She giggles."

Hill chuckled. "You know very well which Fraser girl I mean." He nudged Evans in the ribs, or perhaps it was an accident as they stepped closer together to let some ladies walk by. The chancellor's residence was overflowing with visitors and university faculty and local notables bumping elbow to elbow. Evans preferred wide-open spaces; he was used to vistas under hot blue skies. The room was hot all right, but from being too full of people. And it was too noisy, full of bright chatter and intense academic debate.

"I like the fire in Cleo's eyes," Hill went on quietly, leaning closer to Evans.

"She's a hellcat," Evans whispered back.

Hill's faint smile turned into a lascivious grin. "Then there's the graceful way she moves."

"Years of dancing practice," Evans muttered. Hill didn't know the half of it, and he certainly wasn't going to hear it from him.

"And the way she appeared yesterday—like Venus rising out of the foam . . ."

"She was fully dressed, as I recall." Though she had looked enticingly unassailable dressed in bustles and corsets and high collars and heavy skirts and all the other armor of a proper lady. Different.

"Beautiful as Venus, I meant," Hill rushed to explain.

Beautiful? Yes, Cleo was always that. "I didn't notice," he answered, and added loftily, "I appreciate Miss Fraser for her mind."

Hill laughed. "Appreciate a woman for her mind and you'll never get anywhere with her. Compliment her on her hair, and her pretty shoes, but never on her mind."

Evans wanted to take Hill outside and pound him into the ground. "You don't know Miss Fraser."

"I think I know her better than you."

"I seriously doubt that."

"I know how to win her." Hill's superior, amused expression turned quite serious and assessing as he looked over his rival. "Because, my friend, if you've known her for years and haven't won her, then you're a blind fool."

A fool? Him?

"The woman hates me!"

"Is that so? Good." Hill gave a low laugh and shook his head. "She certainly has strong feelings for you. And you hate her, of course. All the better for me." He clapped Evans on the arm. "That's all right, I like women with strong feelings. No milk-and-water misses for me. She and I will deal quite nicely. And her father will approve of *me*."

With that, he turned and made his way

through the crowd. Getting closer to the door, Evans supposed. Hill wanted to be the first to greet Cleo when she finally made her entrance. Where was the redoubtable Miss Fraser, anyway? And why did Hill have to remind him of—

"Marry her? What do you mean, marry her?"

"Just that," he told Fraser. "I'm asking you for your daughter's hand in marriage."

The older man laughed. He stood there in the lantern light in the hot confines of the tent, and laughed in Evans's face. The sound burned through Evans's soul like acid.

"Do you honestly think you're good enough for my daughter? You? An American nobody disowned by his own father?"

"My father—"

"Cleopatra is the great-granddaughter of the Earl of Bothen. Who the devil was your great-grandfather?"

"A soldier in the Revolutionary War," he answered, hating the arrogant superiority of the man. "We won, you know."

"You'll not win with me. Get out. I want you gone tonight. Don't talk to my daughter again; don't try to communicate with her. She's only sixteen, and I won't have you exploiting a girlish attraction for your own purposes."

The world stopped. He had to catch hold of the

tent pole to keep from falling. All he could do was croak one unbelieving word. "Sixteen?"

The girl he'd made love to and wanted to marry was only sixteen?

He'd been so stunned that he'd given in to Fraser's demand to leave without further argument. He'd known it was a wretched, cowardly action by sunrise. But it was too late then, of course. Cleo went back to Scotland with Pia. Years passed. It was too late then. Now it was ten years too late.

"But damn it," he muttered as his gaze found Hill again, "he's got no business sniffing around her."

Cleo paused outside the garden gate of the chancellor's house and consulted her pocket watch. "I hope I'm not too late." She found the rules of proper society more difficult to interpret than Egyptian hieroglyphs—and far less interesting. But she had to do it. "You'd think the aristocratic blood in my veins would make it all come naturally." She sighed. Well, it didn't, and she was tired from hours of hard work at the museum. She hoped she was only fashionably late, rather than unconscionably, rudely late. Well, she'd better go inside and find out.

Except that Angel was in there.

She'd almost not come at all, and could have used her work as an excuse. But she'd promised Annie. And she'd be damned to every circle of hell at once if she'd show any weakness to Dr. A. David Evans. Of course, it was more likely that he wouldn't even notice her absence. That thought scratched at old wounds she didn't want to examine, though she knew she shouldn't care.

"Oh, do stop dithering, Cleopatra."

She looked at the house's tall front windows, aglow with warm gold lamplight, and could faintly hear the buzz of conversation even from the edge of the front walk. Someone was playing a piano inside, badly, and women's voices were joined in a song Cleo didn't know. She suspected that most of the singers didn't, either, but they were making an effort. The place seemed cheerful, inviting.

She put on her most pleasant demeanor and resolutely marched up the walk and clapped the brand-new brass doorknocker. She thanked the maid who let her in and took her shawl, and walked with head high into the chancellor's overcrowded drawing room, where she saw Angel's tall, broad-shouldered form immediately. A swath of raven-black hair fell across his brow, and his dark eyes bored into her, flashing lightning while his frown was thunderous. She felt his wrath, but didn't understand it.

As always, she was tempted to stride forward to confront it. Tempted to be near him. She was such a hopeless fool. *Had been. Never again.*

Steady, girl, steady.

She had work to do here tonight, people to speak to, situations to handle. Angel Evans was *not* on the agenda.

Nor was the man who stepped in front of her and said, "Good evening, Miss Fraser."

She had no idea what Professor Hill had to be so cheerful about, and almost stepped impatiently around him. Then it occurred to her that the man might be genuinely glad to see her, and she managed to wrench her mind away from her tasks and give him a warm smile. "Hello," she said, and held out her hand. "I tend to get distracted. I need to speak to my sister and Lady Alison and Sir Edward—is Sir Edward here?"

"He's coming, I believe." Hill held her hand instead of giving her the brief social handclasp she expected, and led her farther into the crush of people. "You look fetching this evening, Miss Fraser."

She *had* been fetching—and carrying, and unpacking, and arranging. She had aching muscles from it all. And she had to return to the museum when she was done here to continue the work for the next night's party.

"Thank you. There's Lady Alison on the sofa. I must speak to her."

Hill stuck to her side as though attached, as she started across the room. She knew that Angel was still staring, could practically feel his gaze burning into her back. She honestly had no idea what was the matter with the man, but she was not going to be provoked tonight. That was it: he was trying to embarrass her, trying to get her to repeat her performance from yesterday where everyone could witness her having a fit of temper. That would be fine for him. He was leaving at the end of the week, but she had to live here for months, possibly years. Her whole family could easily be ostracized if she made a fool of herself. She couldn't afford social gaffes, and he well knew it.

She hadn't been prepared to see him yesterday. Her armor would not slip again.

"Your dress is lovely," Hill told her.

"Thank you."

His smile widened. In fact, he shot a triumphant glance to someone over his shoulder. Cleo had no idea what he was so pleased about; she was surprised that he'd even noticed what she wore. Her attire consisted of the same midnight-blue skirt she'd worn the day before, with a different, more formal, matching bodice. It was not as if she had an endless wardrobe, after all.

"Doesn't Miss Fraser look lovely?" Hill addressed Lady Alison as they reached the sofa.

As the laird's widow looked her over with a tolerant smile for Professor Hill, Cleo took the opportunity to say, "Fashion is exactly what I need to talk to you about, Lady Alison."

"Indeed," Lady Alison, a vision in lavender satin and cream lace, answered. "I have heard all about The Dress." A group of women was gathered around her, like handmaidens in attendance to a queen. Lady Alison gave a glance around. "We all have."

"Shocking," said Davida MacLean. "Your aunt and sister have every right to be devastated by this terrible news."

Her words and mournful tone were echoed by many others. Aunt Jenny, with her eyes still faintly red from earlier tears, was standing behind the sofa. She sniffed, and her lower lip quivered threateningly. Annie, standing between Professor Carter and Spiros Tskretsis, looked pale and mortified.

The London dressmaker had made a mistake, sending the wrong gown halfway across the country, and there was no hope of retrieving the lost one in time for the ball.

It was not as if someone had died, or tomb robbers had reached a pharaoh's burial chamber before the scientists. But Cleo managed not to point out that the matter was hardly worth all the drama—because, of course, to any proper woman, it was. If it didn't matter so much to Annie and Aunt Jenny, Cleo wouldn't be standing in front of the arbiter of local taste to ask for a boon.

"I hate the notion of my sister not being able to attend the Highland Ball. It would be tragic for a girl to not go to her very first dance. I've been puzzling over the solution all day," she said carefully, and looked around at the attentive group of women before she turned a pleading look on Lady Alison. She hesitated. Everyone leaned forward expectantly.

"Go on, my dear," Lady Alison urged.

What the devil is the woman doing? Evans wondered. Cleo was playing the crowd like a good fisherman played a trout, but he seemed to be the only one who saw that she was up to something. She was always up to something. And Hill was standing too close to her. Evans hated the proprietary way Hill gazed at Cleo, as though she was a precious and rare gold statue of a goddess he'd just discovered. He sneered at the other man, whose complete attention was centered on Cleo Fraser. Along with everyone else in the room. The woman should have been an actress instead of a dancer, he thought sourly.

"Annie and I are much the same size," Cleo said.

Evans glanced between the sisters, both blond, short, and slender. Annie's eyes were brown, while Cleo's were a rich, warm, lively, snapping golden brown. Annie's complexion was a perfect pink-and-cream tint, while Cleo's still bore the bronzed kiss of the Mediterranean sun that even gloves and wide-brimmed hats couldn't prevent.

And, oh, yes, Cleo's breasts were a bit larger than Annie's. Beautiful, high, firm breasts. He remembered their enticing swell in a dancing costume, the perfect fit of them in his large hands, their satin smoothness on his lips and tongue.

He couldn't help but smile at those memories—a feral, possessive smile aimed straight at that smug bastard Hill.

"If you don't think it would be improper or forward of me, Lady Alison," Cleo went on, "the dress sent for Annie could be altered a bit, and I could wear it. While the Highland Ball is also my first formal dance, I am hardly a girl of seventeen." She looked around at the crowd of local biddies again, charming them the way a street magician charmed a cobra.

Evans didn't know why some of the women looked shocked, or why others looked approving or thoughtful. He exchanged puzzled glances with some of the other men. Chancellor Jackson shrugged his massive shoulders, and Mitchell lifted his eyebrows. Evans was relieved that they had no more understanding than he did. It seemed they were witnessing a women's mystery of some sort. The folklorists in the group should be taking notes.

There was a pregnant pause while Lady Alison considered this grave matter—whatever it was. It seemed to Angel that the world held its breath, the faint strains of very bad singing and piano playing in a distant room was the only noise in the universe. Finally, Lady Alison nodded gravely and said, "Very generous of you, my dear. I see no harm in it."

"Thank you," Cleo said in a girlishly grateful tone that set Evans's teeth on edge.

Everyone sighed and began to breathe again. Annie squealed in delight and clapped her hands. She rushed forward to hug Cleo. Aunt Jenny beamed proudly, as though she'd arranged the solution to this thorny problem herself, and much feminine babble started up. The men turned back to their own far more serious conversations. Except for Hill, Evans noted with great annoyance. Hill stood at Cleo's side, looking worshipfully at her, as though he was ready to nominate the woman for sainthood.

Or the position of Mrs. Hill, which he no doubt thought was an infinitely more suitable position for Cleo Fraser to attain. A snarling wave of fury stabbed through Evans at the thought. When the interloper leaned closer to her to speak, Evans moved swiftly forward to put a stop to this impertinence, but the crowd shifted around him, blocking his way for a few moments. There was a flurry of excitement by the door, and greetings were called out as Sir Edward came bustling in.

By the time Evans spotted Cleo again she was across the room, gliding with graceful purpose toward Sir Edward. Hill followed like a pilot fish in the wake of a sleek, magnificent shark, his presence clearly forgotten with the sighting of this more important prey. Evans knew he should be ashamed of the unkind analogy, but his blood was boiling. Even a hint of her with another man drove out anything but the need to grab on to what was his.

He had a brief, brave vision of sweeping her out of the room, throwing her over the saddle of a magnificent Arabian stallion, and riding into the night under the bright full moon. But his gelding was no doubt peacefully asleep in its stable in Cairo, the moon was a little past full, and it was a cloudy night. And what was he to sweep her away from—normalcy?

He was in Scotland to save Cleo Fraser, all

right, but not from safe, bland mediocrity, or even from the attentions of eager suitors. She didn't want him, and she was certainly better off without him. If she wanted to approach Sir Edward Muir wearing that determined expression Evans knew so well, it was none of his affair. Which didn't stop him from drawing closer to find out what it was Cleo wanted with Sir Edward. It wasn't the determination he minded so much as the flattering smile she turned on her father's patron when she reached his side. She never smiled at him like that.

Sir Edward basked in that look. Hill saw it and sighed. Evans understood both the men's reactions very well. Cleo hadn't a clue as to how beautiful she was, no awareness that her smile could stun a man at a thousand paces, that the tilt of her head or her hand on her hip could enflame unquenchable lust. She could dance like Delilah and not know she practiced seduction itself. She could move like the sultriest of temptresses and speak in a low, purring voice that drove a man to his knees when she did nothing more than ask him to have a look at a potsherd. And her smile—God, her smile!

She was made for sex.

Made for sex with me.

Evans caught the thought, and forced down the yearning that never died in him.

"I'm so happy to see you, Sir Edward."

Cleo's voice, bright, brittle, and cheerful, set his teeth on edge. She sounded uncertain and rather false. She did not sound like Cleo. Which piqued his curiosity and helped calm his frayed self-control.

"And I am delighted to see you, Miss Fraser," Sir Edward replied. There was nothing at all false in his enthusiasm.

"Cleo, please," she said, and laughed in a feminine, breathless way Evans had never heard from her before. "Certainly we know each other well enough by now for you to call me that. Or Cleopatra, if you prefer."

"Cleopatra." Sir Edward nodded. "What a lovely name. I imagine you take some pride in being named for the most famous lady of the ancient Egyptian race."

There was a moment of silence, which was even more significant to Evans than Cleo's performance for Lady Alison about the dress. Yet all Cleo did was continue to smile upon her father's patron. This was not the Cleo he knew, and he didn't like it one bit.

Finally, he couldn't take it anymore. "Cleopatra is a Macedonian name. The Cleopatra who ruled Egypt was a Macedonian Greek, a descendant of Alexander's general, Ptolemy. After Alexander conquered Egypt it was ruled by Macedonians for several hundred years after his death." Cleo gave him a familiar annoyed look. He *basked* in it, and went on. "Our Cleo Fraser here was actually named for another Cleopatra, Alexander's sister. Alexander had his father assassinated at that earlier Cleopatra's wedding," he added with a sharp smile.

Cleo rounded on him, as he knew she would. "Alexander did no such thing! Alexander would never have stooped to the assassination of his own father. The murderer acted alone."

"Oh, yes," Sir Edward said before they properly got going. Cleo turned her attention back to Sir Edward, who nodded wisely. "Dr. Fraser has explained all about Alexander the Great to me. How his small mountain kingdom in northern Greece was not unlike Scotland. How he led the Macedonian army across the known world, conquered Persia and Egypt, and marched on—to India, wasn't it? Amazing man. Died young, I believe." He waved a hand. "I built the museum to bring the glory of the past to my homeland, but if it's not Scots history, I'm afraid I can't keep it straight."

"That's all right," Cleo said, fluttering her eyelashes in a most flattering way. "Remembering history is what you have Father for."

All Evans could think of for a moment was

that Cleo never fluttered her eyelashes at *him*. Of course, he might have laughed at her if she did. Or kissed her. He wanted very much at this moment to kiss her. Come to think of it, he *always* wanted to kiss her; he was simply closer to the edge of losing control at the moment. If she were to turn to him right now, chances were good he'd draw her into his arms and kiss her in front of Aunt Jenny, Professor Hill, Sir Edward—everybody. To hell with propriety!

But she didn't turn to him. She concentrated on Sir Edward. No doubt that was her assigned task this evening.

Evans understood the need to court wealthy patrons, and Everett Fraser was a shameless huckster. It was the one thing Fraser was any good at; Evans granted him that. Cleo, however, had never been involved with the fundraising part of the hunt for Alexander's tomb. She'd been too busy doing the actual research that her father built *his* reputation on. He did not need Cleo's field expertise right now, so she'd been relegated to go begging hat in hand in Everett Fraser's place.

Evans had no idea why this should infuriate him, but before he could do anything to put a stop to it, Apolodoru appeared at his side. The older man's hand clamped around Evans's arm like a vise, and he drew Evans away from the group around Sir Edward. "Your young lady's defense of Lord Alexander is eloquent and fervent," the leader of the Hoplite Order murmured quietly. "It would be a shame to lose such passion."

Evans heard the icy threat beneath Apolodoru's words and met the man's gaze. "She is *mine*," he answered with quiet intensity. His to protect, he told the furious, green-eyed monster that was trying to take over his thoughts and actions.

They stopped by the entrance to the music room. The singing had resumed, and covered Apolodoru's whispered, "Her fate is in your hands."

"Cleo would not agree."

"But you and I know the truth." Apolodoru gave a worried look around. He paused long enough to give a gracious nod to Aunt Jenny, who smiled fit to light up the room at this small attention before she went back to dancing attendance on Lady Alison. Then Apolodoru looked back at Evans. "Your time grows shorter, my friend. I am a moderate man, and I can keep Spiros in check. But several less moderate members of our order have arrived in Muirford. They are not so patient. They question my leadership. They will not stand by and allow Fraser to exhibit what Lord Alexander took with him to the grave."

Evans heard Cleo's throaty laughter even

over the sound of music, because he always listened for her voice, no matter how hard he tried not to. The very sound pressed hot against his skin. The air sparkled with her presence. He must be going mad. He could go for months without thinking of her, couldn't he? Weeks, at least. Why was it that while they roamed the exotic lands of the Middle East he could control his attraction to her, but here in plain, prosaic Scotland being near her drove him mad with lust? He had to keep his head clear. He would not look at Cleo, but awareness of her was everywhere around him. He was drunk with it.

"Whoa." Evans gave a low, bitter laugh, and fought his way back to face the delicate, dangerous situation with the Hoplites. The truth was, he'd never been able to keep his head clear around her, not when they spent more than a few minutes together. He was just able to put more distance between them in other places. So he'd better keep away from her in this room. He focused on Apolodoru. "Those grave goods were plundered hundreds of years ago. You told me so yourself."

"Our ancestors dealt harshly with those grave robbers," Apolodoru answered. "Their blood soaked the sacred ground of Lord Alexander's resting place in sacrifice, but we never found the stolen treasure."

"Then the Frasers aren't exactly grave robbers, are they? They found the treasure fair and square."

"In your opinion, Dr. Evans. We see the situation differently. Our duty is to guard the tomb *and* all it once held. We will have the treasure returned, and the Frasers will halt the hunt for that which shall remain hidden."

"Or they die." Evans spoke before Apolodoru finished. "I've heard it before: you won't stand by and allow what your people have spent hundreds of generations protecting to be stolen away to enrich and entertain imperialist foreigners. You're right. I agree with you."

"Then you had better do something about it, Dr. Evans." Apolodoru glanced over Evans's shoulder toward Cleo. "Before it is too late."

Evans gave the man a tight nod. "Time for me to leave the party, then." He heard Cleo laugh again. "I wasn't having much fun anyway."

with the mummy case the centerpiece of the impromptu exhibit. Cleo had returned to the blessed quiet of the museum to begin filling the display cases. She'd found her father napping in the little room behind his workroom and persuaded him to go home to his own bed. She was happy to be alone with the past in this dark and shadowy place illuminated by the pools of light shed by a few scattered lamps.

"People like mummies," Cleo told the cadaver as she finished writing out an information card on heavy, cream-colored stock. Her handwriting was bold and easy to read. Those who stopped to read the information on the card would find that they were gazing on the withered visage of Princess Mutnefer, a royal lady of the Twelfth Dynasty. "Or possibly not," Cleo said to the late princess. "We'll keep your dubious background a secret between us girls. Lord knows, I understand dubious pasts.

"And just between us girls, tonight was one of the most boring evenings of my life. Except where Angel was concerned," she went on, content to be alone late at night in the museum where she could safely confide her feelings—at least air them aloud to herself. She used to go out into the desert sometimes to do that. Or pick a camel to talk to on the evening picket line.

"I stayed as long as I could stand it, I really did. Made the rounds. Danced attendance on Sir Edward. A good man, if a bit stiff. You'd like him. Quite intelligent in his own field—but I'm not interested in business, and even ancient Scottish history is too recent for my taste. I did say something nice about Robert the Bruce." She touched a small gold brooch pinned to the lace at her throat. "I even managed to bite my tongue when that Carter idiot came up and offered to translate the hieroglyphs on this. If Annie hadn't been with him I might not have been so nice. And did you see the way that handsome young Greek and Annie looked at each other all night? I'm going to have to have a talk with her. Or maybe Aunt Saida should—the talk she always says she should have had with me but didn't until it was too late, and then sadly shakes her head and pats my hand and looks guilty, as if she somehow failed me. I mean, really, the woman's husband had been murdered by grave robbers and she was pregnant—as if she had the strength to look after anyone, even herself, at the time."

Cleo finished polishing the thick glass top of the cherrywood case and glanced up over her head. "This is a cool and cloudy land. The dampness isn't good for you, I know," she apologized to the mummy. "But you won't have to worry about the sunlight damaging your wrappings, either. A lady of your years has to be careful of her complexion. Besides, it's only for tomorrow night. We'll have you safely stored away as soon as the party's over." She patted the side of the case. "Believe me, I understand. Being trotted out for parties isn't something I'm comfortable with, either."

Cleo yawned, but she resisted the temptation to check her pocket watch. She *knew* it was late, and she'd only feel even more tired if she found out just how long it had been since having breakfast at the hotel. Come to think of it, she couldn't recall if she'd eaten since then. Lack of food as well as sleep might explain her light-headed chattering over the last few minutes.

"Of course, it's Angel's fault." She nodded decisively. Being near him always rattled her—muddled or sharpened her thought processes, and filled her senses with all sorts of incoherent yearnings. It was easy to blame him for almost every inconvenient or unjust thing that had ever happened to her. She gave a soft, slightly hysterical laugh. "It usually *is* his fault." In fact, there was only one thing she had never blamed him for.

A pity it was the one thing he wished had never happened.

162

"Bastard," she said. She looked down at the mummy once more, and saw her own haggard reflection superimposed over the mummy's head in the glass. She felt almost as old as her ancient companion, and certainly more world-weary. "And we'll keep my using such language a secret between us girls, too, won't we, Princess Mutnefer?"

She should be ashamed of her actions on that long-ago evening, but she wasn't. She never had been. That was what no one would understand—not even Angel Evans.

Cleo gave the thick glass top of the display case one more swipe with a chamois cloth, then moved to a smaller case that rested on a tall wooden stand. Many small objects had already been carefully placed within this case. There was a small beetle-shaped scarab carving in lapis lazuli, an elegant little gold statue of a seated cat, tiny rock crystal makeup and perfume jars, a pair of dangling gold lotus earrings. Cleo was particularly fond of all these small, feminine objects. They put her soul very in touch with the ladies of ancient Egypt. Thousands of years separated them, but she didn't think they were very different from her, those women who'd lived and loved so long ago. She'd read the poetry and the letters they'd written. The women of that time had no qualms, no restraints. They could speak openly and shamelessly, and with words of scorching sensuality, of love and longing.

Given a choice and the chance, Cleo's heart would ever be on the banks of the Nile. And her memories would ever turn back to those precious few weeks when she and her father's gloriously handsome American assistant had talked, and touched, and shared swift, stolen glances as they unearthed these small precious objects side by side.

She knew bloody well what he'd been up to now, from a decade's distance. He'd always been a mercenary and opportunist. When he saw something he wanted he did whatever was necessary to obtain it. She frowned and reminded herself, as she always did when she was tempted to be flattered by the work he'd put into seducing her, that he was a man of strong sensual appetites and she'd been the only available female in the delta camp.

She laughed. "There I go, living in the past again."

"Well, you are in a museum, Cleopatra."

Evans loved her laugh. He might not have spoken if she hadn't laughed, but the sound drew him out of the shadows, and talking to her had always been the most natural thing in the world. "And it isn't *always* my fault," he added as she whirled to face him. She didn't scream, of course, nor did she demand to know what he was doing there.

She said, "How?"

He smiled. Direct as ever, that was his Cleo. And she *was* his, despite anything she, Hill, or anyone else might think. This was something he hadn't realized until he'd been exposed to the ugly sight of someone else courting her. He hadn't adjusted to the revelation yet, or to the possessive jealousy that still raged through him. She put her hands on the enticing curves of her hips, and the movement drew his gaze down the length of her body.

"Well?" Cleopatra demanded.

"Third-floor back window. The front guard was asleep. I used my belt to go up one of the columns to the roof. Making the skylights too small for a man to go through was a very good idea. The back windows, however, aren't as small as you think. And the painters left one conveniently cracked open. To be fair, the door to the room I came in was locked."

"You always carry lockpicks."

He lifted an eyebrow. "Don't you?"

"Certainly not."

"You left them at home this evening?"

"Yes." She folded her hands demurely at her waist. She had lovely, long-fingered hands. She

165

looked the ideal picture of a proper young lady, with perfect posture and a schoolmistress's primness in the stern line of her mouth.

Only she was not a lady at all, except in having noble blood in her veins. He remembered kissing the small scar on her right palm, the keepsake from a snake's bite. His lips had moved up to her wrist, then to her shoulder, and there had been nothing of the cool-blooded aristocrat in her fiery response. Even when she stood perfectly still he was aware of the lithe strength of her perfect little body, of the fluid gracefulness of her slightest movement. He knew that her grace was the result of exotic dancing practice. The disapproving way she pressed her lips together was equally deceptive. He knew her lively smiles and frowns, and how hot and sweet her mouth could be when pressed to his. The wariness in her eyes was familiar, though, as were the dark shadows beneath. She drove herself too hard. She always had.

"You look tired," he told her. Concern sometimes got in the way of his constant desire. He waved a finger sternly at her. "If you're going to be the belle of the ball you need your beauty sleep."

This caused her to stand straighter than he thought possible and to tick several points off on her fingers. "I am no beauty. Annie will be the belle of the ball. I require very little sleep."

"Wrong on all counts, my dear." He paced closer to her as he spoke, soft-footed, stalking. He wanted more than anything else to erase that forbidding expression from her lovely face. Good God, but she was lovely, wasn't she? Sometimes he forgot to properly *look* at the woman. Tonight was not one of those times.

"Will you dance with me at the ball?" His smile turned feral. "Dance *for* me?" That was what he wanted more than anything in the world. Certainly more than making her smile. Possibly as much as he wanted to save her from the Hoplites. Perhaps that was the price he would exact for saving her. No, it would be the price for saving her father.

There was one ancient, feverishly erotic dance he'd heard of in which a woman swirled and swayed and gyrated in front of a man with complete abandon. As she danced, she shed layer after layer of shimmering veils until she offered herself, completely naked. He could imagine a faint sheen of sweat gilding Cleo's skin, the sleek length of her thighs, the soft roundness of her belly, and the golden curls marking the juncture of her thighs. He could imagine the sway of her naked breasts, her nipples taut with excitement, the scent of desire rising like perfume from her flushed skin. What a dance that would be, and only for him. Afterward, when the music died, passion would begin and—

"Don't be ridiculous."

It took all his effort to focus his attention on the woman in front of him rather than the lascivious image in his mind. He wasn't completely successful. "If I told you I was thinking of you naked, what would you say?"

Her cheeks and throat colored bright pink. He very much wanted to stroke them, to feel the warmth brought out by his words.

"I would say that you are attempting to distract me. And that I ought to box your ears for such presumption."

"Box my ears." He moved closer to her still, so that she had to crane her neck to look at him. He'd never used his size to dominate her, but he wanted her to be aware that he was big, red-blooded, and dangerous; the male of the species; and that she was small, delicate, female, that he could have her if he wanted. She'd never understood that, and it was time she did. She had a lovely, long throat, and he wanted very much to stroke it. He put his hand near her throat, close enough to feel the heat of her skin. "It might be interesting if you tried boxing my ears, Miss Fraser."

Angel was acting distinctly oddly this evening. Cleo would have backed away from him, but that would show weakness. A lamp behind him outlined the breadth of his shoulders and the silky black sweep of his hair, leaving his face shadowed but for the angry, hungry spark in his dark, dark eyes. His presence surrounded her, heightened her senses. Energy throbbed between them at the spot where his palm did not quite touch her. The wool sleeve of his jacket brushed her neck, sending heat stabbing through her.

"Yes, yes," she said after a hot, breathless moment. "You've made your point."

He smiled. It was not pleasant, but it was enticing. His voice was a low purr when he asked, "What point is that, sweetheart?"

Her senses reeled from the hint of danger in Angel's voice. Cleo had to swallow before she could answer. "That you're a big boy," she told him.

The evil smile widened. "I'm glad you remember."

She lashed out, her hand stabbing a sharp, hard blow to his stomach. It had no effect on the arrogant glint in Angel Evans's eyes, but Cleo's fingers hurt like the devil from the futile gesture. "Back off!" she ordered.

She was almost surprised when he did as she demanded, and she was shocked at the ache of disappointment that went through her. The man had no trouble confusing her.

I should not let her get away with this! Evans told himself furiously. *She commands; I obey. Ridiculous.*

But he'd trained himself too well never to take advantage of Cleo again. He'd seduced an innocent girl, wrecked her life. Half the time he denied his responsibility, blamed her for leading him on; the rest of the time guilt ate at him. Constantly, she was a part of him.

"Do you think there's a cure?" he wondered.

"For you?" she spat angrily.

"For you." Her sharp silence followed him as he turned to the display case. He looked at the delicate objects within rather than face her, but the sight of the relics brought back bittersweet memories. He felt her gaze burn into his back. After what seemed a long while she moved up to stand beside him. Her shoulder brushed his arm. Her skirt touched his leg. He wanted very much to put his arm around her waist and draw her nearer.

"You kept the cat, I see."

"It is a valuable historical artifact."

"Hmmm. I still say you'd look pretty in the earbobs."

"They are not mine to wear."

"The princess wouldn't mind."

"You said that when you first found them."

"Meant it then. Mean it now."

"Hmmm."

"What, no 'You're as irresponsible as ever, Dr. Evans'? You're slipping, Cleo."

"I see no reason to preach a sermon to deaf ears."

"Such asperity!" He put a hand over his heart. "I'm cut to the quick."

"Of course you are. May I see the blood, please?"

"You want me to undress for you? Right here?" He gestured around them, and she spun to face him. His hand caught her arm as she moved. He drew her closer without thought. "In front of the princess?"

"*She* wouldn't mind. You are trying to distract me, Dr. Evans."

"Is it working?"

"Yes." She backed out of his grasp. When there was some distance between them, Cleo added, "But you won't find what you're looking for in here, so stop trying to chase me out into the night."

"How am I doing that?"

"By flaunting yourself before me."

He lifted an eyebrow. "Flaunting. What an interesting word." He spread his arms wide and turned slowly around. He reached up and tugged off his tie, then undid the first three buttons of his shirt, revealing hard muscles and dark chest hair. She didn't modestly look away. "I suppose it is my turn. You did the flaunting last time." She blushed deeply at the reminder. "I must say the audience in that nasty little café in Cairo was most appreciative. Very few dancing girls have fights started over them."

She waved this away. "Oh, it wasn't me they were interested in. I paid them to start a distraction. I was perfectly safe; Aunt Saida and Walter Raschid were in that awful place with me."

"Of course," he said, realizing suddenly whom her musicians had been. He chuckled. "You were half naked—"

"Nowhere near to half."

"—but you were properly chaperoned."

"I never find it wise to be alone with you, Angel."

He looked around the shadowed hall. "At least we have the princess with us now. Propriety is served."

"You are almost being charming and amusing, but you're still not going to find what you're looking for."

"Maybe I have found what I'm looking for right here." His voice was a low, persuasive rumble.

"Oh, bother!" Cleo snarled back. She was shaking, and not out of fear or anger. Was her world so small and empty without him that all he needed to do was stand a few inches too near? How could she be so weak and needy after all these years? Anger fueled her next words. "Of all the distasteful, disgusting . . ."

Her words were as much for herself as they were for Angel. She could see in his eyes that he knew it, too. His laughter bit into her like the stinging blast of a sandstorm. "Disgusting? Distasteful?" His sharp gesture took in the display in the museum hall. "You know what's disgusting? That nobody but you and I know the truth about all this. He's ruined your life, Cleo, just as he's tried to ruin mine. You prop him up and keep his secrets—"

"And he keeps mine," she interrupted this unexpected diatribe. "How can I do anything in my chosen field without his help?"

"Do your own work in your own name. You're a brilliant researcher."

His words sent a secret shiver of pleasure through her, but it was her turn to give a bitter, hard laugh. "I'm a woman!"

"Don't I know it, sweetheart."

She put up a hand to halt him when he took a step toward her. "You are trying to use that to distract me."

"Am not."

"Then fasten your shirt."

"I'm more comfortable this way."

"Deny that you broke in here trying to find something you have no right to."

His gaze swept over her, hot, possessive, and wholly unexpected. "I know what's mine, Cleopatra: you. Then. Now. Forever."

If the nearest object to hand hadn't been a three-thousand-year-old Cretan wine vessel, she would have picked it up and thrown it at him. She was still very tempted. "I know why you're saying these things, but you're not going to manage to rattle me enough to find out anything."

"I broke in"—he assumed a lecturing air— "as a help to you. I felt that your security required testing before the complete collection was in place. And who better than a man of my considerable experience in these matters to conduct that test?"

"Who indeed?" she responded.

"Your sarcasm wounds me."

"If I had a weapon to hand, you would have to worry about far more than sarcasm."

"Ah, but words can hurt."

She went very still, her face losing all expression, but the pain in her eyes made him bleed.

He put out a hand. "Cleo?" She said nothing. The fire was gone out of her. Somehow, he'd done it, and he hated himself for it. He struggled on, the words a mixture of truth and the way he wished things to be. "I'm here to help you, Cleo. That's all I want to do. I owe you my life. I want to do something to pay that debt. You think I came to Scotland because of what you found on Amorgis, but I came here because of what happened to me there." He sighed and ran a hand through his hair. "I have a chance here to reclaim my academic standing. To regain some of the respect your father's been undermining for years with the lies he's told about me."

"Why would my father lie about you?"

She'd asked that question before. He'd merely told her that her father would do anything to shore up his own reputation, that he was jealous. That their early disagreements on methodology and interpretation had escalated into personal dislike. All those things were true, but this time he gave her the underlying truth. "Maybe because he thinks I raped his daughter."

The blunt words didn't shake Cleo from her cold, distant demeanor. "Don't be ridiculous. He knows what happened."

"I'm glad he does, sweetheart, because I'm not sure I do."

What did you tell him? Evans wondered. *I never spoke a word of what happened between us in my tent. All I asked for was your hand in marriage. All I got was shown the door—or in this case, the nearest sand dune. Later, years later, he came to me in Cairo, half drunk and carrying a gun, threatening and cursing me for having ruined his little girl. You don't know about that, do you, sweetheart? How did he explain the black eye and bruised jaw I gave him? Fell off a camel, maybe?*

"The old fool loves you in his own way," Evans told Cleo now.

"And I love him."

"But you need to fly away."

"And where, Dr. Evans, could I fly to?" She made a sharp gesture. "This discussion is quite irrelevant."

He found himself moving closer to her again; he couldn't help himself. He couldn't bear her coldness. Who knew better than he did how to fire her senses? The true reason he had let her know he was alone with her in the empty building was the deep, hungry need to remind them both no other man had any claim on her.

"What are you doing?" she demanded, her voice rising nervously as he stalked her.

"Teaching you that talk is irrelevant between us."

"There is nothing you can teach me."

He smirked. "Sweetheart—"

"Stop calling me that!" She backed up as he came toward her, but he kept coming, and eventually she backed into a pillar.

176

"—we barely got started last time."

"Last time— Oh!"

He put his hands on her shoulders and pinned her against the cool, smooth marble. Her palms came up to press against his chest, skin to skin. She gasped, her mouth forming a delightfully shocked *O*, and he smiled as fire rushed through him at the point of connection. He pressed his weight against her soft, sweet curves, felt her trembling along the length of his body. He bent his head until they were eye to eye, mouth to mouth.

"Trust me." He whispered the words against her lips. "This once, Cleopatra, trust me."

She knew it would be wiser to trust a pack of starving jackals, but she was aware of him in every fiber and molecule of her being. He was as close to her as her shadow, equally dark, but infinitely more substantial. Sometimes she dreamed that they were together like this, feverish, futile dreams that burst inside her in fiery glory—only to wake alone and lonely. He was here now—huge and commanding, reckless and ready to abandon every scruple. She could scream. She could fight. She could beg and plead.

Or she could kiss him.

Either way, she'd be alone and lonely in the morning.

But the morning was not now.

She cupped his face in her hands and drew his mouth down hard onto hers.

Within moments, Cleo discovered that Angel was right about one thing: he had a great deal to teach her about kissing. And she was eager to learn. Memory and instinct only went so far, but from the instant their lips touched, arousal slid through her and hunger inexorably took control.

Her hands caressed him in a long, slow slide from his face across his wide shoulders and down the tight muscles of his back. Angel was hard and smooth as marble, but she felt his muscles quiver beneath the shirt, sensed the leashed power of the man. She was being wild and reckless while he held on hard to the control she wanted him to lose. It wasn't right or fair that he not share in this moment of abandon with her. So she slid her hands up under his shirt.

He moaned against her mouth, his tongue thrust deeply, and she answered with an equally needy sound. His arm came around her waist, pulling her tightly against—

"Ow!"

Angel whirled away. Cleo stumbled forward, her senses reeling. She fell to the floor in a pool of skirts and barely caught herself from falling flat on her face. She heard the sound of blows above her head. Shadows swirled as Angel dodged his attacker. Cleo could barely hear over her ragged breathing and pounding heartbeat.

"Ouch! Stop that!"

"Stop it yourself! Take that!"

Cleo's head came up sharply as she recognized the voice, just in time to see a large black folded parasol land a sharp blow across Angel Evans's backside.

"Ow! Quit!"

Cleo might have laughed had circumstances been different. As it was, she jumped to her feet and threw herself between Angel and his attacker. "Aunt Saida!" She put her hands up in front of her. "No!"

The parasol just barely missed her, but raindrops flew off it and splattered across her face.

"You should be ashamed!" Saida Wallace proclaimed, letting the parasol drop to her side. "Can't leave the two of you alone for a moment. I'd rather see you shooting at each other. Then at least I know you're safe from hurting each other."

Cleo discovered that she and Angel were standing side by side, shoulders equally hunched. They shared a contrite glance and looked quickly away. Cleo didn't know what had gotten into her. It had certainly been insane and wrong and—

"Good thing I came to fetch you. I grew worried when the rain started and you weren't yet home." Aunt Saida grabbed Cleo's hand. "You are coming home with me right now, young woman."

Cleo had wanted her aunt to get out more, but this was not exactly what she'd had in mind. The small woman tugged her forward, and Cleo was too embarrassed not to go along meekly. *I'm a woman now,* she thought. *Why am I obeying like a child?* Then she remembered Angel and pulled free of her aunt. She turned swiftly back to face him and pointed toward the museum's front entrance. "Out. Get out of my house."

Angel threw back his head, his laughter filling the dark, echoing hall. Lord but he had a magnificent, strong throat. Then he bowed and snatched up his tossed-aside coat and tie. "Shall I see you ladies home? Show that I *can* act like a gentleman? I am reforming my ways," he added to Saida.

"There is nothing wrong with your ways," Saida answered him. "It is your timing that is always wrong."

"As you say, lady," he answered, and this time he gave her a graceful, Arab bow before walking briskly to the door and out of the building.

"And don't come back," Cleo murmured after him, not meaning it at all.

Chapter 11

"Aunt Saida's right. We really are safer shooting at each other," Cleo mused aloud, as she walked through the village.

"What did you say?" Pia asked.

"Nothing, Pia," Cleo answered. She hated getting caught talking to herself. She might have given Pia a daunting look, but a yawn interrupted any attempt at being repressive.

"Did you sleep at all, Cleo?" Annie asked with concern. "I heard you pacing long after you finally came in last night." Annie glanced up at the sultry pewter sky, where rain threatened. "You don't look much better than the weather."

"Worse," Pia contributed brightly. "She's mad at Angel Evans again, I'll wager."

"Ladies don't wager," Annie informed Pia.

But Pia ignored this etiquette lesson. "Cleo always looks like a thunderstorm ready to hit when she's angry at Angel. What did he do this time, Cleo?"

"I don't like his being here."

"But you don't want him to be anywhere else. They have a complicated relationship," Pia explained to Annie.

"We have no relationship. Dr. Evans is a fraud and a cad. He's here to make trouble for me—for Father, that is."

"Maybe he just wants to attend the conference like everybody else. I think you're picking on him."

"I am not." Cleo realized she risked descending into childish bickering, so she looked at Annie and said, "Nor am I overly tired. I merely have a great deal to think about."

Pia did not look convinced, but Annie fortunately turned her attention to the display in a shop window, and they all halted so she could look over a selection of hats. Aunt Saida, dressed in black bombazine and a huge bonnet that did a credible job of hiding her face, stood silently and watchfully behind them. She had left her isolation—and nine-year-old Thena, at home happily reading a book—to play chaperone to her three nieces. Cleo understood that this implied mistrust of her but didn't complain. She had even smiled sweetly when Aunt Saida donned one of her Western-style walking dresses and made a pleasant comment that a little activity would do them all good. If it took a threat to her virtue from Angel Evans to get Aunt Saida out of the house, Cleo was grateful for it.

It was market day in Muirford, with outdoor stalls lining the narrow main street. Country folk were there to do their shopping, as were townsfolk, people from the university, and visitors staying at the hotel. To Cleo's eyes the hustle and bustle of Muirford's market day was more exotic than the great bazaar of Cairo. And thinking of shopping in the bazaar gave her the urge to pull her shawl across her face, modestly like a veil. She shook her head at such an impulse here in her native land and breathed in the damp Scottish air. Perhaps this wasn't the Khan el-Kalili, but the detour through town on the way to the conference hall had been worth the extra walk. Her attention slipped inward once more as the Fraser sisters and Saida Wallace started on their way once more.

Cleo considered the night before as she walked along between her sisters. It was all one long nightmare. One that was far from over, as she could still taste him on her tongue.

The texture of his skin was pressed into her lips and palms. How could he have done this to her? How could she have done it to herself?

She had thought she was in control of the situation. She'd thought kissing him to be a logical decision. As it turned out, all the man had to do was unbutton his shirt and what little sense she had flew out the window. How had she let it be so easy for him? And what was he really up to? If he was desperate enough to use seduction to achieve his ends—well, he might play rough, but he'd never played so unfairly before. They'd had unwritten rules over the years, cultivating indifference, speaking of their shared night only obliquely until—had it been only yesterday?

What had gotten into him?

Worse, what had gotten into her?

And why was she blaming herself now? Because of the lecture Aunt Saida gave her on the walk home? She hadn't actually listened to what Aunt Saida said; she'd been concentrating too hard on purging the scorching need that sang through her blood. Even the cold rain and Aunt Saida's stinging annoyance had done little to help. Hours later, desire still coursed through her. That and a lack of sleep did nothing to help her mood this morning.

The point she needed to concentrate on was that whatever Angel Evans claimed he wanted, no matter how he tried to get around her, what he was really after was the Alexandrian treasure.

You don't want respectability, and you certainly don't want me. You are a craven cur to try to use me so. Do you think I was born yesterday? That one kiss will bring me 'round to doing whatever you want? Even at sixteen I was not so naive!

"She's thinking hard," Pia leaned around her to say to Annie. "Can't you smell the smoke coming out of her ears from the effort?"

"You're not amusing," Cleo told her youngest sister. "Not at all."

"And grumpy besides."

"You could be exercising Saladin right now, you know," Cleo pointed out. "No one's making you attend a historical lecture."

"I'm trying to improve my mind," Pia said. "And it was either attend the lecture with you or spend the day with Aunt Jenny. She wants to teach me how to tat."

"Tatting is a womanly art," Annie said. "It's kind of her to offer you lessons."

Tatting, as Cleo recalled from her own long-ago lessons, was a deadly dull form of lace making that women practiced to help fight off boredom as they gossiped. She knew some women actually enjoyed such activities, and the results of handicrafts were lovely and useful, but such things were not for her—or for

Pia, who shared Cleo's unladylike tastes in almost everything. *And is being like me a good thing?* Cleo wondered with a guilty look at Pia. What good did a love of history, languages, and adventure do a woman when the world offered so few opportunities to express that love?

"Maybe you *should* be home tatting," she said. "Perhaps we all should be."

"And miss out on the fun of watching Annie make sheep's eyes at eligible young men?" Pia replied. "Not for the world."

"I," Annie said with a toss of her head, "am too discreet to make sheep's eyes." She gave a girlishly wicked smile, confident in her power. "I certainly expect to distract Professor Carter, though. And all I shall have to do is sit demurely in the visitors' gallery with my hands folded in my lap and pretend that I don't know he's worshiping at my feet. I wonder if Spiros will be there?" she added, sounding far more excited at that prospect. Cleo wondered what it was like to feel various degrees of attraction to several young men. Normal, she supposed, and she was delighted in Annie's normalcy. She, however, had been cursed by a relentless fixation on one man.

She wanted to protect her sister from the dangers of courtship on one hand, and for Annie to experience ordinary life on the other. She dreaded the girl's making mistakes, but then, perhaps Annie was a far better judge of men than Cleo was. Cleo certainly hoped so, for the sake of her sister's young and tender emotions. One case of permanent heartbreak was enough for any family.

Oh, Lord, she was being maudlin, the one thing she'd promised herself she'd never be. She glanced back at Aunt Saida. "Why should I be maudlin when I have so many other people to do it for me?"

Saida gave her a sharp look, then her expression softened into a half-smile.

Cleo felt that smile like a blessing, and walked on through the town and onto the university campus almost with a sense of contentment. Today would be a good day, she promised herself. A good, quiet, day, during which she would immerse herself in the world where she belonged—even if it was up in the visitors' gallery with the rest of the "petticoats."

Several people were outside the entrance of the lecture hall when the women reached it. "Good morning, ladies," Samuel Mitchell greeted them. "Good to see you again, Mrs. Wallace," he said to Saida. He gestured toward the thickset, gray-haired man at his side. "May I present Dr. DeClercq?"

"I knew your late husband, Mrs. Wallace," DeClercq said after everyone was introduced all around. "And, of course, I am familiar with

189

your father's sterling work," the famous Belgian historian said to Cleo. "We look forward to his presenting his paper."

Pia made a noise that would have gotten her sent to her room if they'd been at home. Annie and the men took no notice of her, and Aunt Saida stifled any further comment from the girl with a look.

"Our father greatly admires the work both of you have done," Cleo told the men. "And he asked me to convey his regrets that he has to attend an unexpected faculty meeting rather than today's conference session." The truth was that Father had to spend the day fending off yet another whim of Sir Edward's. Though the curriculum in ancient studies had already been set, he'd taken it into his head to name a chair in ancient Celtic Scotland studies. This threw the whole history department, which Father was to head, into chaos. "I, too, admire the work you've done in Egypt," Cleo told DeClercq, who was one of her heroes. "And I'm so glad you survived the awful attack on your expedition."

DeClercq brushed his side-whiskers. "Why, thank you, young woman."

"Will you be presenting a paper today?" Cleo saw Annie frown warningly at her eagerness, but she couldn't help but go on. "On your interpretation of the tomb drawings at Iribidi, perhaps?"

"I'm afraid I have no lecture prepared," he answered. "I am here only to learn from the work of others and to show support for a young colleague of mine who deserves far more respect than he receives." He brushed his whiskers with the back of his hand again. "You know his name, I think, though I doubt your father would wish me to discuss the gentleman with his family."

"Evans?" Cleo burst out before she could stop herself. "You defending Evans?" Why did everything always come back to Angel Evans? "After he disposed of half the Iribidi find for his own gain?"

DeClercq looked appalled. "Where on earth did you hear such nonsense, my girl?"

"I saw him selling looted treasure in Cairo with my own eyes!" she shot back.

She was suddenly aware of the small crowd gathering around them—scholars who had arrived for a quiet morning of intellectual pursuits, drawn instead to the sight of a world-famous historian's being faced by a silly woman who dared to argue with him. Oh, God, what was she doing? What was she thinking? She *wasn't* thinking, of course. Angel was involved.

Dr. DeClercq rocked back on his heels, looking both amused and bemused. "And how is it *you* saw Evans disposing of the relics?"

"That isn't important. What is important, sir, is that he seems to have somehow convinced you that he's a honest man."

"Honest and honorable," DeClercq answered. "But I understand your concern, child. You see, the truth that neither he nor I could reveal, in the political climate of Egypt, was that our expedition was taken captive, and not by any ordinary bandits. I and several other members of our group were held in the stronghold of a high official in the Khedive government."

"Shocking," someone behind Cleo murmured. "Such corruption!"

DeClercq looked over her head at the man who'd spoken. He smiled as he said, "You have not done fieldwork have you, young man? One learns to deal with corruption and demands for *baksheesh* soon enough if one wishes to work in Egypt and the Levant."

"And one easily becomes corrupted," Cleo murmured.

DeClercq's attention returned to her. "I'm afraid you misjudge the young man badly, Miss Fraser."

"I've known him for ten years, sir," she responded.

"And I nearly as long, and better. We worked well together, unlike his relationship with your father. I hope to work with him again quite soon. I know his insightfulness, his daring and intelligence. I also owe him my life."

"He's a brave man," Cleo conceded. "But personal bravery hardly excuses his—appropriations." She could not bring herself to call Angel an outright thief in front of all these people.

"He used the money from those so-called appropriations to save lives, young woman," DeClercq told her. "He used the sale of a hidden cache of artifacts to free me and others from a rather unpleasant imprisonment. But the brigands wanted even more. Providing the ransom they demanded was a slow process, involving dealing with some unpleasant characters."

"Haroun," Cleo said. "That's why he worked with Haroun?"

"Just so," DeClercq went on. "There were five people to be freed, one at a time, with no government authority he could turn to for help. Had he not been discreet, we would have died."

"But—" Cleo's head reeled. She did not believe she was hearing this. Blood pounded in her temples and lights sparked behind her eyes. She realized that she was holding her breath, and let it out in a rush as DeClercq went relentlessly on. He was warmed to his subject and pleased to have an audience.

"A. David Evans is the reason I am here today," he told them all. "No matter what you have heard about him, he had good reasons for it all."

Good reasons, she thought, everything she'd believed for nearly a decade crumbling to dust. *Good reasons?* "Oh, good Lord!"

"I wasn't *that* discreet," a familiar Yankee voice drawled, practically in her ear.

Cleo whirled to face him. From the corner of her eye she could see that others in the crowd were smiling, but Angel looked tense and deadly serious.

"You!" Her fists bunched tightly at her sides. He retreated as she took an angry step forward. *"You!"*

"What?"

She quaked with fury as she shouted, "How *dare* you be a hero?"

"I'm sorry!" he shouted back. "I promise that next time I'll do worse! Will that make you happy?"

"Yes! What? No!"

"Cleo?" Annie put her hand on Cleo's arm.

She shook her sister off, but Saida stepped between them. "I think," she said, firmly drawing Cleo toward the door, "that the session is about to begin." She gestured for Pia and Annie to join them. "It is time we took our places in the women's section."

Cleo went, almost blind and deaf with reaction. This was the worst moment of her life. Absolutely the worst.

Or so it seemed until Angel called after her, "It's not as if I haven't tried to tell you before."

He hadn't. Not really. Had he?

Cleo drummed her fingers nervously on the dark, smooth wood of the gallery railing while someone at the podium droned on about something or another that she would have found fascinating before the world came crashing apart. She felt as shattered and scattered as shards of broken glass. She hated that she felt at all, and wished she could simply stop. But words and images flew relentlessly through her mind, a catalog of memories without order or logic. Impressions came and went, and she developed a hideous, throbbing headache. She was already exhausted, groggy from too little sleep, her senses stripped down to aching, feverish nerve endings from a few moments of forbidden passion the night before.

And now this.

It was intolerable.

Impossible.

Of course, he hadn't tried to tell her. What had he said in all those years? *I'm not as bad as you think, sweetheart.* That could have meant anything! Or nothing. Besides, Father had said . . .

And how long had it been since she'd put complete faith in the words and deeds of self-righteous, self-involved Everett Fraser? She was not blind to the man's faults—but he was her father. Surely he wasn't capable of outright lying to her. When all was said and done, Father was a good man—just a grossly oblivious one with a love for Alexander the Great and an abstract but possessive attachment to his children.

The point here wasn't what Father had said and done, the point was Angel Evans. It always was, and always would be. He was somewhere down there in the audience of grave-faced, dark-coated men. Only an hour ago she'd questioned his right to mingle with the elite in the history field; now it looked as though Dr. A. David Evans was exactly where he belonged. In a perverse way she was proud of him, though it stung her that she was the outsider and interloper here, relegated to being a mere observer of the discussions of learned men.

And there was no use her pouting over the unfairness of life, either, when she very well knew it was only a way of directing her thoughts away from facing the unpleasant pleasant truth DeClercq had laid before her.

"You stole it and I want it back!"

She faced Angel across the width of the inn's stone-tiled terrace. A trellis of grapevines arched over her head, giving comforting shade from the Mediterranean sun. A basket of lemons was on the table beside her, and huge painted pots of bright red geraniums decorated each corner of the terrace. It had been a bright, pleasant place where she'd been sipping tea and reading until Angel came storming up the dusty road to shatter the early-morning peace.

"You stole it first," she pointed out to the large, angry man before her.

"I discovered the existence of the papyrus independent of you."

"That isn't what Father says."

"He's a liar."

His words stung, so she stung back. "And you are a tomb robber, a mercenary, a thief."

He sneered. "It's a living, sweetheart."

"Disreputable cad."

"If you say so."

"And please don't shout; you'll wake everyone in the inn."

"And you have a hard day ahead of you," he added before she could. "I've already been out to the site. The diggers are opening a tomb I should have discovered today."

"It's not Alexander's tomb, so I don't know what you're making a fuss about." They hoped they'd found the resting place of a captain of Alexander's bodyguards. It was possible that there was information buried with the guard that would lead to Alexander's resting place.

"I'm not making a fuss over the tomb. The fuss, sweetheart, is over your stealing the map that led to the tomb."

He only called her sweetheart when he was at his most mocking and angry. His dark eyes sparked with a fury that sent an electric shiver through her. "Stealing from a thief is hardly a crime," was her haughty reply.

"Isn't it?" was his furious response. "Which one of us has gotten her ethics a little twisted, sweetheart?"

"Don't call me—"

"Cleo?"

Cleo turned her head toward her sister, and Annie thrust a handkerchief under her nose. She sniffed. "What's that for?"

"You're crying."

"Oh." She took the square of embroidered linen.

For a moment her thoughts lingered on that last argument before the accident, on the flash in Angel's dark eyes, on the raven's wing fall of hair across his forehead, and on how the morn-

ing sun had bronzed his skin. Even furious at
him—and when was she not furious at him?—
her fingers always itched to brush through the
satin thickness of his hair.

She dabbed at her eyes and cheeks, sniffed
again. She must look a fright. Several faculty
wives and Spiros, accompanied by another
pair of foreign students, were also in the
gallery, but fortunately her sisters and her aunt
were the only people seated nearby. Spiros was
looking at Annie, but only Annie was looking
at Cleo.

How long had this sniffling been going on?
"I have something in my eye," she told her sister.

"Of course you do," Annie answered.
"Something about the size of an obelisk, I
should imagine."

"Just about." Cleo noticed that the speaker
had left the podium, and the audience was
taking a break while waiting for the next person to be announced. There were people
standing in small groups, others were moving
toward the door. This was a good opportunity
to make an exit herself. She turned to Aunt
Saida. "I do have a great deal to do," she said.
"There are still finishing touches to be put on
the exhibit for tonight, and Aunt Jenny is
bringing Dr. Apolodoru to dinner before to-

night's reception. Cook wants me to look over her shopping list before she starts a meal for a 'foreign gentleman.' "

"I can do that," Annie offered.

"With a great deal more domestic skill than me," Cleo agreed. She rose. What if Angel were to take the podium next? There had been a great many changes and additions to the conference program since she'd helped work out the schedule, and she wasn't ready for any more surprises today. She wasn't ready to look at him right now, even from the distance of the visitors' gallery.

"I have to go," she said. "I simply have to go."

Chapter 12

"This is terrible." Reverend McDyess stood in the middle of the hallway downstairs, blocking the door and wringing his hands. Dean Smith and Professor Mitchell were with him, looking sympathetic. "I knew no good would come of bringing strangers here," proclaimed the minister, who'd opened this morning's session of the conference with a prayer. Whatever his bad news might be, Cleo was not interested. She only wanted to get away. But she had to get past the men to make her escape.

No one budged at her approach. In fact, all three men looked her way. She suspected that Smith and Mitchell looked upon her appearance as a chance to make their own escape.

As much as she wished it, Cleo could not avoid pausing to say "Good morning."

"There is nothing good about it, young woman." Reverend McDyess shook a finger under her nose. "You're that historian's girl, aren't you? Your father persuaded Edward Muir to build his temple of Satan right here in our godly village. And look what's happened! Corruption already settling in, and this so-called seat of higher learning not even officially open yet. Desecration!"

The man was red-faced and very agitated. Cleo noticed that Smith and Mitchell had already inched away. Why was she always left to deal with every blasted crisis that came up? She would like to brusquely brush past the man and go about her business, but that was not politic. Nor was it possible, McDyess was as round as he was tall, and he was a tall man. Might as well try to get around a mountain as get past him before he was ready to move out of the way. Cleo sighed and gave him her full attention.

"Desecration?" she asked. Was there something in the presentation you disapproved of?" She didn't recall who had spoken or what his paper had been about, but if it had seemed at all blasphemous—

"I'm not concerned about some fool speech, girl! I'm talking about my graveyard!"

Cleo's heart and stomach lurched painfully. "The cemetery next to the church?"

"Of course, the one next to the church! My sexton's just brought word of the outrage! I can't bear the thought of seeing what's been done to the resting places of our righteous dead." He gestured wildly, taking in the entire university with the sweeping movement of his hand. "A stranger's work. The Devil's work. I kept my peace about my misgivings until now, but I knew no good would come of Edward Muir bringing outsiders into the town where he was born. Aye, I knew no good would come of it."

"Get out of my way."

McDyess bridled at Cleo's cold, commanding tone. "What?"

"Move." When he did nothing but stare at her, Cleo put out her hands and shoved against his huge belly.

It was outrage more than anything else that pushed him backwards. "Wha'? Yon strumpet, what de y'think you're doin'?"

Cleo slipped past the mountainous cleric, hiked up her skirts, and ran, leaving him erupting invective like an outraged volcano as she sped away.

"What's all the shouting about?" Hill asked.

The vicar's colorful swearing had drawn everyone out of the lecture hall to the entrance foyer. The commotion was a fine diversion from Professor O'Neal's droning discourse on Etruscan musical intruments.

"I'm not quite sure, exactly," Mitchell answered as Evans and Hill joined him at the edge of the milling crowd. "At first the vicar was upset about an act of vandalism at the church, but he seems to have gone off on a new tangent."

"Impudent *sassenach* wench!"

Evans's attention was more on the men who'd come out of the hall with Spiros than on the angry giant, who was mad as a wet hen at somebody. This was the second mob scene of the day, and Evans suspected Cleo was somehow again involved.

"What's a *sassenach?*" he asked.

More important, who were the men with Spiros? Were they the Hoplite fanatics Apolodoru had warned him about? As if the existence of a two-thousand-year-old secret order didn't imply fanaticism in all its members. There was a certain amount of honor and trust built up between him and Apolodoru, and Spiros had convinced Evans that he would never do anything to harm Pia or Annie Fraser. That wasn't very reassuring when it came to Cleo's fate, but knowing the girls were safe gave Evans less to worry about.

And he knew Apolodoru would give him at

least a few more days to find the treasure. Before he'd completely lost his head last night, Evans had come to the conclusion that the treasure was not hidden anywhere inside the museum. He'd carefully explored the central display room Fraser was setting up to hold the treasure, but the crown, cup, and other grave goods were not in the building. That was not good news for Evans, meaning it might ultimately be very bad news for Cleo. She was too clever by half. He couldn't help but smile at the thought—and be furiously frustrated, as well.

Above all else, Apolodoru wanted to keep his secret society secret, but the newcomers stood out like sore thumbs. The men who flanked Spiros were large, furtive-looking, and obviously out of place in their ill-fitting suits. They looked like street toughs, not university students. The Hoplites' ancestors had been members of Alexander's elite bodyguard, and this pair looked to be direct descendants of a couple of very hard-bitten soldiers.

"Presumptuous slut!" the minister ranted on. "Daring to strike a man of the cloth."

"What's he on about?" Hill asked Mitchell.

"I believe that at first it was because some vandals knocked over some gravestones in the cemetery. He tends to slip into the local dialect when he's excited."

Carter ventured to approach the angry vicar. "Sir? Reverend? Perhaps if you could—"

"The chit struck me! What do they teach women in the outside world? I won't have loose women invading Muirford."

"Miss Fraser was deeply upset about the desecration in the graveyard," Mitchell explained.

"Cleo has firm opinions about grave robbing," Evans agreed, half his attention still on the Hoplites in the back of the crowd. So, Cleo was not safely ensconced up in the visitors' gallery.

"Miss Fraser was a bit brusque with Reverend McDyess when he wouldn't allow her to leave the building."

"So she pushed him out of the way," Evans concluded.

"The man was rude not to let the lady pass. Poor Miss Fraser probably needed some fresh air after hearing about such gruesome matters," Carter suggested.

"The woman's been excavating graves since you were a pup," Evans snapped. "I'll thank you to give her the respect she deserves, you young fool."

"Wicked strumpet!" McDyess raved on, red-faced with fury.

Evans stepped up to the huge vicar. "Strumpet?" he asked, voice low and dangerous. "No one calls my woman that."

Piggy eyes focused on him. "I'll call—"

One hard punch to the jaw laid the big man out.

Many people in the crowded foyer gasped. DeClercq, Mitchell, Duncan, and Carter hooted with laughter and clapped in approval. Evans shook his bruised hand and gave his supporters a wry shrug.

Hill stepped up to him and said quietly, "I haven't a snowball's chance in hell with Miss Fraser, have I?"

Evans looked him squarely in the eye. "None whatsoever." He glanced away from Hill and into the crowd. Spiros was still there, but his companions were gone. Evans swore under his breath, stepped over the supine Reverend McDyess, and ran from the building.

"Thought I'd find you here."

"Hello, Angel."

"It's an old graveyard," he said. He came up behind Cleo and put a hand on her shoulder. She was looking down into a disturbed grave. There were quite a few moss-covered headstones scattered about. It was hard to tell which ones had fallen over by themselves and which had been pushed down by the vandals. The place had an abandoned look to it, tucked away as it was in a stand of woods near the old stone church. Mausoleums stood on either side of the cemetery. The one to the left was a worn, abandoned-looking little building that could have dated from the Middle Ages. The tomb on the right was of brand-spanking-new polished white stone with a bronze door flanked by carved figures of weeping angels. A statue of a kilted warrior brandishing a claymore stood guard on top of the roof. Sir Edward's future resting place, Evans presumed.

After silence stretched out a few seconds more, and Cleo's shoulder grew tense beneath his touch, he spoke again. "Not as old as we're used to, perhaps . . ."

She didn't answer, and he tried to not concentrate on the spot of smooth, bare skin that showed at the nape of her neck, between the collar of her dress and the thick twist of hair firmly pinned behind her head. Had he ever kissed her on that lovely, vulnerable spot? No, he didn't believe he had. There were a great many places he hadn't kissed. Her ears, for example. She had lovely, small, pink ears. He wondered if the arch of her foot was erotically sensitive, or the base of her spine. It had been a waste of ten long years, when he could have been exploring the sweet secrets of her lovely body.

He shifted his gaze carefully around the silent graveyard, alert to any noise or movement. He'd half hoped there'd be a crowd of outraged villagers here investigating the damage, but the entire community seemed to be shopping at the village market. Of course, if he hadn't cold-cocked the vicar, the man might have gone off and informed his flock of the outrage to their ancestors. Evans hadn't seen either of Spiros's friends on the way to the cemetery, and he couldn't see them lurking among the trees or headstones now, but that didn't mean they weren't there.

"And why are you here?" he asked Cleo.

She sighed and slipped from his grasp to turn and face him. "I wanted to see the damage for myself. All this vandalism is starting to worry me."

She looked almost frightened. He put his hands on her shoulders and drew her closer. He wanted to put his arms around her and draw her closer still. "You haven't accused me of the vandalism yet. You might feel better if you did."

He'd hoped she'd laugh, but his words managed to draw only a faint smile from her. "You're not on my list of suspects, Angel."

"Angel." He answered her smile with a gentle one of his own. "Do you know you're the only person who calls me Angel? You and Pia," he added.

"Pia—the little scapegrace—is fond of you."

He wanted to ask if *she* was fond of him, even just a little, but was afraid of the answer.

"Angel seemed like the right thing to call you," she went on. "For several reasons."

He cocked his head teasingly to one side. "Like what?"

Her pale cheeks took on a bit of pink. "Well—you never looked like a David to me."

"No good at giant slaying," he agreed. "Can't play a harp. No qualifications to be a king."

"You always seemed larger than life to me." Her blush deepened, and her gaze shifted away from him. "Heroic."

"Angelic?" He gave a soft, bitter laugh. "Hardly."

"I was rather young when my first impression of you was formed."

"Too young to know better," he agreed, and decided to move to safer ground. "You're the one who's the hero, Cleopatra."

Evans hadn't let a little thing like not being wanted at the Amorgis excavation get in his way. He went to the dig site, and had been getting nothing but hostile looks from Cleo all day. Fraser didn't dare try to have him expelled from the area

210

in case he made a scene in front of the man Fraser depended on for financing. So Fraser tried his best to pretend that he didn't even exist. The first thing Evans had done was strike up a conversation with Fraser's rich patron, of course. It turned out Sir Edward Muir was a smart, hardheaded businessman, and Evans was from a family of hardworking, practical businessmen. They had far more in common than an aesthete nobleman with pretensions of scholarship. So, when the workers cleared the last of the rubble away from the tomb entrance, and Fraser approached his patron to invite him to be the first to enter, Evans managed to wrangle an invitation to join his new friend in his moment of triumph.

Fraser looked like he was ready to explode, but he didn't complain.

Evans was gleeful—for about six seconds. That was how long it took before he looked at Cleo and saw how his vindictiveness had spoiled this moment for her. He might have backed down, made some excuse to Muir, but Fraser sneered and Cleo turned her back on him, and he had to go through with it.

So he and Muir took up lanterns and made their way into the dark, stone-lined underground chamber. The trap they walked into had been laid two thousand years before, but it was triggered with exact precision all the same. The noise was horrendous when the walls collapsed and the darkness

211

came down, but Evans could have sworn he heard a distant voice call out, "Angel!"

It was the memory of that voice that he hung on to all those painful, terrifying hours later, trapped in absolute darkness.

And when the last stone was pulled away and the light came back into his world again, the first thing he heard was "Angel."

The first things he felt were her hands soothing the hair off his brow. His first taste was of her tears. The first things he saw were the bloody cuts on her gentle hands.

"You saved my life," he told her now, coming back from that nightmare that had ended with the heavenly bliss of Cleo Fraser's holding him in her arms. He owed her his life, and far more—she, who had never asked him for anything.

He didn't know when he had moved so close to her, but her face was tilted up appealingly as she answered, "I was not the only one involved in your rescue."

"But you're the one who wouldn't let the diggers stop even after two days, when they insisted it was hopeless."

"I knew you weren't dead."

He found that he held her face cupped in his hands. Her skin was warm satin against his palms. "How?"

"I . . . just knew." Her words were whispered, her lips very close to his.

You couldn't die, Cleo thought, remembering the desperate pain and terror. *I wouldn't let you die!*

There was a look in Angel's dark, beautiful eyes that she had never seen before. Familiar but strange, raw and honest. Terrifying. Alluring. Lord knew what he saw in her eyes. She had never felt so naked herself, not even on that long-ago night when she'd gone into his tent. Her limbs felt oddly heavy, her heart ached, her lids drooped languidly closed. Caught in a dark spell, she could only succumb to undeniable need. Angel's lips brushed hers, a gentle, feather-light touch—almost a memory, almost a wish.

It was not wishful thinking when he pulled her tightly against him. They fitted too perfectly, yielding and firm in all the right places. The kiss moved swiftly from gentleness to hunger, sweet, deep, and frantic.

And over far too quickly.

They both heard the noise from behind a nearby headstone, and both reacted with equal swiftness, whirling out of their tight embrace, their already heightened senses alert for danger. They stood back to back a split second later, their gazes scanning the graveyard.

"See anything?" he asked, his breath ragged but his tone sharply alert.

"No."

"Probably a stray cat."

"Or the sexton returning, more likely," Cleo answered, remembering where they were and what had happened. She stepped reluctantly away from the solid protection of Angel's broad back, then walked to the rusty iron fence surrounding the churchyard and gazed up the lane toward the village. "Reverend McDyess and his flock approach."

Cleo stood stiff and still while Angel did a quick circle around the headstones and mausoleums. "Time we were gone, I think," he said when he joined her by the gate. "The good reverend might sic a lynch mob on both of us if we're here when he arrives."

"I was rather rude to him," she admitted.

"You and me both, sweetheart."

Cleo stepped through the gate. Angel lingered just inside the graveyard. With some distance between them, she said, "We really should not have done that."

He put his hands behind his back and contemplated her. His expression was serious, but there was a twinkle in his black eyes. "There are several things we should not have done. Which are you referring to?"

This was hardly the time for conversation.

Besides, she wanted very much for both of them to be away from the cemetery. "I have duties, Dr. Evans. And you have a paper to give. Go dazzle the masses, Angel. I have to go home."

Chapter 13

"**Y**ou don't look good." Evans realized what he'd said even before Cleo turned a cutting look at him. "That's a nice dress, but it doesn't suit you at all," he added hastily. She was wearing a very feminine pale yellow and blue print frock with ribbon-and-lace trim.

His bluntness drew a smile from her. "Annie will be happy to hear that. It's hers."

Evans had told himself that he was not going to bother with the party at the museum. He was going to spend the evening searching for the treasure. The sooner it was found, the sooner Cleo would be safe. And the sooner he could leave.

But when his dinner companions at the hotel—Carter, Hill, Duncan, and DeClercq—asked for his company, he had come along to the museum with them. They were all anxious to see this preview exhibit; he only wanted to see Cleo. And she was the first thing he saw, standing by a column near the door, looking weary and distracted and utterly lovely—even if he preferred her in the simple, severe, practical garb he was used to seeing her wear. The sight of Cleo Fraser standing in the sun always sent a shiver of desire through him. She'd be wearing a plain brown walking skirt, her slender waist and high, round breasts outlined by a tailored white shirt, and a wide-brimmed hat would be shadowing the precise angles of her cheekbones, her jaw and the lovely width of her mouth. Wearing that plain outfit, she was the sexiest thing he'd ever seen. The way she looked in a split riding skirt and a pith helmet was devastating. Especially if she was carrying a rifle. There was something utterly scorching about a heavily armed Cleopatra Fraser. No matter what she did or wore, Cleo of the perfect posture and brisk, economical movements, Cleo the unconsciously graceful, was a glorious sight that left him more in awe than any view of the Pyramids.

I should have told her, he thought, regret boiling in him. *I should have just opened my mouth and told her.*

Except she wouldn't have believed it. Hell, a

good part of the time he was too much of a fool to believe it himself. He'd let anger, hurt, and pride get in the way early in their relationship, and it became habitual, almost comforting. It was easier to work at provoking her ire than at redeeming the sins of the past. It was a pity they had no future together. Fate was a bitch with an ironic sense of humor, and fate dictated that in order to save Cleo he must betray her. Again. The worst, damnably painful irony of all was that this final betrayal came when he was finally man enough to acknowledge the passion for her that had never died.

It was a good thing that they were in a crowd, he decided, even if they were on the fringes of it. He gestured toward the center of the hall, where Everett Fraser and Sir Edward stood at the head of the mummy case. Fraser was holding forth importantly while his audience stared at the shriveled, linen-wrapped figure inside the heavy glass. "The princess is attracting most of the attention, I see."

"She hasn't gotten out much in the last few millennia," Cleo answered. "She deserves a bit of fussing over. She *is* a princess, after all—or so I've decided to believe. We didn't find her with the grave goods, if you recall, but in a separate tomb nearby."

"Rather like you didn't find Alexander's

grave goods with him, but you did find them? That was the rumor I heard on Amorgis while I was recovering. But let's not talk about the treasure," he added as her expression went blank and her eyes turned hard. He put his hand over his heart. "I don't want to talk about your secret find. I'll be content to wait for the grand exhibit at the end of the conference to see what you really found."

"Father," she said. "What Father found."

"We don't have to lie between us, Cleo."

She opened her mouth, and he was certain she was going to say *Yes, we do*, but she closed her mouth and took a deep breath instead. When she did speak, it was to say, "Dr. DeClercq admires you a great deal."

"And you admire him. So now you think you have to admire me." He stepped closer to her. She backed up a step, and they ended with the pillar between them and the crowded center of the hall. "You don't have to admire me if you don't want to, Cleo. You really don't."

"I can't very well take back what I heard this morning, can I? I can't take back the whole day, though I wish I could."

"Should I apologize for kissing you?" he asked. "Would that help?"

"No."

"It wouldn't change what happened," he

agreed. "And I'm not sorry I did it. You ought to be kissed more often, Cleo."

"Why?"

Her genuine puzzlement made him smile. It was not a mocking smile, despite the thunderous frown she gave him. "What's the matter?" he asked her. "You seem too tired to even get a good argument going. Just how bad a day has it been?" He stepped back and ticked off points on his fingers. "No sleep. DeClercq. The rude reverend."

"You know about that?"

"More than you realize. Let's see, you're worried that the history department will somehow be blamed for the vandalism in the graveyard. I kissed you. What else went wrong with your day?"

"Something much worse than being kissed by you," she confided.

Fear shot through him for a moment as it occurred to him that she knew the Hoplites were after her. Then he had a moment's hope that the Hoplites had recovered their treasure and she was upset because it was missing. No, if the treasure was gone, she'd have accused him of the crime by now. A quick glance around the pillar assured Evans that none of the Hoplite contingent was nearby. Spiros and Apolodoru were with the rest of the guests.

The group was on the move, following Fraser the short distance from the center of the hall to the tall case holding the jewelry and other small treasures.

Evans turned his attention back to Cleo. "What's worse than kissing me?" he asked. "Did dear old Dad find out about our indiscretion in the graveyard?"

She put her hand across her delicious lips for a moment, hiding a smile, but he saw a faint bit of humor in her eyes. It faded too fast. "For a moment I thought he had," she admitted. "When he came storming into the house and demanded to see me in the library, I thought, *Oh, dear, it's the convent for me!*"

"Good thing you're not Catholic. What was his problem?"

"MacBeth."

"The play?"

"The king. The real one."

"MacBeth's real?"

"Yes. Apparently he was king of Scotland sometime in the eleventh century. Ruled from the Hebrides or the Orkneys or some other cold, remote islands up off the north coast."

"Really?"

"Yes. According to Sir Edward, MacBeth and his lady wife were great rulers, much maligned by the English in recent centuries.

They never murdered anyone they didn't absolutely have to."

"Fancy that."

"I don't. At all. I could not care less about MacBeth. And Father certainly has no interest in leading an expedition to find artifacts and evidence of MacBeth's kingship." She leaned back against the pillar and sighed tiredly. "But Dr. Apolodoru suggested to Sir Edward that he fill the museum with Scottish historical treasures, since, after all, the museum is in Scotland, Sir Edward was so taken with the notion that he wants Father to leave for the Hebrides or the Orkneys or wherever the bloody hell MacBeth lived as soon as absolutely possible."

"Oh, dear."

"So while finding out that you are a fine upstanding citizen is a disaster of monumental proportions, it pales in comparison to discovering that I am about to be exiled to a remote island in the North Sea, where I will conduct research I care nothing about on a period I know nothing about, where the sky will be constantly gray, where it will snow on Midsummer Day—" A tear spilled from her eye and rolled slowly down her cheek. Evans brushed it away with a gentle forefinger. She sniffled and he handed her a handkerchief from his coat pocket.

"And you will never see Egypt again," he finished for her. "Or Greece. And you will hate every moment of this exile."

She sniffed, but no more tears came. "Precisely."

From Apolodoru's point of view, this was a brilliant move. Evans might have thrown back his head and cackled in glee at the notion of Everett Fraser's being exiled to the Hebrides, except that for Cleo this was indeed a disaster. The Fraser family lived on the income from a bit of property, a small legacy from the great-grandfather who'd been an earl, and whatever salary Everett Fraser secured by procuring antiquities for Sir Edward Muir. What little they had was completely in Everett Fraser's control, and his daughters were dependent on him. Where he went, they went, especially Cleo. Oh, yes, most especially Cleo. Even if she would be loathe to admit it, Everett Fraser had known for years that he was nothing without his brilliant eldest daughter.

She crumbled the square of linen in her fingers. "What am I to do? Angel, what am I to do?"

Her desperation tore at him. So did the realization that this was the first time she'd ever asked anything of him. Everything in him cried out with the need to help her, to hold her, protect her. It clenched a fist around his heart and burned like a fever in his brain. Only one solution immediately presented itself, and he blurted it out before he could stop himself.

"Professor Hill likes you. You could do worse."

She looked at him strangely. "What are you talking about?"

He didn't know. The words were coming out, but he didn't feel in control of them. The impulse to protect Cleo had taken over and was running riot with his tongue. "Marriage," he said, firmer now, more assured. "Have you ever thought of marriage?"

She stared up at him in confusion. "For who?"

"For you, of course."

"I don't have time for marriage! And who would want to marry me?"

"*I* wanted to marry you."

"When?"

Before he could answer, Lady Alison, on the other side of the room, shouted, "That's my necklace!"

"What is it?"
"What's going on?"
"Do you see that?"
"Modern work," someone commented. "Seventeenth century at the latest. What was it doing in with proper antiquities?"

"It's the missing necklace. The one that was stolen a few days ago," Mrs. Douglas explained.

"Well!" Aunt Jenny's voice rose above the hubbub. "I think this has gone too far!"

"Indeed," Cleo heard Dr. Apolodoru answer, quite coldly. "It most certainly has."

"Please let me through." Why Cleo was rushing toward the center of trouble, she really couldn't say. Possibly because it was easier than confronting the naked pain in Angel Evans's eyes.

Finally getting close to the case, she caught a glimpse of Annie, pale with mortification and big-eyed with surprise. Spiros was comfortingly holding her left hand, Dr. Carter her right. Annie would be all right.

Father, however, looked like he was about to faint. "I—" he said. "I—"

Lady Alison was brandishing her cane under his nose while holding up a sapphire-and-diamond necklace in her other hand. Sir Edward stood behind her, next to the open glass door of the relic case. From this tableau and the comments she'd already heard, Cleo surmised that the missing necklace had been found on display among the Egyptian artifacts.

"I'd very much like to know how Lady Alison's valuable family jewelry got in among this rubbish!" Sir Edward demanded.

"R-r-r-rubbish!" Father sputtered.

Cleo heard echoes of her father's indignation from the historians gathered in the crowd. "The necklace is a modern trinket," someone called out. "Not at all comparable to the priceless relics in that case!"

"How'd it get there?" Sir Edward demanded.

"Another student prank," Dean Smith declared darkly.

"Perhaps someone left a reminder that one culture's trinkets are another's priceless family jewels?" Dr. Apolodoru suggested wryly.

The already hostile muttering in the crowd grew even louder after this.

"Well!" Lady Alison declared, pounding her cane hard on the floor.

Just what I need, Cleo thought with growing resentment. *Another crisis.* "Oh, Lord, I'm tired." She pressed a palm to her aching forehead.

Then she took a deep breath, smiled confidently, straightened her spine, and put herself into the fray. "Congratulations," she said, stepping up to Lady Alison. "It seems your missing necklace has been recovered." She put a calming hand on her father's shoulder and turned her smile on Sir Edward. "We can all be thankful that whatever young fool pulled this prank meant no true harm. The necklace has been restored to its true owner, and no damage has been done to the valuable property that you worked so hard to bring to your country." She raked a calm gaze over the gathered academics and dignitaries. "It would also seem that there is something of a security problem with the museum. Nothing serious, but I'm sure my father would like some privacy now to make a necessary investigation of the rest of the building."

"Well." Lady Alison tossed her head. She met Cleo's imperious glance, well aware that she and everyone else had just been dismissed. "Blood will tell," she murmured low, so that only Cleo heard her. "*Noblesse oblige* comes naturally for an earl's great-granddaughter."

"Actually, it comes from giving orders to camel drivers," Cleo whispered back. "You have to learn to be more arrogant and stubborn than a camel if you want to get anything done."

The old lady laughed, and her reaction broke the tension that had grown in the room. Lady Alison addressed the crowd. "I say let's all return to the Dower House. The lass is right; I've got my own back. I think that calls for a celebration." She held out her arms and gestured toward the wide main door. "Come along. Port and sherry and currant cakes are waiting for everyone at my home."

Lady Alison was not to be denied. They went, every last man and woman of them, faculty, local citizens, and visiting professors filing out into the night. Cleo longed to follow them to the door, slam it shut, and lock it behind them. Instead she waited in quiet dignity at her father's side, her hand on his arm, until they were alone. Her head was splitting, her aching heart was in even worse condition, her soul was torn to shreds, and she was ready to drop from exhaustion and reaction, but she refused to let any of that matter at present.

"Why don't you go home?" she suggested to her father. "Pia and Saida and the others miss your company."

"But, security measures . . ."

"It's all right. I'll have a look around. There's really nothing much we can do tonight."

"Evans." Everett Fraser's eyes blazed with hatred. "I'll wager it was Evans who staged this little scene."

Cleo pinched the bridge of her nose, but that did nothing to ease the pounding in her head. "Oh, do leave Angel out of this. Such childishness is not his style."

"Don't you defend him to me, young woman. Not after what he did to you."

She had to bite her tongue to do it, but she managed to hold back the hot retort that danced into her mind. She was not going to

Chapter 14

"**W**hat's that smell?" Cleo asked.

"It's tea," Angel replied.

"I'd rather have whisky."

"There's whisky in the tea."

"Oh."

Evans stood back and watched with the tin mug cradled in his hands while Cleo, eyes still closed, lifted her head an inch or so off the thin pillow. She gave up after a moment's effort and settled back with a heavy sigh.

He thought that she'd gone unconscious again, but after a minute or so, she asked, "Where am I?"

"Your father's room, I think."

"My father's—"

"Never mind. Rest."

"I'm dreaming that you're here, aren't I?"

"Yes."

"Where am I really?"

He'd found this small space tucked off a large workroom when he'd searched the museum the night before. It contained a daybed, a camp stove, some supplies, a teakettle, and a few dishes. He surmised it was Everett Fraser's home away from home. Though hardly a luxurious haven, it had been the logical place to bring Cleo when she collapsed.

"You fainted," he told her as her eyes slowly opened.

She stared up at the dark ceiling. He'd lit a small lamp as well as the stove. The room was warm, but there was very little light beyond the circle cast by the lamp. "I do not faint," she said.

Evans sat down beside her on the narrow bed and helped her sit up. The blanket he'd covered her with fell around her waist. He'd unfastened several buttons of her high-necked bodice to make her more comfortable; now he tried not to notice the generous amount of cleavage peeking above the lace edging of her white cotton chemise.

He held out the cup to her. "I made you some tea."

"I've been asleep," she said. Her fingers brushed his when she took the cup. Cleo's hand was cold, but the touch sent warmth through him. "Soundly asleep, if you've been bustling about while I . . . rested." She downed a long gulp of the warm liquid. After a brief coughing fit, she handed the cup back and said, "There is indeed whisky in this tea."

Even with all their clothing and the blanket between them, Angel was aware of the feel of her body pressed to his. He glanced inside the empty cup. "Good stuff, too," he added. "At least your father has taste in that."

"It was a gift from Sir Edward. I believe he owns a distillery."

"Busy man."

She nodded, and said, "That makes me dizzy."

"Then don't do it again."

"All right. You're sitting very close, Angel."

"It's a small bed."

Angel was a big man, it was a small room, and yet she knew that *not* having him close would be worse. As usual, he was doing a good job of confusing her, but it wasn't just his nearness that made her light-headed. She recognized where they were, knew that they should not be there, but felt no desire to flee the room's cozy confines. Despite the impropriety and her consternation at finding herself alone with Angel, his nearness was comforting. She couldn't bring herself to ask him to move, any more than she wanted to move herself. What she wanted to do was draw him down beside her and go to sleep, comforted by the closeness of his embrace. She had never gone to sleep in anyone's arms before, not even with Angel after the one time they'd made love. It might be nice to simply be held, to hold Angel in turn, to rest her head on his heart, breathe in his scent, and sleep.

"I have no idea how I got here," she told him. "None at all." She touched her hand to her forehead. "I have some vague memory of forming a plan to run off and become a governess—and then everything went black."

"A governess?"

"It seemed logical at the time. It's not as if I haven't considered running away before. This time I thought I'd run off to the moors and become a governess and the master would fall in love with me, but then it would turn out that I was heiress to a great fortune and I could go off and do anything I bloody well wanted without having to depend on any man at all. The master would be heartbroken, of course."

"Of course." Angel put the cup on the floor and took her hand. It was large, warm, strong, and very gentle. His touch comforted her, yet it didn't make her feel in the least bit safe. "Have you been reading *Jane Eyre* by any chance, Cleopatra?"

"Yes. Before I go to bed every night. Not that I've had a chance to go to bed recently."

"Fiction is not like real life, Cleopatra."

"I know. Most of it is far less exciting than the sort of life we're used to." And it made more sense, generally, and people got what they deserved, one way or another.

"Most people prefer a quiet life."

"I can't think why."

"Nor I."

He sat very still, gazing off into the small room's shadows. "Is that why you were crying? Because you have to give up your exciting life?"

"Was I crying?" She really didn't remember.

"You don't want to remember."

He knew her too well—for someone who really didn't know her at all. Of course, the same could be said for her knowledge of him, couldn't it? So close—especially now, as they shared the width of the small bed—yet so far from each other. She could reach out and touch his face, stroke her fingertips along the square line of his jaw, and feel the rough texture of masculine skin in need of a shave beneath her fingers. But she wouldn't. What good would it do her to touch his body when his spirit and heart were unknown territory to her? Once she had thought flesh was enough. It had been a hard lesson, learning what a mistake that was.

"You were crying. I saw you." He slowly turned his head to look at her. "You were crying because of me."

Evans did not want to look Cleo in the eye as he said this, but she deserved that much from him. She deserved a great deal *more* from him, after all he'd done to ruin her life. He'd stood deep in the shadows after everyone else had gone, and it had cracked his heart open when Cleo, his strong, capable, resilient Cleopatra, sank to her knees in a pool of pastel silk and pressed her face into her hands.

He hadn't stayed behind to spy on her but to protect her, fearing the Hoplites would break in to cause even more mischief after leaving the necklace as a warning. Then her father threw what Evans had done to her in her face and left her to sob out her shame alone. How was he to protect her from the crime he'd committed against her? She'd fainted dead away and he'd rushed to help, and now here they were, and it was time for him to face up to everything. Trying to save her from the Hoplites was not enough.

"An apology, I think, dearest Cleopatra, is in order."

Cleo saw Angel's muscles tense and the

almost fathomless pain in his dark, dark eyes. She could not help but reach out to brush the raven wing fall of hair off his forehead. "Apologize? Surely I'm the one who needs to apologize for having misjudged you for so many years."

She'd been stroking her fingers across his brow without knowing it. He grasped her wrist and pushed it away, then stood to face her. "Don't pretend you don't know what I mean. It's time we stopped avoiding the issue, Cleo."

Cleo crossed her arms. "Oh. That."

"Yes. That."

"There is nothing to discuss."

"It wasn't *nothing*. I saw tonight how your father uses it against you."

"That's my fault. I shouldn't have told him. One should keep some things to oneself." She gave him a warning look. "Don't you agree?"

"Not anymore."

"It was a decade ago. I doubt you remember the occurrence all that well. You've had so many others since," she added bitterly.

Oh, dear—what deep well in her soul had *that* bubbled up from? Possibly the same place where a small flame of anger burned at his suggestion that she marry a stranger a few hours before? As if she would ever consider any man other than—

"Jealous, Cleopatra?"

"Don't flatter yourself."

His moment of teasing faded instantly. "I have nothing to be flattered about. I have wronged you."

"Frequently, but not that night."

"Why won't you let me take responsibility for having destroyed your life?"

"If you had, I would. But you didn't."

"You were an innocent virgin. I despoiled—"

"Must you be so melodramatic about it?"

"You're exhausted to the point of sleepwalking. You think you're too tired to argue, but we have to get this out in the open."

"I am perfectly wide awake." The merest mention of sleep made her want to yawn, but she fought the urge.

She was *not* going to allow him the advantage of looming over her. She swung her legs over the edge of the bed and got unsteadily to her feet. He was still far taller, but it was a size difference she was used to. Her lips lifted briefly in an ironic smile, recognizing that this was their usual confrontational position—and she took some comfort from the familiarity. She couldn't help but run her gaze over him, from the tips of his highly polished shoes up his long, strong legs, his broad chest, wide shoulders, and the sharply angled planes of his face. He was still and would always be the handsomest man in the world, even though the painful intensity of his expression made him look almost a stranger to her. It was far better for her to face him down when he was arrogant, cocky, and teasing.

"Your being solemn and serious is disconcerting, Angel. Please stop."

He held out a hand, stopping just short of touching her cheek, but close enough for her to feel the heat radiating from his palm. "I am so sorry, Cleo."

She took a deep breath and drew in his scent with it, a potently masculine mixture of whisky and rich spice. She wanted to step closer, to breathe in her fill of him. She saw that he was so tense that he was faintly trembling, and hated seeing him that way. She wanted to brush her lips across the downturned line of his wide mouth and coax a smile from him. But her pride was deeply stung by this sudden contrition, as well.

"I do not want your sorrow. And stop looking at me with such pity."

"I ruined your life, Cleo. How can I—"

"Oh, for God's sake!" She slapped his hand away. He backed up a step and she came angrily after him. She couldn't have stopped if she had tried. "It was one night! One. Ruined? Am I the only one who—"

"I took your innocence."

"I *gave* you my innocence." She stabbed a

sharp forefinger into his chest. "It cost me, but you *took* nothing. How can you be so bloody self-important? It was not robbery, you bloody fool, it was a gift! I never thought I'd see you again."

Angel's eyes were wide open in shock. "You were a child. I seduced you."

She gave an emphatic nod. "I'll grant those points."

"I pursued you like the selfish, lascivious animal I am. I took something I had no right to take from you. I shattered your innocence, ruined you for any decent—"

"We had sex, you mean." She put her hands on her hips. "Stop trying to sugarcoat the act. Speak like a man or get out of my sight."

"I truly did not realize you were a virgin. I'd seen you dancing and—" He gave a wild shake of his head. "That was long before I knew the customs of the country, before I understood that what Saida taught you is an art form practiced by the most respectable of women. I saw how you ran the camp, how you dealt as a mature woman taking care of everyone. I assumed—because I wanted to—that you were a woman who knew what she was doing and what she wanted."

"I did know what I wanted. No," she conceded after a moment. "I knew I wanted *some-*

240

thing, and I knew that what I wanted was bought with a high price. What *we* did was inappropriate; it should not have happened. But I knew that at the time."

She wrapped her hands around the lapels of his jacket and would have shaken him like a terrier if she could have, but she was a small woman and he was a very large man. Instead, she pulled him to her so that their faces were inches apart. When she spoke, distinctly pronouncing each word, she looked him unflinchingly in the eye.

"What I also knew was that it was *my* choice. That what I did, *I* did, of my own free will. I wanted you. I had you. It did not ruin my life. Changed it, yes. And I have lived with the consequences. I have not complained; I accept *my* responsibility. While I have many regrets for what happened afterward, I have never, ever, regretted coming into your tent, unfastening my clothes, lying down on your bed, and—"

"Stop!" Angel pushed her back and swung away from her. She stumbled and landed on the bed. His breath came in ragged gasps as he stood with his back to her, his hands balled into tight fists. "I remember what happened. I remember it every day of my life."

"Good Lord," she said, genuinely amazed. "Why?"

She did not recognize the wild, feral creature who turned back toward her. "Because I have never stopped wanting to do it again."

He moved forward with the speed of a desert jackal. She didn't recognize the look in his dark eyes as desire until he was on her, pressing her down beneath him on the narrow bed.

Chapter 15

Angel had held tight rein on his response to the images conjured by each of her blunt words, but he was not made of stone. Need set his imagination on fire, lashed hotly down his spine and into his groin. He'd locked away his lust for this woman for years, only to have her step up to its cage and mercilessly provoke the wild thing inside.

When the caged animal finally broke free, there was nowhere either of them could hide. He descended on her with the fierceness of a desert sandstorm.

A soaring rush of panic went through Cleo as Angel's mouth covered hers, hot, hard, and demanding. His weight bore her down, crushed her against the thin mattress. His touch was harsh, urgent, making her feel small, helpless, and fragile. He caressed her, her breasts, her throat, without subtlety or gentleness, branding heat into her flesh. He combed his fingers through her hair, drawing her head closer to his. Somewhere in the distance she heard the faint metallic ping of hairpins scattering and heavy strands of hair fell in wild disarray around her face. He surrounded her, covered her, heavy and unyielding, blocking out the light; his demanding kiss turning the very air, her skin, her blood, to fire. All she could do was close her eyes and ride the storm.

He wanted to taste her skin, every inch of it. He buried his face against her throat and breathed the sweet scent of her skin. A soft cloud of gold hair caressed his cheek. His lips brushed across her collarbone and down across the very top of the round swelling of her breasts. His hand cupped her breast, his thumb seeking the bud of her nipple beneath her bodice, chemise, and corset. It was a long time since he'd touched and tasted a woman, and none had drawn his desire like the one he held now. He'd dreamed of her. Dreamed of her dancing, dreamed of her beneath him. Imagined her mouth pleasuring him and her hands caressing.

She was his. There was no escape. No turning back.

Cleo had worked her hands from beneath

her and her small fists pummeled at his shoulders. His pleasure was piqued by her struggles, but there was no escaping this bed until he'd had his fill of her.

"Ten years of payback, sweetheart."

"Revenge?"

She put all the fury in the world into that one breathless word.

"Oh, yes." He nipped at her bare shoulder. "Talk dirty to me, sweetheart."

She bucked beneath him, the desperate movement only serving to heighten his desire. Her nails dug into the back of his neck, and he laughed. "Draw blood if you want. Do anything you want. I intend to."

He remembered the skilled sway of her hips, the jingling of the coins and bells decorating the belt worn low over the delicious curve of her hips, drawing attention to the secret, hidden place between her legs. Heaven would be her moving like that beneath him, with him buried deep inside. Heaven would be his tonight.

"Pelvis of a camel, indeed," he murmured, breathing the words against her half-bared breast.

He kissed her again, reveling in the softness of her lips. His tongue delved into sweet heat while his hands continued to explore, hunting for treasure. She writhed and arched and his leg slipped between hers. He pressed closer, letting her feel his excitement. She moaned against his mouth. Her tongue tip touched his and a sudden darting dance began, but she threw her head back and turned away, denying even this small declaration of desire.

"Dance for me," he rasped with his lips against her ear, and kissed the spot just below it.

She couldn't breathe, couldn't think. The man was driving her mad. Fear coiled inside her. Fear and heat. And fear of the heat. Fear of his strength; fear of the darkness in him, which threatened to overwhelm them both. Part of her wanted to beg for her freedom, for the whirlwind to stop. How do you beg a storm? How do you put passion back in a bottle? They'd done it once before, but—

"Angel—"

His kisses drifted down her throat, melting skin in their wake. "No angels here, sweetheart."

"I . . . hurt." The ache was always there, deep inside, but now it throbbed, grew, spread . . . She was weak, so weak. So lost and lonely and in need of the searing touch she'd always longed for. Sixteen or twenty-six, there was only Angel. *I—want*.

But not like this. Not overpowered, aching, controlled and helpless. Never. Never. *Never*.

"If there's going to be a fate worse than death here, it isn't going to be mine."

She took her hands off his shoulders and slammed her fists against the sides of his head. He howled. When he jerked his head back, she grabbed the thick fall of hair over his forehead and tugged with all her might.

"Ow!"

"Get off me," she ordered. "Get off me right now." She shoved against his chest with her free hand.

"Let go of my hair!"

"You're not going to rape me."

"I want you!" he shouted back.

He heard the petulance in his voice, and that, more than anything, brought him back to his senses. Desire still rushed through him, his balls ached, and he was hard as a rock—his conscience had jumped ship, and ethics and morals had splashed in right behind. He'd never been happier than to have them gone. Who needed them when he could have Cleo? Have her, take her, use her any way he wanted. Sweet, God, he still wanted to drive into her, to bury himself deep inside her body! But she'd gotten his attention, started him thinking, and he couldn't go through with it.

"Damn it, Cleo, I want you!"

"Am I supposed to be flattered?" she shouted in his ear. She rapped him on the head.

"You'd never forgive yourself if you took me this way."

"Stop trying to save me from me."

"Someone has to save us both, you damn fool. Now, get *off* me."

This time, he obeyed. He moved to sit on the end of the bed, his head buried in his hands.

Cleo's skin still sang with their shared body heat, but cold emptiness would take that warmth soon enough. She moved slowly, rising to her feet, all too aware of throbbing tenderness on her throat and chest, and of the swelling tenderness of her lips. The taste of his frantic kisses lingered, and his scent clung to her. She trembled with reaction, with desire.

I'm not a child anymore. I'm a woman.

Soon she would go into exile on a cold island in the North Sea. This time, she really would never see him again. She couldn't live on a girl's memory of one night of awkward lovemaking forever. The choice was hers—and her choice was to take a woman's memories of loving Angel Evans to sustain her.

Cleo licked her lips. "Help me," she said.

Angel slowly lifted his head. She was standing in the lamplight, her disheveled hair backlit and shining, framing her pale face and falling all the way to her waist. Her eyes were enormous. He expected to see hate and contempt in them, but her expression was unreadable. Why hadn't she bolted from the room yet, like a sensible woman?

"Help you?" he asked.

She reached for the buttons of her half-undone bodice. "Help me," she repeated.

He bolted to his feet as she unfastened a button. "What do you think you're doing?"

"Getting undressed."

"*What*?"

Her bodice was mostly undone by now, revealing the lacy white embroidered chemise beneath. His heart pounded hard against his chest at the hint of the high rounded breasts beneath the thin cotton garment. The tension in his groin tightened harder than ever. He fought down the urge to go to her.

"I thought you wanted to have sex," she said.

"Of course I want to have sex! I'm a man. But—"

Her fingers moved to the fastening of her heavy skirt. "Then you can help me take my clothes off. They're not my clothes, you see," she explained reasonably, though he noticed that her hands were shaking. "This is Annie's dress. One of her best. She'll kill me if anything happens to it."

"I see," he said, though he didn't.

"It's quite an operation for a woman to become naked," she said. There was a tremor in her voice, and her gaze was anywhere but on him now, but she went on with dogged practicality. "There's the skirt, the bodice, a half dozen petticoats and this silly bustle contraption, then the corset and the chemise and the drawers, stockings and garters and shoes, as well. You could dress an Egyptian village with all the layers I've got on." She held out her hands to him. "Come here, Angel, and make yourself useful."

He put his hands behind his back, the sight of her making him sweat. "Cleopatra, you're trying to seduce me."

"Yes." She smiled. "You've gotten to seduce me."

"I remember."

"It's about time I had a turn."

"Fair's fair," he agreed, his voice cracking on the words.

She slipped out of her bodice, folded it neatly, and laid it across the chair. "The corset's laced up the back." She turned around, and with her usual unself-conscious grace flipped her hair away from her back, revealing the graceful line of her spine and neck and slender waist. The gesture nearly drove him to his knees.

Cleo held her breath. It was far too late for her to reach for the knob and walk away from this man, who might or might not touch her at any moment. She wanted to stomp her foot and demand that he succumb to her charms, whatever those charms might be, but she waited. She'd made her choice; it was up to him to make his.

"Oh, God."

The hoarse words were whispered directly into her ear. She felt his presence now, and leaned back against the broad width of his chest. He let out a sigh and ran his hands slowly down the length of her bare arms, until his fingers twined with hers.

"Sweet, sweet, Cleo."

"There is nothing sweet about me. You know that for a fact."

"You've never kissed you." He wrapped his arms around her waist, cradling her close. "You're blushing. I can feel it."

She felt the smile in his voice as well.

A spot on her throat stung where he'd bitten her, but there was a hint of pleasure overlaying the small pain. The mark made her feel claimed, wanted. She wondered if he'd noticed doing it. He had been so wild then, and seemed so gentle now as he moved—with more skill than she liked—to help her off with her skirt and unlace her hated corset.

His hands lingered and explored as he slowly removed each piece. When she wore nothing more than chemise and drawers, she turned slowly in the circle of his arms and pressed herself close to rough wool, smooth linen, and hard muscle. She put her arms around him and rested her cheek above his heart. "Hold me," she said. "For a while."

"As long as you want," he whispered back, voice rough with desire. "I'm not going anywhere."

For a peaceful while she was silent, her eyes closed and the only noise in the world the murmur of his breath and heartbeat. It was warm in his embrace, and safe. "You'll go away," she said at last. She raised her head to look into his dark, hooded eyes. "But that's all right. You're here now."

"I'm here now."

"So am I. Kiss me, Angel."

He did, slowly and gently, for a long, long time, holding her as though she were a fragile piece of priceless alabaster. She reveled in this courteous building of desire. It was heaven to kiss him. He tasted so very good. Delicious. Sensation worked slowly through her, intensified languidly at every spot where their bodies met and melded together. Time melted, she melted, and for a heady moment it seemed he and she became one.

When she came back to herself, she smiled a teasing, wicked smile against his mouth. Then she began to dance, moving ever so slowly against him. Her knees flexed; her hips shifted in slow, sensual circles against his.

His head came slowly up, his hands moved to her waist, and a low, needy moan escaped his lips. "Good God, woman."

"You wanted me to dance for you."

His breathing was hard and sharp. "You're killing me."

"You like it." She could feel very well how much he liked what she was doing, as his erection pressed against her belly.

"Don't stop. Ever."

"No?" She eased off his jacket, undid his already loosened tie. Then, one by one, she undid his shirt buttons, pausing to delicately kiss the widening line of flesh as it was revealed. She traced a fingertip slowly down the vee of black hair that arrowed down his hard stomach. "You're not wearing an undershirt," she observed. "How very improper."

His breath caught. "Indeed."

Her breasts felt tender and heavy, and her stomach clenched, but there was no nervousness or hesitation in her body's responses. Her hands were sure and steady as she continued to undress him. She'd never truly explored his body before. Caution and pride were gone. Everything was burned out of her but pure desire. Passion was like gold: time wore down and tarnished everything else. But no matter how you shaped it, or whether you hid it away for centuries out of sight, gold remained gold.

Wanting him was a state of being.

Tonight it didn't have to hurt.

"Help me, Angel." *Make love to me. I'll call it sex tomorrow, but name it love tonight.* "I've never undone anyone's trousers before."

By the time he was naked, she had shed the last of her clothing. A cool draft sent a shiver of goose bumps over her bare skin, tightening her already hard nipples. She shivered until he looked at her, hot-eyed and greedy, and every other sensation was unimportant. They stared at each other in the faint gold glow of the small lamp. There was not a great deal of light in the room, but there was enough.

"God, you're beautiful."

"Lord, you're handsome."

He laughed and she smiled, and they came together once more. Her hands smoothed over the muscles of Angel's arms and shoulders. His hands glided over her skin, cupped her breasts and buttocks, then drew her closer. His mouth moved to cover the tip of her breast. Her hand closed around the thick base of his penis. He spun them around and they landed on the bed once more.

"Where we started," she murmured.

"Where we've never finished." He gave her a hungry kiss before he started a long, erotic exploration of her body.

He loved the roundness of Cleo's breasts, so perfect in his hands and covered by his mouth. Her skin smelled of some subtle iris-scented soap with a deep undertang of feminine musk. She tasted like a creamy pink pearl should taste: sleek, smooth, rich. He stroked and kissed his way over every inch of her. She had long, shapely legs for her height, a narrow waist, and supple hips.

Then she said, "Let me," and he rolled them. Cleo straddled him as he lay flat on his back, her knees on either side of him. He moaned with need as her sex pressed hotly against his stomach. He would have grabbed her by the waist and thrust up and into her, but she shifted position before he could move. She leaned forward, and his head strained upward to suckle her breasts while her fingers took a long, sweet time trailing fire across his chest and throat and belly. She kissed him then, her tongue as talented a dancer as the rest of her. He moaned low in his throat, and the sound turned into a demanding growl, and he shifted them again.

"I've always wondered about these," she said, and gently cupped his testicles.

As ripples of pleasure shot through his loins and up his spine, his fingers stroked between her legs, teasing her moist, soft folds and the sweetly swollen nub.

Cleo forgot everything but the delicious waves of sensation overwhelming her. She'd never known pleasure like this, yet her body yearned for deeper, more intense passion. Her hips lifted with the building hunger; her legs fell open before this gentle onslaught. "Please," she said.

"Yes," he answered, and loomed over her, thrusting deeply, smoothly, completely into her.

Thunder rolled through her and lightning consumed her, but she was part of the storm this time, equal to him in fervor. Her need was terrifying, exhilarating, devastating, wonderful.

As Angel's weight pressed Cleo down she strained upward, meeting each thrust as their bodies fitted perfectly together, skin gliding against skin in sweet friction. Her legs went around his waist and she clung there, muscles straining, urging him into her. The universe came down to the two of them becoming one, and the universe was a living beautiful swirling firestorm, and she was a spark thrown up into the wind. The searing storm caught her up, twisted her around, took her higher into the burning night, and all she wanted was more and more and more and—

"Angel!" she cried, and the spark that was her burst and blossomed and shattered and fell in a long-fading, glorious descent into the dark.

Chapter 16

"**C**leo?" Angel touched her cheek and found it wet, kissed it and tasted salt. He stretched out beside her, wedged between the cold wall and her warm naked skin. Her breasts rose and fell with her soft breathing, the pretty pink nipples still taut. He considered covering them with his hands, for warmth's sake of course, but was too sated and satisfied to make the effort just yet. Soon—but soon had to be now; it was getting late.

Too late for them, he thought, remembering why he was in Scotland. He was there to betray her, not make love to her, and a night of love-making had only made her even more precious to him, making the betrayal all the more necessary. She was going to hate him, and he could never hope to have this closeness with her

again. He sighed. *You pay the price you have to.*
He told himself the melancholy was part of the
afterglow of making love.

"Cleo?"

Eyes shut, she was smiling like a cat with the
cream jar, but her stillness began to worry him
all the same. He brushed damp hair from her
forehead, then gently kissed his sleeping
beauty. This brought a soft, purring sound
from deep in her throat, but she still didn't
move. "All right, I was good," he said. "You
were fantastic, but don't die or anything.
Please."

Cleo cracked an eye and regarded him
briefly, unwilling to return to the world just
yet. "I'm savoring."

"You'll be stiff in the morning, you know,
being almost a virgin, and all."

Cleo could have said several things on the
subject of her status as "almost" a virgin.
Instead she said, "I read somewhere that what
occurred is called the little death. Now I understand why." She opened her other eye. "Have I
been asleep for very long?"

"I don't know. I just got here myself. So to
speak."

"Oh." Her cheeks turned from pearly pale to
bright pink. "I understand. I think."

He yawned. "That wasn't from boredom,"
he assured her with a wide, wicked smile. He

briefly bent forward to kiss the spot between her breasts. "Thank you for this, Cleopatra."

He sounded sad, and for a woman who had been so blunt and wildly experimental a few minutes before, she felt suddenly awkward. "I trust you . . . enjoyed the experience?"

"You'll never know how much."

His words offered enough reassurance to keep her from asking for more. She would not be needy. At least she had enough self-respect not to show it. A confusing memory of a conversation they'd had a few hours ago stirred.

She'd said, *"I don't have time for marriage! And who would want to marry me?"*

He'd said, *"I wanted to marry you."*

"When?"

"When what?" he asked now.

She hadn't meant to speak aloud, and she didn't answer him. This was not the time to bring up the subject of marriage. Even to mention the word would imply there was a price on what had been given and taken freely in this room. Perhaps she would ask him another time, but certainly not now.

What she wanted to do was lie beside him like this forever. Well, lie beside him forever after they shifted to a more comfortable position on this small cot. She wanted to share companionship and warmth, to feel small and protected by his size and enveloping embrace.

She said, "I think we had better get dressed."

"Aunt Saida and her umbrella could be here at any moment," he agreed.

They helped each other to sit up and then to stand. "You're right about the stiffness," she conceded as she crossed to the chair for her clothes. He knew a great deal about women and she knew very little about men, except for what she'd learned from statues, poems from thousands of years ago, and the paintings on fragments of pottery. For such an overeducated woman she was a woefully ignorant one.

The first time she'd made love, she'd thought it was the ultimate experience. The second time had proved to be infinitely more satisfying. Clearly the experience became better and better with practice. She doubted there would be another chance to explore this conclusion, though, as she had long ago decided that Azrael David Evans was the only man she would share her body with. It was one of the prices for her long-ago sin with him, and—

Oh, dear.

Silent laughter suddenly took her, and even though her back was to him, Cleo covered her mouth.

He noticed anyway. "What's so funny, Cleopatra?"

Having finished with the first layer of her

undergarments, she slipped into her corset. "Come help with this, Angel."

He began tightening the lacings. "The air around you is humming with amusement, sweetheart. What did I do this time?"

"It's what we did. Again."

"It was funny?"

She laughed aloud. "You are always confident, cocky, and self-assured. And with good reason," she added, "blast your hide."

"Then you enjoyed it."

His relief stunned and touched her. "You know very well I did."

"Then why are you amused?"

She cleared her throat. "If you must know, I was struck by the irony of thanking God for a second chance at sin with you. I doubt Reverend McDyess would be amused."

"I doubt Reverend McDyess has ever been amused at anything in his life. What's next? The petticoats or the bustle?"

"Bustle."

They didn't say anything else while he acted as lady's maid for her. After she was fully dressed, she busied herself with straightening the bed and cleaning up the dishes he'd used for tea. By the time the evidence of their presence was erased but for whatever hairpins she hadn't been able to find, Angel was done dressing. When she would have put out the lamp and gone to the door, he put his hands on her waist and turned her to face him.

"There's something I need to know, Cleo."

She could not read the look on his face. He had taught her to play poker; she knew how good he was at games of bluff and chance. He gave away nothing of what he felt now—if he felt anything. She was tempted to ask if he wanted to know about the Alexandrian treasure, but gave him the benefit of the doubt that he would not try to coerce that knowledge from her by using his body to pleasure her.

"What would you like to know, Angel?"

"Earlier tonight, you said that my seducing—and abandoning—you was not the reason you had spent a decade furious with me."

She tilted her head, trying to remember. It had been a one-damn-thing-after-another sort of day. "Did I?"

His hand left her waist long enough for him to rub his jaw. "Implied, at least. I received the definite impression that everything I thought I knew about you—about us—was wrong."

Us. Despite their closeness in the last hours, there was still a decade of conflicts that had pulled them apart. What chance was there for the rift to completely heal? Perhaps with a little truth? A little trust? Perhaps a beginning could be made.

Cleo lifted his hands off her waist and took a step back. "It's true I never blamed you for that night in the delta. I never thought I'd see you again, and chose to make love to you before we were separated forever." She shrugged. "I was sixteen. It's a very melodramatic age." His lips lifted in the faintest of smiles. "I thought I had proof that you were an antiquities thief. After the times we were attacked, after Uncle Walter was murdered by grave robbers, believing with all my heart that the treasures of the past should be studied and displayed for public education and appreciation, knowing how brilliant you are and what contributions you could make to advancing the world's knowledge of the past—well, blast and damn you, I thought you were wasting your life!"

He stepped back, his neutral poker face quite gone. "You've been angry with me all these years because I wasn't living up to your ideal of what I should be?"

"Yes."

Angel rubbed his hands over his face. "I—I—"

"As it turns out, I was quite wrong about you. I have no basis for hating you."

He dropped his hands to his sides. He sounded utterly exhausted when he answered, "You have plenty of basis, sweetheart."

Cleo shared his exhaustion. "Let's go home."

She took him by the elbow and directed him to the door, blew out the lamp, and followed after him. After they crossed through the workroom, she led him down the hallway to the rear entrance of the museum. "After you," she said, opening the door and gesturing him through.

"You don't trust me, do you?" He put a hand over his heart. "Even after DeClerqc cleared my name. Even after we—"

"Do I look like a fool to you?"

Angel patted her shoulder. "That's my Cleopatra. You haven't any tangible proof you can trust me." She noted that he didn't give her any promises to provide any proof, either. "Let's go," he said, and preceded her from the building.

"I'll walk you home."

"You'll do no such thing."

What was she afraid of? That her father would see them? That thought infuriated Evans. Was the man's hold on her ever going to break? Or was she afraid of her reputation? Or afraid that such civilized behavior as walking across the campus would bring them closer together? Most women wouldn't fear that— but most women didn't have an adversarial relationship with their lovers.

Lover—he liked that word.

He'd also better not let himself get used to it. There were things out there in the night that

Cleo should fear, men who threatened her safety and her life. For a moment Evans considered confiding in her about the Hoplites, but he had sworn an oath not to reveal their existence. Besides, he wouldn't expect a sensible woman like Cleo to believe the wild truth of the matter.

He did say as they reached the rose garden behind the museum, "I don't think you should be out alone."

He wasn't surprised when she laughed softly. "It's a mild summer night on a university campus in Muirford, Scotland. Unless you're expecting a pack of jackals to attack or a camel stampede that I'm unaware of, I think I'm perfectly safe walking home alone."

Oh, sweetheart, if you only knew! "What about the vandals?"

"A tribe of barbarians that settled in Europe around 400 A.D., I believe."

"You know what I mean, Cleo."

"I'm sure the prankster is safe in bed after triumphantly leaving Lady Alison's necklace in the relic case."

"You can't be sure."

"Oh, I am quite sure."

Her tone was grim, making him wonder what she meant. She walked away from him with a firm, swift tread before he could ask her about it. "You could at least say good night," he called after her.

"Good night, Angel." Her voice floated back over her shoulder.

He stayed to watch her back, and saw two figures that had been lurking across the commons. They appeared out of the shadow of a building and began stalking Cleopatra, flanking her from two different angles.

A little peaceful walk across the commons, hey sweetheart? He moved swiftly to come between Cleo and the men following her. *No danger? Except the danger to your heart of making love to me. And we're both in danger there, aren't we?*

The threat from the Hoplites was a blessing, in a way. It freed Evans from having to think about anything but the peril of the moment. No time now to think about things done and said, lies and truths about each other that they'd once believed and still believed. So much that could and should have been—which could never be now because of the damned fanatics who guarded Alexander's tomb and the promises he'd had to make to protect her from them. *If you only knew, sweetheart . . .*

Which she wasn't going to.

Chances were that the Hoplites were armed. Evans was not carrying a gun—mainly because they were messy and loud, and the wounds they made were too easily fatal. He didn't want anyone to die if he could help it. But the men shadowing Cleo were very likely the hotheaded ones Apolodoru had warned him about.

Knives were not noisy or messy. He slipped the Bowie knife he always carried from the hidden pocket in his jacket, veered to the left, and came up behind the first of the two men.

"I'd rather be out riding."

Cleo glanced across the library. Aunt Saida was seated by the window with her daughter, Thena, quietly teaching the little girl how to embroider a sampler. The lamps were lit and there was a cozy fire in the grate. The wind howled outside, and sheets of water cascaded down the windowpane. The book-lined room was a peaceful haven this afternoon.

"It's raining," Cleo pointed out to her sister. "Hardly a good time to be out riding."

"I could be grooming Saladin, then."

"Better to spend time with your family than with your horse, don't you think?"

"No." Pia threw her pen down on the desk. "Why should I be studying Greek? What use is it? It's not as if we're ever going back there!"

Cleo refused to respond to Pia's adolescent tantrum. She wasn't going to let anything disturb her today. She was going to bask in the wonderful, singing afterglow from last night's lovemaking for as long as possible. She'd think about consequences when she must; today was for herself and a quiet time with her family. She'd spent the morning upstairs with Annie and Aunt Jenny, doing the final fitting for their ball gowns. Annie was giddy with the prospect of attending her first ball tonight, and Aunt Jenny kept making pleasant comments about how Greece was the cradle of civilization, after all, and how Continental men were so much more charming and sophisticated than Britons, don't you think? Even yesterday Cleo might have been amused at the influence falling in love exerted on a person's thoughts and ideas, but love *did* change everything. She was changed, or the decade-old change was fresh and newly polished, to be savored for at least a little while.

The morning had passed quickly and pleasantly, and neither aunt nor sister had paid any mind to Cleo's smiling dreamily and occasionally humming. She'd reserved the afternoon for Pia whether Pia wanted the company or not. Her world was full of many dilemmas, but she firmly put them all in the back of her mind. Cleopatra Fraser felt up to any challenge today. Even Pia.

"It is very important for you to learn Greek," she answered the rebel calmly. "Your spelling is atrocious, for example. Tell me, what is the proper archaic spelling for *crown*?"

Pia considered this question for a few moments. Then she gave up the battle, picked up the pen, and turned her gaze to the language book before her.

Cleo left her to it and moved to stand by Saida. She checked her pocket watch. "We'll have to go upstairs and start dressing for the ball soon."

Saida continued stitching. "Yes."

Cleo moved a basket of embroidery thread from the window seat and sat down. "What dress are you wearing? The green satin?"

"Black."

"You've been a widow for a decade, now. You don't have to wear black anymore if you don't want to."

"I want to. Sometimes it is good to have the reminder that I am a widow."

"Then why'd you have the green dress made?"

"I don't know. A foolish impulse," Aunt Saida added with a sigh.

It occurred to Cleo suddenly that Aunt Saida had been acting oddly even before the family moved to Scotland. There was something different about her. Something . . .

"Who is he?"

Saida finally looked up from her embroidery stand. Her dark eyes snapped with an emotion that was not quite anger but not quite amusement. "You are not as clever as you think you are, niece."

Cleo smiled. "Oh, yes I am. But I am a bit slow, sometimes, where matters of the heart are concerned."

"You were not so slow two nights ago."

Cleo had no regrets about her behavior—except that she hadn't spent the entire last decade kissing Angel Evans. "We're discussing you right now," she informed her aunt. She tapped a forefinger on her chin as she thoughtfully observed the small Egyptian woman. "Now, who—"

"Sir Edward," Thena piped up from beside her mother.

Across the room, Pia's head came up. Cleo stared at her young cousin.

Aunt Saida rose to her feet and said, "I think it's time to dress for the ball now."

In the same instant, the library door opened and Everett Fraser entered. He looked around, his expression angry, and made a sweeping gesture. "Good day." He held the door open and gestured once more. "I have very little time and I need to speak with Cleo alone."

Pia was happy to slam her lesson book shut and hurry out without even greeting her father. Saida took Thena by the hand. "We were leaving anyway, Everett," she said, and followed Pia out.

"Wear the green," Cleo called after Saida as her father shut the door.

"The green what?" Father asked when they were alone. "Never mind." He came over to the window. "Sit down, child."

Cleo resumed her seat and looked up at her father, and her heart gave a panicked jolt at his thunderous expression. "What's wrong?" It was becoming habitual for her to think that he had discovered her assignations with Angel. She hated the thought of how he'd react, even though she told herself that she had every right to even a few snatched moments of happiness. It wasn't as if she held out any hope that anything permanent could be built on a foundation of furtive lust.

"It's Sir Edward."

Cleo had not realized how tense she'd become until she relaxed back in her chair. A smile played about her lips. "We were just beginning to discuss Sir Edward—"

"The man is driving me mad," Father stated. He began to pace back and forth between the desk and her chair by the window. "When he sought me out in Egypt and we formulated the plans for the history department and museum, there was a clear understanding that there would be a concentration on the work I was already doing with Alexander and the Hellinistic period."

"And your Egyptian finds," Cleo added. Father had never viewed the work in Egypt as more than a way to remain in the Middle East as he pursued anything to do with his beloved Alexander the Great.

"Yes, yes, Egypt."

"I'd like to continue exploring ruins in Egypt." She rarely spoke her own dreams aloud.

He ignored her. "But the point is," he continued, "that Sir Edward agreed to finance further
digs on Amorgis. Now he has reneged on that
agreement. I've been puzzling since yesterday
on how to get him to change his mind about
this expedition to the Hebrides in search of
MacBeth." He gave her a canny look. "I *know*
you have no interest in that."

She'd put her fear of exile in the north of
Scotland from her mind since last night, but
now it returned with a stomach-churning rush.
Father was quite correct; she did not want to go
to the north of Scotland. Angel Evans would
not be there. How could she live in a place that
offered no chance of seeing him, even from a
distance? She knew the answer to that desperate question, but had no idea what she could
do about it.

"Surely the reaction from the scientific world
when you reveal the treasures will be enough
to turn his attention back to Amorgis," Cleo
offered. "What will be on display will rival
anything found by Schliemann at Troy. Amorgis will become the center of the scientific
world. Sir Edward will *have* to send you back.
You are the one who is the expert in the search
for Alexander's tomb." Cleo sincerely hoped
that what she said would prove correct. "Sir
Edward's pride—"

"That's it!" Her father grabbed her hands

and pulled her to her feet. "My dear, you are a golden-tongued beauty!"

Cleo looked at him suspiciously, afraid of the desperation she saw in his eyes. The last thing she'd ever expected from him was a compliment on her looks. "It is getting late," she said. "It's time I got dressed for the ball."

Her father stepped back and looked her over in a way that started her blushing. "A definite beauty. I forget that about you sometimes."

She gave a tight little nod. "Thank you, I think."

"You don't believe me, but it's true. You think too much, and you have too many pretensions to scholarship."

"Pretensions?" She heard the dangerous edge in her voice, even if her father didn't. Cleo deliberately made her tone mild as she said, "I do my best to help you when and where I can."

His wide grin told her that her comment was a mistake. He patted her cheek. "Clever girl. Always so clever. I'm sure I don't need to tell you what you must do."

Cleo clenched her jaw and her fists. She searched her father's face, looking for the mild, well-meaning, but absentminded historian she loved. What she saw was not that man. He was tall, and still handsome in a faded, fair way, but had a lean and hungry look about him. The craving that consumed him was raw in his eyes, making him totally unaware that he was hurting her. She'd always told herself that she loved him even when he was weak and petty, but she didn't love him at this moment.

"I see," she said. "So we are about to openly have the conversation I have been avoiding for the last several months." She took a deep breath. "I've done a very good job of telling myself that when you told me to be nice to Sir Edward, you were not implying that I seduce him. I hoped you did not mean for me to use sexual tactics to persuade him to give you a fortune and a free hand to pursue the hunt for Alexander."

Everett Fraser's fair complexion grew redder and redder under his tan as she spoke. He replied, "Well, you aren't the marrying sort. So, I thought—"

"That I would be willing to be a man's mistress for the sake of Alexander?"

A thought took her by devastating surprise. *I could be* Angel's *mistress.* Then she recalled Angel's words, which had not been far from the surface of her mind all day: *I wanted to marry you.* "Father." She was not sure she wanted to know the answer, but she had to ask. "Did Azrael Evans ask you for permission to—"

"You're too good for him!" Everett Fraser cut her off. "You were too young when he asked. And he only asked out of guilt for what he did to you. I didn't know he'd dishonored you when he came asking for permission, but I would have refused even if I'd known."

Guilt? Perhaps it *had* only been done out of guilt, but at least Angel had asked. It pleased her to know that he'd thought that much of her. She wondered why he had gone away without bothering to say good-bye. Perhaps Father could answer that as well, but she didn't want her father's explanations. She wasn't sixteen anymore. Everything that needed to be said would be said between the two adults involved.

"Whatever gave you the foolish notion that I'd be willing to go to bed with Sir Edward?"

She saw from the hunch of his shoulders that her blunt words disturbed him, but he blundered on, "Why not become Sir Edward's lover? You're already a whore."

She answered precisely, "I am not a whore. I am a fallen woman. There is a difference."

"You've been dishonored," was his answer. "Why not use it to your advantage?"

"Yours, you mean."

"Ours. You long to return to Greece as much as I do."

"Not exactly."

"I have great work waiting for me in the Greek isles. It is up to you to persuade Sir Edward to let me finish what I've started."

"Why is *everything* always up to me?"

Her father absorbed this with lowered brows and a puzzled expression. "Well . . . because . . . you're so very good at managing things."

"Managing." She chewed the word over for a bit. "Managing. Yes. That's an interesting euphemism, isn't it? The word encompasses raising Pia, trying to keep up a long-distance relationship with Annie, helping Saida with Walter Raschid and Thena, running a household that is constantly on the move in foreign countries, organizing your research expeditions, and running the encampments when we're in the field. As well as doing most of the fieldwork myself." She ticked her duties off on her fingers as she continued. "Then there is the family finances. When was the last time *you* signed your name to a letter to a bank manager, Father?"

"Well, I—"

"Plus the work for the Egyptian collection that you ignore while searching for Alexander. How many papers published in your name have I actually written?"

"You've been a great help with manuscript preparation."

"Yes. I am quite particular about what *I* write." He flushed a deep, choleric red, but didn't contradict her. For the first time, Cleo resented just how much she was responsible

281

for. "*I* found the Alexandrian papyrus. *I* found the key to translating it. I've kept rivals from getting their hands on the information." *Oh, Father, if only you knew the cat-and-mouse game Angel and I have played all these years.* "As far as I can tell, all you've done for a decade is catalog and reconstruct artifacts, cultivate Sir Edward's patronage, and blacken Azrael Evans's name to anyone who'll listen. No wonder I have no life."

"You're my eldest daughter—and a spinster. Caring for the family is life enough."

"No, it isn't!"

"And you've done a wonderful job. There, there, my dear," he added, as though the words were some sort of soothing balm on her open wounds. "It's seeing Evans again that has you distressed, isn't it?"

"Evans? What's Angel—"

"I don't blame you; the man is infuriating. But he'll be gone soon and everything will be back to normal."

"That's what I'm afraid of!"

He was either totally oblivious to her fury or doing an excellent job of pretending that she wasn't quivering with outrage. He moved across the library and held the door open for her. "We'll talk again about Sir Edward when you're feeling more yourself. Time you dressed for the ball, now. You'll feel much better once you're wearing a pretty frock."

I can't kill him. That would be patricide.

She kept her hands very close to her sides and preceded him out of the room.

Chapter 18

"What did you think you were doing?" Apolodoru whispered angrily, leaning close to Evans so that no one around the punchbowl overheard.

Evans kept his gaze on the door of the manor house's great hall. The huge room was awash in flower garlands and huge drapes and bows of plaid ribbon bunting. A small orchestra brought in from London played softly in one corner, while bagpipers and harpists awaited their turn at the other end of the hall. Buffet tables were set up once again below the stained-glass windows, and chandeliers and great brackets of candles set the room aglow. The huge room was packed to overflowing. Evans hadn't seen so many male knees since— well, he'd never seen so many men's knees before. He, Apolodoru, Divac, and a few others wore the standard black-and-white formal wear, and they stood out like sore thumbs. This was, after all, a Highland Ball. Any man who could lay claim to a tartan was dressed in full Scottish highland regalia, including kilt and sporran. The Scottish ladies wore their family plaids as well with their ball gowns, in scarves and shawls and ribbon decorations. It was all very different from anything he was used to. Very interesting. Almost enough to distract him from the angry Greek at his side, but not enough to divert his attention away from watching the wide doorway.

"What were you thinking?" Apolodoru insisted, tugging hard on Evans's arm.

Evans gently extracted his sleeve from the man's nervous grasp. "I thought I was protecting a lady."

"Your actions have caused nothing but more trouble. How am I to control the young, hot-headed ones when you, our ally, my own chosen one, cut up two of the ancient order?"

"Your boys were trying to hurt Cleo."

"They said they were only going to question her."

"They got in my way."

"They didn't realize you were also following her. They might have been some aid to you," Apolodoru added, almost apologetic. "But they were not acting on my orders. I trust you. They don't. Now that you've cut up two of them—"

Evans turned a narrow-eyed glare on Apolodoru. "Two of them? There's more than two Hoplite renegades running around town?" The older man gave a grave nod. Evans barely restrained himself from grabbing Apolodoru by the front of his formal coat. "How many loose cannons are out there?"

"I cannot tell you."

"I'm on your side, Apolodoru."

"The injured men would not agree."

"They were threatening Cleo."

"Miss Fraser may have knowledge we require."

"She's a defenseless woman," Evans answered. "Comparatively. Why don't you pick on her father?"

"Because you assured us that the woman is more of a threat to us."

Damn. Why hadn't he been more careful in what he told the Hoplite leader? Had he been boasting about Cleo's brilliance? Or had his loose words slipped out during one of his fits of frustrated longing for the woman? That's what all his annoyance and teasing and pestering of her always boiled down to—wanting her. And that wanting was even stronger after their lovemaking last night.

"I'll get your treasure back."

"Tonight," Apolodoru insisted.

Evans looked around them. A dozen people noticed him and smiled and nodded his way. "We're kind of busy tonight."

"There is danger in the air," Apolodoru warned. "And very little time. The reckless ones are planning something. Spiros will not join them, but I cannot promise to stop the rest."

"More vandalism?" Fear slashed through Evans at the other man's closed, hostile expression. "Are they planning to harm Cleo? What are they up to?" He wanted to run out and find the men who lurked in the shadows this instant. "I came here to solve your problems, Apolodoru. We had a deal."

"You still have an agreement with me, Evans, but the others . . ." He shook his head. "Bring us the treasure tonight, or the young woman and her father will die. And they may not be the only ones. The Hoplites are prepared to do whatever they must to protect our sacred trust. I cannot give you any more time."

"I'll go to the authorities," Evans threatened.

"You took a vow. You are one of us." Apolodoru put a hand on Evans's shoulder. "There are papers that will be discovered linking you to whatever violence may occur. You, my friend, would take any blame. You would be proved to be the leader of a gang of thieves who raided this poor, defenseless village."

Evans didn't laugh in the man's face; he knew it would be foolish to give any sign that this blackmail meant nothing to him. If anything happened to Cleo, what did he have to live for anyway? He gave Apolodoru a tight nod. "Tonight," he agreed. "You'll have your damn treasure back tonight."

What was he going to have to do to fulfill that promise? He had a good idea: lose the one thing he treasured, of course. Until he'd found her in Scotland, a sensuous woman finally ready to love and be loved, he had not truly realized how precious she was to him. In their usual setting she'd been a part of the landscape, as important as air, but the scintillating give-and-take of tension between them had seemed as common as the sight of the Pyramids in the desert beyond Cairo—and as eternal. Last night had changed everything. Tonight would end it.

Last night had been pure, spontaneous passion. Tonight he must practice seduction, deception, tell lies and make promises he couldn't keep to wrest the necessary information from her. This would be the greatest, grandest betrayal of Cleo of all, totally unforgivable. He would break her heart, and his, and he would do it because he must.

"A grand and glorious night, is it not?"

A hand clapped him on the shoulder, and he turned a bleak look on the smiling Sir Edward. "Grand, indeed," he agreed, with the taste of gall on his tongue.

Like most of the men, Sir Edward was dressed in full highland rig, wearing a dark blue, military-cut jacket over his kilt, a white shirt with a lace jabot at the collar, and a huge cairngorm brooch anchoring the plaid draped over his shoulder. The laird of Muirford looked every inch the wild highland chieftain this evening. He was accompanied by a group of cheerful young men dressed in kilts of the same tartan plaid. "Kevin, Joseph, Wally, Terrell, and Anthony. They're to be some of the first university students," he introduced the group proudly. "My clansmen, one and all."

Evans shook hands with each of the hearty, bonnie lads, happy to have a diversion from his conversation with Apolodoru. The young Scots were enthusiastic in praise of their history and their art, though they conceded that the Welsh were fine singers and Wales could lay claim to Merlin, even if King Arthur really was a Scot the medieval poets mistook for a Welshman. Apolodoru listened to all this with great interest, as though it had never occurred to him that anyone but the Greeks might have a history worth defending.

"My ancestors came from Wales originally, but I'm an American," Evans said after a while.

"Many of our ancestors were sent to North America," one of the lads replied. Evans had trouble telling them apart. "During the Clearances."

"The what?" Apolodoru asked.

"The lairds and landlords were corrupted by the English," one of the other Muir lads answered. "It was more profitable to run sheep on the land than to let their clansmen farm. So—"

"They packed their own folk off to America or Australia, or anywhere that wasn't Scotland," another bitter Highlander explained.

"It's only now that some of those wrongs are being righted," Sir Edward chimed in. "We Scots are finally coming into our own."

"We Greeks suffered greatly under the yoke of the Ottoman Empire," Apolodoru said. "Our people were oppressed, our treasures scattered."

"The English stole away the Stone of Scone," a Muir said. "The sacred throne of the kings of Scotland was robbed from us hundreds of years ago." He sounded as though the insult to the Scots nation was as fresh as yesterday. "We'll have it back someday." He looked around. "Will we not, lads?"

There was a hearty chorus of agreement.

Someone signaled a servant and soon they were all holding silver cups of punch. Sir Edward called for attention, and everyone nearby paused to lift a cup. "To treasures returned," one of the Muir boys announced.

"Hear, hear," Apolodoru said heartily, seconding this sentiment with a dark look at Evans.

Evans drained his cup and would have moved away from the group, but Sir Edward looked at him and said, "Think she'll be here soon? The Frasers, I mean." Sir Edward's attention was on the door, so he didn't see the look of pure jealousy Evans turned on him. Sir Edward cleared his throat. "Handsome woman," he went on.

"Beautiful," Evans corrected before he could stop himself. The possessive streak that had come out in the last few days disturbed him, but he didn't try to push down this primal reaction. It had always been part of him, though no rival had ever appeared to challenge his claim to Cleo before. It was a claim he'd never acted upon, it was one she didn't even know about, but she was his all the same. Except that he was going to seduce and abandon her a second time tonight, and there'd be no chance of their ever being together no matter how possessive of her he was. He was such a fool.

"Of course you've known her for years," Muir said, "while I've only met the lady a few times. She's very shy and retiring, but kind. Very kind. Makes a fine cup of tea. A wonderful homemaker. I feel . . . comfortable around her."

Shy? Retiring? And how could any man feel comfortable around Cleo? Energized, yes. Stimulated. Completely enraptured. Frequently furious. But comfortable? "Is there a side to the lady I don't know, Sir Edward?" Though he'd witnessed how attentive Cleo was around her father's patron, how deferential and accommodating. It was disgusting.

"Mrs. Wallace is quite comforting," Sir Edward responded. "And a fine mother to Thena and Walter Raschid. I think perhaps she's been widowed too long. I do hope Professor Fraser persuaded his sister-in-law to attend the festivities tonight. She's the widow of Fraser's late wife's brother, you know."

"Yes. I vaguely knew Walter Wallace before he was killed." He was delighted to hear that Muir's attention was not on Cleo. "She *is* a kind, charming woman." *And has a fine aim with a parasol*, he added to himself.

"Sad story. She couldn't return to her own family because she'd married a foreigner."

"I believe it was because she converted to Christianity, and she comes from a family of Islamic scholars."

"A good, upstanding Christian woman. That's another thing I like about her. We've discussed the Bible—" Sir Edward's eyes lit as he added, "They're here."

Evans spun to face the entrance. He and Sir Edward were not the only ones whose attention focused on the doorway. In fact, it seemed as if the whole room had been waiting for some grand entrance—and the whole room was not disappointed. The Frasers had arrived.

Everett Fraser stood in the center of the wide, arched doorway to the great hall with Saida Wallace, wearing a green gown, on his right arm. His sister Jenny, dressed in dove gray, was on his left. Beside her stood Annie Fraser in a pastel frock with fresh flowers twined in her pale hair. The lovely girl would have been the center of attention but for one thing: Cleo.

She stood slightly apart and ahead of the others, her head high, crowned with elaborately arranged gold hair. Even standing still she was the most graceful woman Evans had ever seen. She was dressed from head to toe in scarlet but for white gloves and a plaid ribbon of green, blue, red, and white Fraser tartan fastened high on her long throat. Even the beaded reticule she carried was a matching shade of vivid red. It was not just a passionately red dress, it was—

"Oh, my God," one of the Muir lads whispered hoarsely.

—the way she wore it.

Evans wasn't imagining that the temperature in the room went up significantly as the male population reacted to Cleo Fraser's entrance. And it wasn't just the men. There were looks of disapproval and outright jealousy on the faces of many of the women present. When he saw the way the tight-fitting, low-cut, sleeveless bodice revealed most of her shoulders and rounded breasts, and how the sweep of the heavy skirt molded and enhanced her already flawless figure, Evans understood why she'd taken the trouble to get permission to wear this frock.

"Designed for an opera singer, I hear," a woman nearby whispered to another. "Delivered by mistake for the younger girl."

"Miss Fraser *volunteered* to wear *that* in her sister's place?" a shocked voice spoke behind a fan. "Brave of her, I must say."

"I wouldn't have had the courage."

"Nor the figure, Fiona," someone else said, and was answered by soft laughter.

"Clever girl, to head off a scandal beforehand," he murmured as Cleo let the pause go on just long enough, then moved into the hall ahead of her family with her usual incredible grace.

A stampede of men nearly tripped over each other in the rush to be the first to ask for a dance, offer to fetch her punch, exchange a greeting, or simply be near her. Evans held back, enjoying her surprise at this masculine reaction to her blatantly displayed feminine charms. There was the faintest hint of color at the base of her long throat and across her elegant cheekbones. He knew he was not the only man there with the urge to delicately kiss each tender spot. The dress made her look sophisticated, worldly, and available, but her expression was charmingly vulnerable and unsure. The combination was irresistible. She looked like a rare scarlet rose suddenly surrounded by honeybees in kilts. He smiled at the analogy until he recalled that flowers were pollinated by honeybees. And if anybody around her was going to do any pollinating with Cleo Fraser, it was him.

Well, no, that wasn't exactly what he meant . . .

"Indeed!" he heard Reverend McDyess huff. "So this is what the world is coming to!"

"Aye. Isn't it grand?" Sir Edward answered him.

Then the laird of Muirford went off to kiss the hand of an exotic Egyptian widow named Wallace. Meanwhile, Apolodoru had gone up to Aunt Jenny. Everett Fraser spared one blistering look at Evans, then joined a conversation with Divac, Mitchell and some others. Carter and Spiros concentrated their attentions on the gentler charms of Annie Fraser. Other conversations resumed. The band tuned up, and a waltz was announced as the next dance.

It was time to make his move. Evans stepped into the crowd around Cleo, elbowing Hill aside. He wondered what she would say when she saw him, what she would do. Would her expression soften with the memory of their lovemaking last night? Would her pulse quicken, her body sing with desire? Would they share a secret smile, a subtle touch?

"There you are," she said when her gaze finally settled on him.

There was a spark and flash in her light brown eyes, hitting him like lightning. *Her eyes are brandy*, he thought. They held the same color and richness, and looking into them went right to his head. He wanted to warm her with his hands the way one cupped a snifter of brandy. He wanted to drink her in. "You make me drunk," he whispered, surrounded by the other men around them who still vied for her attention.

Had she the power, Cleo would have swept the room clear of everyone but herself and Evans. She'd held her breath when she first walked in, afraid to look around in case he

wasn't there. Aunt Jenny had fussed about
what she wore the whole way to the ball, while
her father, for once noticing her mood, kept
trying to draw her into inane conversation.
Both Saida and Annie had wanted her opinion
on how they looked. She'd ignored them all
and walked away from the demands they put
on her when they entered the manor house.

All she wanted was Angel. All she'd ever
wanted was Angel.

All she'd been able to think about on the
short carriage ride up to the manor house was
what she would say to Angel. But there was
nothing but a blank spot in her mind, only the
glowing core of desire that burned like the
desert sun. Outside the carriage the rain had
stopped and the evening was clear, the stars
overhead bright and lovely, but for the occasional scud of a cloud across the waning
moon. It was a beautiful night for a ball, but
her only reason for walking into the party was
because it was where Azrael Evans was to be
found.

When she saw him at last, her breathing
stopped. In a room full of fine, bonnie Scots-
men, she saw Azrael Evans and her mind filled
with the dark, sleek, and predatory image of
Horus the Hawk. This impression cleared
quickly enough, but Angel remained, a tall,
black-haired man with intense dark eyes, a

confident, scoundrel's air, and a sinful mouth. He was also graced with a brilliant tailor whose work had done a fine job of setting off Angel's wide shoulders and chest, narrow waist, and strong, long legs. He was impeccable, perfect. There wasn't a man in the room, or in the world, to match him in looks and style. She doubted there was a woman at the ball who could resist such temptation.

Not that she was going to give them the chance.

She smiled faintly. She had been jealous of Angel before. She'd written off her reaction to rumors that circulated around the small European community in Cairo as disgust at his wasting his life. The truth was, she admitted, she'd been a green-eyed monster whether she'd known it or not.

Then all of a sudden she was surrounded by people, smiling, laughing, complimenting her, kissing her hand and offering to fetch her punch, a plate, the stars. That was Professor Hill, being facetious. She didn't want any of them near her. It felt as if she might have to claw her way through a pile of people to get to the one man in the room who meant anything to her. Then Angel sauntered over to the rear of the crowd at last, and loomed over the lot of them, tall man that he was, and she looked up at him and said something inane.

"I'm here," he answered. "You're fashionably late."

Music began to play on the other side of the room, and Cleo became aware that Professor Hill was holding out his hand. He gave Angel a triumphant glance before he said, "Remember that I asked for you to put me first on your dance card at the reception the other night, Miss Fraser?"

She vaguely remembered a conversation about the ball. "I've had lessons, but I've never waltzed with a man before," she told Hill.

"Her dancing master was a eunuch," Angel said.

"Aunt Jenny isn't a—" Hill was still waiting for her to take his hand, and she wasn't going to embarrass Annie now. "Are you sure you want to take the risk of my tripping over you, Professor?"

"She has large feet for a woman of her size," Angel interjected from a safe spot behind, looking over the shoulders of two young men in highland dress. "But she is the finest dancer I've ever seen," he added when she flashed a look of outrage at him. His glittering black gaze was full of teasing humor. She thought there might be pride in his look as well, and was that a hint of jealousy?

Good Lord, him jealous of *her*? How delightful.

She let the historian from Edinburgh lead her out of the sea of young Highlanders surrounding her.

A few moments later she saw Angel on the dance floor with Davida MacLean held confidently in his arms. *He* had obviously danced the waltz before, and so had Davida, from the easy way she fitted into Angel's embrace and followed his lead in the heady, swirling steps. Cleo forgot all about making Angel jealous and concentrated on hating him and the Honorable Davida MacLean equally. The music did nothing but serve to emphasize Angel's masculine grace and power as he guided another woman around the small space set aside as a dance floor.

Nor was Cleo the only woman who couldn't take her eyes off him. She was too aware of all the others who took note of the handsome American, of how they exchanged looks and talked behind their fans as he went by. He would be considered quite a catch by some of the young women, she supposed, with a taste of bitterness in her mouth. What if he returned interest toward some proper woman from the academic community who could help advance his career? It had never occurred to her that anyone might set her cap for him, but why not? He was not only handsome, he was brilliant, with an exciting hint of mystery and adventure about him. Perhaps he might want a woman of good family and moral purity to make a home for him and have his babies.

Have his babies? *No* woman could have Angel Evans's children but her.

"Miss Fraser?"

"What?"

Hill's gulp was audible. "You're snarling."

Cleo became aware that her lips were drawn ferociously back in fury.

"What's wrong?" Hill asked. "Did I step on your foot?"

"No." Cleo did her best to smile at the man she was dancing with. "I always look like this when I waltz."

"You said you'd never waltzed before." When she turned a fierce look on him, Hill added, "Perhaps it would be safer if Dr. Evans and I changed partners."

"Is it that obvious?"

She realized how handsome Hill was as he smiled and told her, "To everyone who has met either of you in the last few days." He sighed. "Still, I'd heard of your feud when I was in Aleppo. Evans got drunk and told me some of your history. He was convinced you hated him."

"He was right." He thought about her when they were apart?

"But that didn't stop you from loving him. Very similar emotions, love and hate." He sighed again. "Still, when I met you I nursed some hopes."

Cleo's brows came down in puzzlement. "Of what?"

He shook his head. "You've never considered another man but him, have you?"

"Not since I was sixteen," she admitted, and looked over Hill's shoulder to get a glimpse of Angel and Davida MacLean. "But it looks like he has other ideas."

"If I'm lucky, he does." Hill's smile was bright and hopeful. "But I'm afraid it's only one dance."

"That's how it starts," she said, remembering the night before. "With a dance."

"We're dancing."

She smiled at him. "This isn't dancing."

"You're breaking my heart."

"Ladies named Cleopatra have a reputation for doing that."

He laughed. "Why don't you run off with me, Miss Fraser, in your lovely scarlet dress and your head full of more wit than any dozen men in this room?" The music stopped and they came to a stop in the center of the crowded dance floor, but Hill did not release his hold on her waist. "Would you like to come away with me?" he asked. "Or would you rather I fetch you some punch?"

"Neither," she answered, and stepped back.

She heard him say, "I was afraid you'd say that," as she turned in search of Angel.

She was just in time to see Lady Alison introduce him to a beautiful red-haired young woman wearing a sash of Leslie tartan over her white gown. Cleo marched up to his side before the introductions were finished. She put her hand on Angel's arm, and when he looked her way she said, "We're at a Highland Ball, Dr. Evans."

"I have noticed that, Miss Fraser."

"You are a historian, are you not?"

He rubbed his jaw, his expression both amused and puzzled. "I like to think I know some history."

She hated that they were constantly surrounded by people. Egypt contained far more sand, rock, and ruins than people, and holding conversations was so much easier when they were the only ones around. But she had things to say to Dr. A. David Evans and she was going to say them now, before her courage deserted her. "Do you know any highland history? The Fraser clan motto, perhaps?"

"I'm afraid I've never heard your family motto."

" 'I am ready.' "

Evans was warmed by the fire in Cleo's eyes and by the determined look on her face. He lived for that familiar light of battle in her eyes. "You are ready? For what?"

"That's the clan motto," Lady Alison explained.

Cleo was the most amazingly beautiful woman in the room—in the world. It wasn't just the vivid, daring dress and the way it showed off her high, round breasts and molded her slender waist. It was everything. He forgot that he had decided to seduce her for the sake of finding the Alexandrian treasure, and simply decided to seduce her. "And *I am ready* means . . . ?"

"Exactly what you think it does," she answered, and took him by the arm. "Let us have a look at Sir Edward's garden, and I'll explain more about the Fraser clan to you."

She gave a firm tug and he went without any protest, barely aware of walking through the crowded room and out the open French doors with her. He was aware only that they were arm in arm, that his heart was racing, and that his body was tight with need—and that was as much as he could handle until he found that they were alone together in the fragrant shadows of a thick rose arbor.

305

Then he pulled her to him and kissed her, and she fitted her body against his and matched his ardor in a way that scorched away the last vestiges of coherent thought for a very long time.

Chapter 19

❧

"**Y**ou might be ready, but I'm not sure I am." Evans held Cleo close and laughed breathlessly into her loosened hair. He didn't recall running his hand through it to tumble it down around her head, but there it was, soft as a satin pillow against his cheek and smelling of flowers and spice. He wasn't sure when they'd stopped kissing, or why. Where the devil were they? He breathed in the scent of roses and rain-damp earth. There was music in the distance, if one could call bagpipes musical. Oh, yes, Sir Edward's garden, the Highland Ball.

He had a mission: seduce Cleo to wrest the secret of the hidden treasure from her. Retrieve the treasure and get it and the Hoplites who threatened her out of the country. Break her heart, but leave her safely settled in her homeland away from any foreign danger. Break *both* their hearts.

Cleo moved subtly against him, sending a bolt of need through his loins. "You're ready," she whispered back, a deep, sensual huskiness in her voice.

"This isn't quite the time and—don't stop that!" He skimmed his hands up her back and bunched heavy handfuls of rich fabric in his hands as he cupped her lovely round bottom. He kissed her throat and she arched her back to give him access to all that marvelously exposed cleavage. "I love your dress," he said between kissing the tops of her breasts and the sweet valley in between. "I'd love you to take it off." She giggled, and the sound set off sparks all through him.

This is going too fast. An image of backing Cleo against the flimsy wall of the rose arbor, hiking up her skirts, and entering her in a hard, quick coupling flashed temptingly through his mind. But light spilled out across the lawn, and other couples strolled in the garden—he could hear voices not far away. They could be discovered at any moment, and their current position was compromising enough. He didn't want to ruin her reputation completely. He loved her too much to destroy her chance of leading a respectable life in this small university town. She deserved better from him than that. She deserved the wide world at her feet, damn it, to explore and conquer and—

"Let's run away," she said, her lips brushing against his ear.

Her words jarred him so much he took a step back. "What?" he heard himself ask over the wild pounding of his heart.

"You heard me." Cleo stepped back as well, her hands going to the round curves of her hips. Her breathing was as ragged as his. There was a wild glitter in her brandy-brown eyes.

This was indeed moving too fast. And wasn't *he* supposed to bring up the idea of running off together? "Let's talk about this."

"Oh, Lord, haven't we talked enough?" Her frustrated words were close to a shout.

"Shhh." He moved closer to her and put his hands on her bare shoulders. The feel of satiny bare flesh beneath his hands was damnably, delightfully, distracting. "We always have a lot to talk about," Evans answered her. "Why on earth would you want to run away with me?"

"Do you know that you once asked to marry me?" She blinked a couple of times at the unexpected tangent.

"I was there when it happened," he answered. "The bastard never told you, did he?"

"Why on earth did you want to marry me?"

She wanted to know; he wanted to tell her;

and time was running out. It wouldn't be long before the Hoplites did something vicious and violent. But there were things he wanted her to know before he severed their connection forever. "I seduced a virgin, remember?"

"I was there when it happened."

He smiled. "You could have the grace to blush, you little wanton."

"I'll take that as a compliment."

"As it was intended, for the woman you are today. But ten years ago you weren't a wanton; you were a tired, frantic girl who hadn't a clue what the desire that had been building between us for months would lead to. Making love to you was—unexpected—wonderful, but it was so very wrong. I wanted to make it right. So I did the honorable thing and asked your father for your hand."

"Ah." She nodded tightly. "So it was only because your conscience was bothering you."

"Yes." He took a deep breath and offered her the truth. "It wasn't because I loved you. Desired you, yes, but would desire have been enough? The wisest thing your fool father ever did was tell me no. You were a child and I was an arrogant fool." His hands slid down her arms and he twined his fingers with hers. Her hands were cold. "It would have been a miserable mistake. We wouldn't have had the chance to . . . become us." In all the years that followed he'd never stopped thinking about her or stopped wanting her, but the vibrant girl he desired then was not the magnificent woman he shared this moment with. "I blamed you for what happened, sometimes. I managed to twist my desire for you into something you did to me—while telling myself that you coolly dismissed me from your thoughts except as a rival for your father's damned treasure. The last thing I wanted was for you to forget me—"

"Why?"

"Because I couldn't forget you."

"And that was my fault?"

"Sometimes I told myself that. I'd also go on binges of guilt for having taken advantage of you."

"What nonsense."

"Then I'd blame you for making me feel guilty. Then you'd outsmart me, and the thrill of getting the better of you would consume me. Our rivalry's been the spice of my existence." He loathed knowing that it would be over soon. He looked into Cleo's eyes and said, "It's taken me years to work through it all and simply accept that the attraction between us will never go away. Of course, it would have helped if *you* had explained sooner than last night why you were always so annoyed with me."

She squeezed his hands. "I suppose it might

311

have. And here I thought you simply wanted to torment Father."

"That was only a pleasant side benefit in the quest for Alexander's tomb. You were the reason I kept up the chase. I'm not even that interested in Alexander," he confided. "The fourth century B.C. is a bit modern for me."

"Me, too."

He saw the light of their shared enthusiasm reflected in her eyes. She also looked thoughtful, disturbed by his explanations. If she was hurt she didn't show it, but he now knew how well she could mask her deeper feelings from him. A few days ago he'd thought any attempt to make love to her would be unwelcome, rebuffed, possibly even simply ignored. Only the memories of how she'd reacted when she pulled him out of the rubble of the collapsed tomb gave him any indication that she felt anything but furious contempt for him. And then there was that time she'd rescued him from the brigand's prison. And then—

Of course, he'd been there for her a few times, too. "We can count on each other," he said, lifting his hand to stroke her cheek. "We can always count on each other to come to the rescue." It was more than many couples ever had. He would need those memories to live the rest of his life on.

"We have that," she agreed, her eyes closed,

absorbing his touch. She pressed her face into his hand, languid as a cat, then turned her head to kiss the center of his palm. The contact sent a thrill of heat through him. "I don't want you to rescue me now," she said.

But I'm going to anyway. "Then what do you want, Cleopatra?" He laughed softly, regretfully. "I've asked you that before, haven't I?"

"And my answer is the same." She looked him in the eye and said with frightening determination, "I want you." After a moment she turned her back to him. He came up behind her and she leaned back against his chest. He took great comfort in holding her for now, with his arms around her waist. "I have a confession of my own," she said after they stood together for a while breathing in the scent of roses and each other. "I didn't want to marry you, either." He knew she felt his body stiffen in surprise, and Cleo gave a small, sad laugh. "Men always think that's all women have on their minds— marriage. Never mind that I was too young to get married ten years ago; I had more important things to do."

"Thank you very much for completely destroying me." He rested his chin on the top of her head. "I bleed from the insult to my masculinity and my honor."

"Nonsense. You'd have been relieved when I said no. That's not to say I wouldn't have liked to have been asked; I was romantic and dramatic enough to pine for a declaration of true love. I *was* sixteen, remember? I knew I couldn't bear never seeing you again if we parted before we became lovers—I thought I could survive the pain of parting if I gave myself to you for just one night."

"Oh, God."

"I know." She dug a sharp elbow backward into his ribs. "Then you had to go and spoil the whole melodramatic tableau by not going back to America. Why didn't you go back?" she asked. "Your father needed you."

"My father *wanted* me in the family business. I needed to be a scientist. We came to an understanding before he died, by the way," Evans told her.

"Good."

"He came over and I showed him the ruins of the ancient world. That hardheaded New Englander needed to see and touch the bones of ancient history with his own hands before he could understand. He became as fascinated with the past as you or I, and forgave me."

"I'm glad."

"And left me his fortune, besides."

"That explains your tailoring."

"Better to live on a legacy than earn a fortune as a relic hunter, Miss Fraser?"

"Much better. I've misjudged you terribly

for years," she added. She turned in his arms and put her hands on his shoulders. "I am so sorry, Angel." The contrition in her voice was a wound in his heart, but Cleo went on before he could correct her new image of him. "Let's return to my earlier suggestion."

"What earlier sugges—"

"About running away and living in sin. That is part of the proposition," she rushed on. "I thought we might indulge in a lifelong passionate affair while digging up desiccated dead people together. I'm so sick of being good. I'm so tired of taking care of everyone. I want a life to call my own."

"And you deserve it."

She drew in a long breath. "I try so hard not to want anything for myself, but what good has it ever done me? If I'm to be a man's mistress I ought to have a say in whose mistress I am, shouldn't I?"

"You want to be my mistress?"

"Yes. If you'll have me. Unless, of course, you would rather be respectable and find a virgin to marry—except that I'd have to kill the poor woman, because I can't bear any woman having you but me. We can have a secret affair, if you like, but if I'm going to live in sin I see no reason to be furtive about it."

Cleo sounded very sure of herself. She looked very determined, as well as ravishingly

315

beautiful in her daring scarlet dress, with her hair tumbled around her shoulders and her lips a little swollen from their kisses. She looked every inch the carnal female, a temptress, thoroughly irresistible, and Azrael Evans was no angel.

He knew he shouldn't be grinning like a child who'd just been let loose in a candy shop, or feel like an explorer who'd stumbled onto a temple made of solid gold. He kissed her—hard, fast, and sweet. "Do I want you? Good, God, woman!" He kissed her again, and ran his hands over her perfect, responsive body.

After a few delicious moments, she put her hands on his chest and firmly pushed him away. "I take it that your answer is yes," she said when their bodies were a few inches apart.

Evans dropped to his knees and buried his head in her skirts. Beneath all those petticoats, he could feel the sleek outline of wonderfully muscled legs. He wanted to kiss his way up and down the length of them, and between them. He wanted her to dance for him, naked on her back, with him hot and hard between her thighs. He was almost too aroused to recall what they'd been discussing.

Cleo's hands combed gently through his hair for a moment. Then she whispered urgently, "We'd better hurry. I hear someone coming. Can we steal a carriage, perhaps? I must go back to the house and pack a few things."

He rose to his feet. "What sort of trousseau does a girl pack to begin a life of sin?" He tugged on a lock of golden hair that fell across her shoulder. "And I drove one of the hotel's vehicles; all we have to do is fetch it and go."

"Well then," she said, and strode briskly from the arbor. "Let's go."

Chapter 20

Half an hour later, Evans paced back and forth in the small walled garden of the Frasers' house where Cleo had left him while she packed a bag. A small light glowed in the second-story window overhead, and he occasionally caught a glimpse of her shadow as she moved swiftly in front of the lamp. While Cleo hurried through her preparations for running away, he rehearsed what he would say and do once she joined him in the garden.

He was so very tempted to simply run away with her. It would be glorious. It would be grand. It would also be fatal. They couldn't return to the Middle East. He thought about taking her back to America with him but abandoned that idea quickly. He'd made a vow to aid the Hoplites, and they would not allow him to abandon his sworn mission. With the Hoplites in pursuit, any sensual interlude between Cleo and him would be intense but short-lived.

So, he was going to have to stick to his original plan. Except he had trouble remembering that the plan was to seduce, then abandon. The seduction part came easily; it was leaving her—

"Hell," he snarled, and punched the nearest tree trunk with his fist. He swore again at the pain, and shook his aching hand. Then he whirled around in surprise as a hand tapped him on the shoulder.

Cleo had the sense to jump back and duck. She'd put out the lamp before leaving the house, so the only illumination in the garden was the moonlight. It was enough to show him that she'd changed into a familiar split riding skirt and jacket. The rucksack she held in one hand was also familiar. She indeed planned on traveling light if all the worldly goods she deemed necessary were inside a bag she could carry on her back. Her eyes were large in her face, and bright with excitement. She looked nervous and skittish and ready to bolt.

He put his hand under her elbow and guided her toward the gate in the back wall. She walked stiffly beside him, and he stared straight ahead. If he looked at her he couldn't go through with it—but he *had* to go through with it. He wanted her to live. They would go back to the hotel first, he decided. There he'd take her to bed, and once he had her fully aroused—

They stopped with silent, mutual accord. Cleo slipped away from his touch and looked back at the house with a deep, heartbroken sigh. "I can't go through with this." Her voice caught on the words. "I simply can't."

Evans smiled. "I wondered when you'd say that, sweetheart."

An hour ago she had been sure. An hour ago she'd been strong, ready to abandon the small, chaotic kingdom that Everett Fraser ruled and she ran, to strike out on a life of sin.

He put his hand on the latch of the gate. When he would have opened it, she covered his hand with hers. "I can't go."

"You can't stay, either," he told her. "Time to burn your bridges, sweetheart." He kissed her cheek, then brushed his lips across hers. He traced her mouth with the tip of his tongue. "You don't want to stay."

"I know very well that I do not want to stay," she answered with her usual asperity. "What does what I *want* have to do with it?"

"Everything."

"Nothing," she countered. She sighed again. "They need me."

"I need you."

"But you aren't fourteen. I can't leave Pia."

"Pia is your father's responsibility."

"I raised her from a chick; I think I know whose responsibility she is. Father likes having her about, when he remembers that any of us are there, but he hasn't raised her. And what about Annie?"

"She has your Aunt Jenny to look after her."

"But Aunt Saida, and Thena, and Walter Raschid . . ." She made a small, helpless gesture that managed to convey that she tried to hold up the weight of the world.

Evans leaned his back against the gate, crossed his arms, and said patiently, "Sir Edward might have something to say about Saida's future, and Walter Raschid is starting university. He's very nearly a man." He straightened from his slouched position. "And if you dare to say your father needs you, I'm walking out of here without you." That wasn't what he was supposed to say! Not if he was going to gently persuade her to go with him. "Leave the man to do his own work," Evans went on, unable to stop himself. "Digging through castle ruins in the Outer Hebrides will be good for him."

"But . . . Alexander . . ."

"Is dead." He snagged an arm around her

waist and pulled her to him. After he'd kissed her for a while and desire was singing sharp and sizzling in his veins, he said, "We're not dead."

She rested her head on his shoulder. "I noticed that."

He simply held her for a time, while a ragged cloud moved slowly across the moon and the world turned a little bit closer toward morning. This felt good. This felt right. But they had to go, somewhere private where he could—

Evans sighed, a deep, heartbroken sigh. "I can't go through with this." He put his finger under her chin and drew her head up off his shoulder.

She leaned back and peered at him. Even in the moonlight, the hurt was clear in her eyes. "You don't want to run away with me?"

"I do, actually," he said. "Very much." He held her out at arm's length and brushed a stray wisp of hair from her forehead. Touching her now made him ache with bittersweet desire. He had never been more lonely in his life. "But not like this."

Tears glistened in her eyes, and her voice shook, but she spoke with her usual logic. "Then you understand about Pia. The poor dear's upstairs sleeping . . . she was so still I couldn't bring myself to wake her to say good-bye. She is very unhappy here and needs me and—"

"This has nothing to do with your family, sweetheart."

"Why can't you just kiss me and sweep me away from all this?"

"Ride up on a white stallion and kidnap you, you mean?"

"I'd appreciate that."

"No. You're a doing-everything-of-your-own-free-will sort of person. You've proved that time and again. And half the time I never noticed. You can't and shouldn't be coerced."

"I know, but . . ." Cleo had never been more confused in her life. It was as if some great storm was buffeting her from both inside and out, tearing her in a thousand different directions. The one thing she was sure of was that she wanted, needed—loved—Azrael Evans. Her heart told her one thing, but her mind roiled with a dozen different needs and expectations, and she damned her mature soul. "One of us needs to be irresponsible, Angel. I was counting on it being you."

He laughed, but the sound was so bitter it terrified her. "I can't coerce you into this. Or seduce it out of you."

She had the scariest feeling that she didn't

know what he was talking about. The darkness of the night seemed to grow darker as he spoke. *It's a cloud over the moon.* "You could try," she told him.

He touched her, brief brushes of his fingertips across her cheeks, her throat. His thumb gently traced her lips. She couldn't stop herself from kissing it and drawing it seductively between her teeth. His breath caught in a sharp gasp of response, and he practically jumped away from her.

His hands clenched into fists at his sides as he leaned back against the garden gate. She'd never seen Angel so tense. "I really was going to do it—but I can't. I thought it would be . . . not easy, but that it would work. Time's running out and I—"

A climbing rose trellis threw a spiderweb of shadows across his face, but his dark eyes were clearly visible. The mixture of stark pain and regret in them frightened her. Cleo stood rooted in place, her heavy rucksack dangling from her hand. She was dressed to run away with this man, to toss all respectability to the winds and—

"I see," she said quietly, calmly, dying. "This has all been the same old game with you. You decided to seduce me, promise me love everlasting, and talk me into giving you the treasure as a token of my devotion to you." It was the one thing she'd trusted him never to do. Angel fought hard, and he could be devious, but she had never, ever thought he would use her emotions, use desire, use the hope of a future together, against her. How could he do this to her?

"Something like that. Exactly like that," he admitted.

"What made you lose your nerve?" The bag fell from her nerveless fingers and she found that she had turned her back on Angel, though she didn't recall moving. She looked up at the now starry sky as his hands settled on her shoulders. "I thought my heart was safe with you, Azrael."

The words were out before she could control the pain. His thumbs had begun to massage the tense knots of muscles between her shoulders, and she hated that it felt damnably good. She doubted he even noticed what he was doing. She shrugged away from his touch and whirled to face him.

He was ready for it, and didn't so much as flinch when her closed fist slammed across his cheek. "Ouch. I was expecting a slap, not a punch." He grabbed her wrist when she swung at him again. "I know I deserve to have the stuffing beat out of me. If we live through this, you can pummel me senseless, but we don't have time right now."

"We have all the time in the world," she snarled back. "Since we're not going anywhere and I'm not telling you what you want to know."

He grabbed her free hand before she could hit him with it, and held on tight. He pulled her closer and looked around, as if he expected to be overheard in a secluded back garden. "You are going to tell me where the treasure is."

"We don't even claim to have a treasure," she answered. "Nor would I tell you even if we did."

"You haven't yet found Alexander's resting place," he told her, "but you do have some of his grave goods. You brought them back to Scotland and they are hidden away until your father presents the last paper of the conference. It's an open secret."

"It's a rumor," she corrected. "Father has made no claims—"

"Because he's afraid of creating the same sort of controversy as Schliemann's find at Troy. By presenting last, no one will have time to raise questions or demand more proof. What your father will get is oohs and aahs and universal praise from his colleagues. Praise that will launch the university with a bang, and practically guarantee that Sir Edward will send him back to Amorgis to finish the search for Alexander's grave. That was the plan."

"That would be a very good plan *if* this treasure existed."

"Except Sir Edward has a bee in his bagpipe about exploring his own country's history. I don't think your returning to Amorgis is likely any time soon—especially since you aren't going to have a treasure to display at the end of the conference. The treasure is going back where it belongs—"

"It belongs in a museum."

"—and you're going to help me return it to its rightful owner."

"Alexander is dead; he isn't missing it—if this treasure exists."

"A gold oak-leaf crown; three gold, ivory, and marble statues; a gold burial chest embossed with the sun symbol of the Macedonian royal family; and a gold wine goblet decorated with a battle scene featuring a portrait of Alexander's favorite horse."

Cleo's mouth hung open in shock for a moment; she shut it with a snap. "No one knows those details but Father and I." Even Sir Edward had only been shown the gold chest. The rest was a magnificent surprise yet to be revealed to the world.

"The Hoplite Order knows. They've always

known. They've been searching for the treasure for centuries."

"The Hoplite what?" As far as Cleo knew, *hoplite* was the archaic word for a Greek soldier. Alexander had won his empire with his hoplite army.

"The Hoplite Order," Angel repeated. He looked around furtively again and whispered, "They're an ancient secret society."

He looked serious. Of course, he'd looked serious when they'd made love last night, when all he'd wanted was some gold baubles instead of her. At least she knew what she was worth to him. "Secret society?" she repeated, concentrating on her outrage at the nonsense he was spouting rather than on her breaking heart. "Secret society! What sort of foolishness do you expect me to—"

"Hush!" He pulled her to him and placed his hand over her mouth for a moment. "You're in deadly peril, Cleopatra. I'm not joking. We'll hold this conversation in hushed tones. Do you understand?" She nodded behind the pressure of his hand, and he released her.

Cleo stepped away from him, glaring, but when she spoke, it was quietly. "Deadly peril, my foot. Secret society, indeed."

Angel held his hands out before him. "I know how it sounds. I made a vow to help them recover the lost treasure stolen from

329

Alexander's tomb. I don't want the grave goods for myself, Cleo—I'm trying to save your and your father's lives. There's a death mark on you for desecrating the tomb if you don't return the crown and other treasures. And I shouldn't be telling you any of this."

"Because you know I'll laugh in your face? Or because spouting such nonsense could get you locked up in a madhouse? You expect me to believe that you're in league with this, this Hoplite Brotherhood?"

"Order. The Hoplite Order. Ancient guardians of the tomb of Alexander the Great. Really."

"Bah. Secret society, indeed. I know everything there is to know about Alexander," she pointed out, "and I have never heard of any secret society protecting his tomb."

Angel pressed the arch of his nose between thumb and forefinger for a moment, then sighed. "Cleopatra, of course you haven't heard of them; they're a *secret* society."

"So are the Masons, and everyone knows about them. I've even seen a Masonic ring on Sir Edward's hand."

"This is different," he told her. "This is dangerous. This is real. They are fanatics who have carried out their sacred trust for thousands of years. They came to me because their leader got to know me when I was recovering from the accident. Before I knew who he really was, we had long discussions about how Westerners are taking far too many treasures from the lands where they belong. They knew you'd found the grave goods they'd lost long ago and spirited them out of the country. They wanted them back. I agree that the objects rightfully belong to them. I believe we need to be careful about what we take and how we deal with people now living in the lands we explore. I don't want to exploit the past."

"Which convinced your Hoplite friend to tell an American outsider all the secrets of his ancient Macedonian Greek society?" she asked with scalding skepticism.

"They're descended from all the soldiers in Alexander's elite bodyguard. Macedonian Greek, Persian, Egyptian, Bactrian, the guard were picked from every land Alexander conquered, all devoted to their emperor—as are their descendants. They spirited his body out of Alexandria when the Romans took over Egypt and took it to a secret hiding place."

"Amorgis."

"I can't say. The head of the order swore me to secrecy and used the precedent that Alexander's bodyguard was always international to initiate me as one of them. He thought I'd be useful in getting the treasure out of a foreign land with a minimum of fuss and bother for the Hoplites. I break my vow to them now because I cannot lie to you. I am trying to save your life, woman. Do you think I'd try to coerce information from you with sex if this wasn't deadly serious?"

"I think you're pathetic." She refused to be touched by any of his earnestness. "I think that you're at wit's end and disgusting. Expecting me to believe such ridic—"

He grabbed her shoulders and shook her. "That's the point!" He was the one who raised his voice this time. "I knew you wouldn't believe the truth! No woman in her right mind would believe this tale." He put his fingers beneath her chin and forced her to look him in the eye. "I should not have told you, but I couldn't go through with taking you to my bed to learn your secrets. When I take you to bed, it is because I want to make love to you, because I—"

It was Angel who looked away first. He let her go and put his hands behind his back. When he looked back at her, he was smiling. "I have proof."

She crossed her arms beneath her breasts. "What proof?" Why was she standing there and listening to the man? Her weakness was that she never could dismiss him out of hand no matter how much he deserved her contempt.

"The Hoplites have been issuing warnings for days now."

"What warnings?"

"The stolen necklace found in the museum case. The graffiti on the university building. The desecration at the graveyard. Can't you see? They were sending a message about how wrong it is to steal and profane other cultures' treasures."

"Oh, yes," she agreed quite calmly. "That was indeed the intended message."

He frowned at her easy agreement, then spoke slowly, as though perhaps she didn't understand. "Cleo, the Hoplite Order is responsible for the vandalism."

Cleo laughed. "Don't be ridiculous, Angel. That bit of heavy-handed foolishness is Pia's doing."

Chapter 21

〜〜◯◯〜〜

"**P**ia? Don't be ridiculous. Of course it isn't Pia. It's the Hoplites!" This was not going well. "How could you possibly think that Pia is to blame, when there's an unknown number of fanatics skulking around town striking terror in the—"

"Spare me the melodrama, Angel."

"But you have no proof—"

"Pia keeps the horse you gave her at Lady Alison's stables. She could easily have taken the necklace. She has unquestioned access to the museum, so leaving the necklace in the display case was easy for her. As for defacing the building . . . I met her on the university commons the night it was done—and while she speaks Greek beautifully, her writing leaves much to be desired. If you will recall, there were spelling mistakes in the graffiti."

"But why would she—"

"The gravestones are a puzzle, though." Cleo touched her chin thoughtfully. "I haven't quite figured out how she managed to topple them. But I suppose a simple lever . . . and then, there's Spiros. I've seen them talking. Perhaps that young Greek helped her." She leveled a stern look at him. "She's a hellion, my little sleeping darling. She wants to go back to the life we left and is acting up because she's miserable here." Cleo glanced back at the dark bedroom window. "Who knows what mischief she's . . . planning . . . in . . . her . . . dreams . . ." Cleo's voice slowed with each word, until she said sharply, "Olympias Fraser is a light sleeper who didn't so much as move a muscle while I packed and—Wait right here."

Alarm bells were going off in Evans's head as well, as Cleo ran into the house. "Spiros," he whispered hoarsely as the door banged shut behind her. He ran a hand across his face. Pia knew and trusted Spiros, a member of the Hoplite Order. "Good God, this could mean anything." He was certain in his bones that it meant trouble.

He picked up the bag Cleo had left lying on the damp grass. The old canvas rucksack was heavy for its size. When he opened it, Evans wasn't surprised to discover that there were no clothes packed inside, no dainty, lacy bits of undergarment in which to begin her life of sin. "Let's see," he said, taking out each item and dropping it on the ground. "Notebook, pen, ink, spyglass, copy of *Jane Eyre*. Ah, here we are." He smiled as he took out the large item at the very bottom of the bag. "One Colt Navy revolver. She does have a fondness for American firearms." He made a quick check. "Fully loaded. That's my girl." He slipped the revolver into his belt.

He was coldly certain that he was going to need the gun an instant later when Cleo came pelting back out of the house. The look of panic on her face terrified him. She'd obviously discovered that Pia was not sleeping in her bed and wasn't anywhere else in the house. He wasn't even sure Cleo saw him as he stepped into her path and grabbed her before she could go rushing out of the garden. He could tell by her fear that she'd begun to believe him on an instinctive, if not rational, level. His only question was whether Pia had gone off for a bit of freelance vandalism on her own, or whether the Hoplite fanatics had abducted her as a bargaining piece. He recalled seeing Spiros at the Highland Ball, but the young man could have left to meet Pia. Had Apolodoru's young lieutenant gone over to the side of his more radical brothers?

"Let go of me!" When Evans didn't drop his

hands, Cleo trod hard on his foot. He ignored this. "I have to go after Pia!"

"Of course we do," he answered as she wriggled, trying to escape his tight grasp. He gave her a small shake. "Look at me and listen. First, fighting me won't do Pia any good." She finally stopped struggling, took a deep breath, and looked at him. The eyes that met his were full of deep terror of the unknown and glistened with unshed tears. "You don't *want* to believe that this is a life-and-death situation," he told her. "But deep down, you know it is."

"She's out raising hell," Cleo countered. "I have to find her before Father finds out. The whole village will—"

"You aren't afraid of what the people of Muirford will think. You're afraid for your sister's life. You have good reason to be."

"You're trying to frighten me—and doing a cursed fine job," she added viciously.

"Good. You need to be frightened." As she sucked in a shocked gasp, he went on. "You think clearly when you're frightened." He closed his eyes for a moment and held her close for a few heartbeats. She was as tense as an alabaster sculpture, but she did rest her head on his shoulder. "Listen to me. Please." He held her out at arms' length.

He could not read her expression when she answered, "I'm listening."

He put everything he felt for her into what he said next. "Trust me now. I know what I've told you sounds far-fetched, but every word is true. Believe me. Trust me. For Pia's sake, and for yours."

Long seconds passed while Cleo silently looked at him.

Finally, she dropped her gaze from his, lowered her defiant chin to a more reasonable angle, and said, "How many of these Hoplites do we have to go through to get to my sister?"

"How many?" Cleo asked again as they knelt side by side behind the meager cover of the largest rosebush in the garden behind the museum. Angel was peering over the top of the bush. She tugged on his trouser leg. "Well?"

"Shh." He ducked down beside her and put a finger gently over her lips. "I'm sorry I didn't have time to do a head count, sweetheart. I think you're right that they'd come here."

"I said Pia would come here." He ignored this correction, and she held on hard to the belief that he wasn't lying to her. "I wish you'd give me back my gun."

"I'm a better shot with a pistol than you are. You're better with a rifle." She didn't argue what they both knew were their strengths. "I didn't see a guard on the door."

This was quite worrisome to Cleo. Both Sir Edward and Father had made quite a fuss after one of the night guards had been caught sleeping a few nights ago, and the man had been sacked. That should have ensured that the men assigned night duties would remain extravigilant for at least a few days. If no one was there, the chances were good that the guards had been overpowered. "The Alexandrian artifacts aren't in the museum," Cleo said.

"But your guns are in there," he informed her, and grinned.

That was right, he'd already had a look around the place. "You are a very wicked man, Azrael David Evans."

"You get named after a dark angel, you have to work with what you're given. What I'm certain of," he went on, "is that the Hoplites are in there, and that they have Pia. The simplest and most secretive course of action is for them to wait for your father to come to his workroom. They'll be waiting for him there, with his favorite child as a hostage."

Her blood froze and her heart sank, as much with fury as with fear. She would allow **nothing and no one to threaten her sister.**

Those people would pay. She tried to sound calm as she asked, "Will they let her go if Father cooperates?"

"If?"

"You know how he is." Of course Father would do anything to save Pia, but he *might* hesitate for a moment when faced with an ultimatum to return relics he'd hungered after for most of his life. He was not a man of action; he would not understand that one could not hesitate at a dangerous, decisive moment. Cleo put her hand on Angel's arm. "We have to get Pia back. Right now."

"Fine," he said. "Where's the secret entrance?"

She looked at him in utter consternation. "There isn't one."

"I was hoping you wouldn't say that."

He didn't have to point out to her that a frontal assault wouldn't work, even if they enlisted every able-bodied citizen of Muirford in the effort. After all, it was Cleo herself who had planned the building's exterior to keep out intruders. "Perhaps we should call in the local magistrate," she suggested weakly, and received a sarcastically tilted eyebrow in response. "I know we're used to handling our own emergencies," she said. "But—"

"How many people do you want to get hurt? This bunch will wipe out as many people as they have to in order to keep their secret safe. Think, woman," he said, stroking her cheek. "How do we sneak into the museum you designed?"

"From the roof," she answered promptly. "Or through that window you found the last time you broke in."

"And how—"

"There's building material and equipment all over the campus." She backed away from the rosebushes on hands and knees, heading toward the university commons. Angel followed swiftly behind her. They stood once they were behind the shelter of a thick tree trunk. "Surely," she said then, glancing toward a building site, "there must be a ladder we can use somewhere around here."

It hadn't been as easy as he'd hoped; it rarely was. The ladder they came across wasn't quite long enough to reach the window they wanted, but for two people who had climbed pyramids and rock faces leading to hidden tombs, scaling a few feet of dressed stone hadn't been a particularly death-defying feat. After he'd broken the window, slipped into the dark room, and pulled Cleo in after him, Evans gave her a tight, hard hug and hurried to try the door.

He grinned back at her. "I think I broke the lock when I visited last time."

"I'll send you a bill," she answered as he slowly opened the door and looked cautiously up and down the hallway.

"If you were a fanatical secret society, where would you hold a hostage? More importantly, how many fanatics are between us and Pia?" She had a feeling Angel wasn't really talking to her as he continued, "How many of them could there be in a small Scottish town? Even with all the foreign scholars and students, a huge group of outsiders would be noticed. I'm betting on no more than a half dozen. Those two I cut up the other night will still be out of commission, so—"

"The two you what?"

"You've already had a run-in with these jokers, sweetheart," he told her. "You just didn't know it."

Pia first, Cleo reminded herself. *Ask questions later.* "They'll have the front and back entrances covered. One of those guards has to go if we're going to get out. Straight exit from the building is through the exhibit halls to the front; the back of the place is a maze of storerooms," she contributed to the battle strategy.

"Front guard goes, then," he agreed.

"And the most logical place to hold a hostage is in the room where we—in the room behind Father's workroom. What we need is—hmm . . ." She stepped back and put her hand on her chin.

"A diversion?" Angel guessed.

"A diversion." She nodded. "Museums in the dark have a haunted quality to them for people not used to dealing with ancient artifacts. This secret society of yours may be dedicated to guarding a tomb, but I'll wager they're uncomfortable inside one."

"I'll clear the exit," he told her. "You get as close to the workroom as possible without getting captured. There's a stack of packing crates near the door to the workroom. Get behind them and wait for me."

All she said was, "I won't wait long."

They left the safety of the upstairs room and silently made their way down the stairs. On the main floor they separated. He went to secure their line of retreat.

Cleo went to fetch the rifle stored in the closet next to the crates.

What's she up to? She isn't the let-me-play-Galahad type, Evans wondered as he moved across the marble floor of the hall. It occurred to him that it might be easier for them to take out whoever blocked the door together. He shook his head in disgust. This was a fool time to turn gentlemanly and chivalrous; it was too late to rethink their strategy.

His luck held in the exhibition hall. The only illumination was from the skylights high over the mummy case, and that light was dim and wavering due to clouds blowing across the moon. The fluctuating light helped make the place look mysterious and spooky. *Haunted by the spirit of a dead princess*, he thought as he carefully removed poor Princess Mutnefer from yet another temporary resting place. He'd helped excavate this mummy a decade before, and not only was it familiar to him, but he found the princess rather attractive for her advanced age. To someone unused to the sight of a partially wrapped mummy, however, the leathery blackened skin sunken onto thin bones, the head with its yellow, gaping teeth and sunken eye sockets, topped by a few wisps of gray hair, might look terrifying . . . under the right circumstances. Evans hated having to use the princess like this, but he had no way of knowing how many men he was about to face. He did know that the Hoplites would be alert, and he needed an edge.

So he hefted the princess in his arms and sneaked behind the pillar nearest the entrance. Once there, Evans threw back his head and did his best imitation of the howl of a hunting jackal. It was a very good imitation, a haunting, hideous call that reverberated chillingly through the dark, moving shadows of the museum.

Within seconds, two Hoplites stepped into the hall from the doorway they guarded. One man was armed with a pistol, the other with a huge knife, and they both looked nervous. Evans let out another howl. Both men spun toward his hiding place. When they did, Princess Mutnefer came flying out of the darkness toward them.

The one with the knife gave a shout of fright. The one with the pistol fired, but the gun was knocked out of his hand as the mummy landed on top of him. Evans dove into the confusion. A punch to the jaw dropped the one with the knife. The other Hoplite took a bit more work.

Cleo wished she'd kept her pistol. This would be much easier with a smaller weapon. Fortunately, the bundles of papyrus scrolls in her arms as she approached the workroom did a great deal to disguise the presence of the rifle hidden among them. At least in this dim light. Of course, there was the possibility that no one was in the room beyond the door. She'd seen no evidence of these Hoplites, but she'd trusted

Angel this far, and she'd carry on until he was proved irrevocably wrong. Besides, if she didn't trust Angel Evans, there wasn't much use in believing in anything in this world anyway.

She heard the jackal call in the deep distance as she reached the door. A muffled noise that might have been a gunshot followed a second howl. She doubted anyone heard the far-off commotion behind the thick door of the workroom. Well, she decided, stiffening her spine with resolve, Angel was doing his bit, it was time for her to do hers.

Don't worry, Pia. We'll save you. Cleo had to duck a bit to reach the doorknob with so much in her arms, but she managed to get her hand around it and pushed the door slowly open. She waited a moment before stepping inside. The workroom looked empty but for the small lamp burning on the table under the high windows. It was a large, cluttered room, full of boxes and cabinets and the odd sarcophagi and painted mummy case, with plenty of shadows for a villain to find lurking space.

The first place Cleo was tempted to look was behind the door, but she controlled the impulse. She quite deliberately did not close the door behind her. She stepped in with her burden of ancient scrolls and modern firepower in her arms, and walked briskly to the worktable. Should anyone be watching her, she hoped they would read her concentration as scholarly distraction rather than notice her scanning the room for any telltale sign that she wasn't alone. She thought she counted four darker shadows in the darkness past the small circle of lamplight, but she couldn't be sure.

The man standing near the spare room door didn't make his presence known until she'd placed the papyrus scrolls on the table near the lamp. "You are Fraser's oldest daughter." He spoke in Greek.

Cleo jumped in surprise and put her hand over her mouth to stifle a startled scream. She leaned weakly against the table rather than turn and face him. From the corner of her eye, she saw a man behind the mummy case on her right move slightly. "Y-you frightened me," she answered the first man weakly.

He took another step forward. "Where is it?"

"I-it? W-wh-whatever do you mean?"

"What are you doing here?" *That's it. Move away from the door.* "Look at me, girl."

"Who are you? I can't see you." Cleo reached for the lamp—and deliberately knocked it over onto the pile of priceless papyrus. Dry, dusty papyrus, some wrapped in oiled skins. They caught fire instantly, and thick smoke billowed up and spread quickly. Cleo jumped back, crying, "Oh, no! Oh, dear! Help me!"

Men rushed toward the table from all sides of the room.

Cleo snatched up the rifle and fired as she turned. The Hoplite behind her went down with a wound in his thigh. Cleo ducked into the back room, and from the light of the growing fire Cleo saw Pia as the girl jumped up from the chair. Her hands were tied and a gag was across her mouth.

"Come on!"

Pia didn't hesitate. The sisters kept low, used the smoke and confusion of the fire as a shield, and were out the door in a few seconds. Cleo took a moment to slam the door behind her. She wished she had her keys with her, and quickly pushed a few crates in front of the door. It wouldn't lock the Hoplites in, but it would slow their pursuit. Part of her was fiercely glad to have escaped the trap; another part of her calculated that the men inside the room should have no trouble dousing such a small fire and were really in no grave danger. She didn't know whether to be exultant that Angel had told the truth or terrified that there really was a fanatical secret society out to destroy them.

Angel came pelting up and helped her pile up the crates. He waited to ask questions until they were running down the hall toward the entrance, Pia between them, guided and steadied by their hands on her arms. "What were you doing, Cleo?"

"Burning down the museum," she answered.

"I told you to wait for me!"

"Is the door clear?"

"Yes."

They didn't talk any more until they were outside and well away from the building. They headed for the shelter of the trees and only stopped when they were hidden deep in the shadows. Then they huddled on their knees behind a boxwood bush. Angel brought out his Bowie knife and made short work of the rope around Pia's wrists, while Cleo worked loose the tight knot binding the cloth around the girl's mouth. Pia's arms went tightly around Cleo the instant they were free. She buried her head on Cleo's breast and sobbed. Cleo was of a mind to deliver a stern lecture to her sister, but she settled for hugging Pia tightly and murmuring soothingly to her for a while.

Pia was made of stern stuff, and stopped crying soon enough. When she sat back on her heels she hung her head contritely and said, "I shouldn't have left the house tonight. Who were those men?"

"We'll explain later," Angel said. He put a reassuring hand on Pia's shoulder and received a bright, worshipful smile. "We need to know how many there are. What did you see, Pia? What did they tell you?"

"They were speaking in a Greek dialect, mostly," Pia answered. "I couldn't make out a lot of what they said, but I think they wanted to trade me for something Father has." She was well aware of the rivalry between Angel and the Frasers and clearly wasn't about to mention the treasure to Angel, no matter how much she adored him. "People came and went. I think there's at least a dozen of them, but I'm not sure."

Cleo and Angel looked at each other over Pia's head. Angel said, "I took out two, at least for a while."

"I wounded one," Cleo said. "I think there's three more in the workroom. It should hold them long enough for us to get Pia to safety and bring back the magistrates."

"No law," Angel said firmly. "That will only make matters worse in the long run." Angel put his hands on Pia's shoulders and turned her to face him. He asked very earnestly, "Do you think you can get away on your own?"

351

"Angel!" Cleo warned.

Pia nodded. "They took me by surprise. That won't happen again."

"We're all getting out of here," Cleo said firmly, and was ignored by the others.

"Everyone is still at Sir Edward's. You'll be safe at the manor house, Pia. You know where that is, right?" Angel asked.

Pia grinned at Angel. "Of course. I know two different shortcuts."

"Then run there as fast as you can." Angel stood and gave Cleo and Pia a hand up. He looked at Cleo. "You and I have another errand this evening. Go, Pia," he ordered.

Cleo didn't know what he planned, but getting Pia safely away was more important than arguing. "Take this." She handed her sister the rifle. "And be careful."

Pia took the weapon, gave a wicked grin, and then was gone, moving as silently as Angel or Cleo would have through the darkness.

She's safe, Cleo told herself. *Pia's competent and confident. She'll be fine.* She sent up a quick prayer that she was right, then rounded on Angel.

"And just what errand do we have to run on a night when we're being chased by madmen?"

He grinned, and his eyes shone brightly in the dim light. His confidence frightened her more than facing the Hoplites in the museum. He took her arm before she could step away. "We're going to fetch those madmen's treasure for them—that's what we're going to do, sweetheart."

Chapter 22

"**O**h, no we're not!" Cleo declared angrily.

Evans looked upon his darling, dangerous, furious Cleopatra and smiled benignly. "Yes. We are. It's the only way to peacefully resolve the issue. Besides, I made a vow to return the treasure. It belongs to them, Cleo."

"It belonged to a dead man."

"And you used to accuse *me* of being a grave robber."

"But—but—Angel!"

"The Hoplites are the rightful owners. We're giving the treasure back."

She shook her head. "Not without my father's permission. I can't."

"We don't have time for that."

She crossed her arms beneath her bosom and

355

planted her feet stubbornly apart. She looked quite adorable when she did that. "I'm not telling you where it is."

He wasn't going to argue. He pulled her arms down and took her firmly by one wrist. "You don't have to tell me where it is," he said as he led her away from the university. "I already know."

"Aren't you going to ask how I figured it out?" Angel asked as he escorted Cleo through the cemetery gate. The old church reared up on the far edge of the burial ground, forming a sort of lopsided triangle with the family mausoleums on either end of the cemetery.

"I have no idea what we're doing here," she responded. She was rather pleased with the precise, cool haughtiness of her tone, but it only earned her a smirk from the ebullient Dr. Evans. "I hate it when you're like this," she added before she could stop herself.

"I do get smug when I win," he agreed with a nod. He marched them to the center of the old graveyard and came to a halt. He snagged an arm around her waist before she could get away, and drew her to his side. When they were standing hip to hip, he tilted her chin up so that they were looking at each other. "It was your doing," he said. "I was a bit puzzled at your behavior when it happened, but it only took me until half an hour ago before the obvious answer came to me."

"Obvious answer for what? What did I do that was puzzling?"

"You constantly puzzle me, my sweet. And delight me." He kissed the tip of her nose. This endearing action melted her insides. "But you're not in the mood for endearments, are you?"

"I might be— No," she corrected herself, and stiffened against him. It was very quiet here among the gravestones. Ancient trees spread their branches over the peaceful earth, and the gentle aroma of moss rose from underfoot. She pressed her palm against his chest but couldn't quite bring herself to push him away. "This is hardly the place for a tryst."

"But it is a good place to bury the grave goods of Alexander the Great."

She felt the blood drain from her face. This was her fault. She had led him here after she first heard about the desecration of the graves, shoving past Reverend McDyess like that in her hurry to get to the cemetery and make sure that the treasure was still safely hidden. She hadn't had a chance to check with Angel so close on her heels, but she had been reassured when she saw which graves had been disturbed.

"Which one is it in?" Angel asked now.

She watched as he glanced from the moss-covered centuries-old McKay mausoleum on one side of the cemetery to the brand-new, empty edifice erected to hold the remains of the Muir family on the other end of the Muirford burial ground. The polished white marble and small stained-glass windows of Sir Edward's crypt gleamed in the moonlight.

Angel thoughtfully tapped his chin with a forefinger. "Logically, you'd have the easiest access to Sir Edward's future resting place." He gave her a narrow-eyed smile. "But you'd expect me to think of that. So, the old mausoleum is more likely. *Except* you're a devious Scot."

"On behalf of my ancestors, I thank you, yon Taffy Yank."

"A devious Scot who knows that I am a devious American of Welsh ancestry."

"I didn't exactly expect you to come calling in Muirford."

He tapped her on the nose. "But you didn't take any chances." He grabbed her hand and marched across the cemetery with her dragging her feet as she was forced to follow.

When they reached Sir Edward's mausoleum, she pointed out, "It's locked, you know."

Angel looked down at the huge padlock that fastened the door. "So it is," he said. "Brand-new lock, expensive, and quite complex-looking." He took out the pistol in his belt, pressed it against the padlock, and fired. "Sir Edward can send me the bill for this, too." He tossed aside the broken lock as the smell of gunpowder filled the air.

"How charmingly barbaric of you," she muttered.

He pushed open the crypt door and glanced over his shoulder at her. "That's me, sweetheart. You coming?"

She glanced down to where his large hand circled her wrist like a band of iron. "Do I have a choice?"

"With me," he said, grinning, "you always have a choice. Maybe it just doesn't always seem that way."

"It's late, I'm tired, we're in a cemetery. Let's get this over with and go home, all right?"

"Cleo doesn't think this is any time for philosophical discussions," he said. "Got it." He stepped into the dark crypt and tugged her in after him. "Tomb with a view," he muttered, glancing at the small, round windows that ringed the upper wall of the mausoleum. "Innovative man, our Sir Edward."

"The stained glass is quite lovely in the daylight," Cleo said.

"So you aren't denying that you've been here before?"

She pointed at the large box wrapped in oil-skin that rested in one of the empty coffin niches against the wall. "It seems rather futile to deny that the treasure is sitting in front of you at this point, Angel. Also, there's a supply of candles and matches in case you'd like to check the contents of the package before we go."

He gave her a slightly disappointed look. "You're being far too cooperative all of a sudden, Cleopatra."

"I know." She gave him a wicked smile. "Infuriating, isn't it?" He released his hold on her wrist, and she went to the back of the mausoleum and lit some of the votive candles lined up on the small altar and the candle stands on either side of it. Warm, gold light filled the clean, unused crypt. Outside, the horses hitched to the buggy they'd come in nickered nervously. A fox? Cleo wondered, but was distracted from thoughts of the outside world when Angel turned her to face him.

He tugged her to him and lifted her hand to kiss it, one finger at a time. "You are magnificently infuriating," he said, each word coming between the touch of his lips to a fingertip. When he reached her thumb he gave it the slightest of teasing nips rather than a seductive kiss. "My own Cleopatra."

His Cleopatra. For how long? She ran her fingers through his silky, raven-black hair while she fought off a sense of melancholy. He sensed it, though, somehow, and drew her into an enveloping embrace. She tilted her head, and his mouth covered hers, demanding and giving at once. Reaction shook her down to her toes, but before she could let desire carry her completely off, she pulled away from him and said, "You'd better check to make sure all the items your Hoplites want back are there. We *should* return the treasure," she agreed reluctantly. "I will not take any artifact that can be claimed as a cultural treasure by a living people. It seems a remnant of Alexander's empire still exists, and his grave is sacred ground to them. The last thing I will ever be is a grave robber."

"I love you, Cleopatra."

He turned away to examine the box before he even seemed to notice he'd spoken. Cleo stared at his back with her mouth hanging open and her heart hammering thunder in her chest. *Love* was a word neither of them had ever used. She would have remembered.

"Good God," Angel said reverently. He'd opened the crate.

Cleo knew what was inside and didn't bother looking. She did move forward, though, after studying his broad back and wide shoulders with longing that bordered on adoration.

She put her arms around him and pressed herself close. Cleo buried her cheek in the finely woven wool of his coat and crushed her breasts against the hard muscles of his back. If she could have melded her body with his she would have, so consumed was she by the longing to become one. *Don't leave me*, she prayed, wild with fear and craving. *Please don't ever leave me.* She was mad, knew it, and didn't care.

"Oh, God," Angel whispered again. This time his voice was rough, filled with unleashed emotion. The long muscles of his back rippled as he moved within her embrace.

Cleo's head came up as he turned around. The swift hammering of her heart shifted from desire to fear, and she moved away, toward the open mausoleum door.

He reached for her. "Cleo?"

"Someone's out there."

Evans was instantly alert. A moment before, he'd forgotten the glorious glitter of the gold and alabaster of Alexander's treasure, completely consumed with tactile awareness of the woman holding him so close. It had been more than her physical touch, it was as if their spirits somehow joined for a moment. He swore under his breath. "The Hoplites must have followed us."

Cleo set about extinguishing the flickering

candles. "And I lit a beacon to tell them exactly where we are."

The self-reproach in her voice hurt him. "You thought we were safe." He peered cautiously around the door frame as his eyes adjusted to the darkness once more. "There's someone moving out there, all right. Several someones." They shared a worried glance.

"Do you think we're making a fuss over nothing?" Cleo asked. "I mean, theoretically we'll be perfectly all right if we give them the treasure. That is why they're here."

He nodded. "Theoretically." He didn't like this situation, not one bit. All his senses warned him that they were in terrible danger. He knew he could trust Apolodoru, but the bunch lurking outside were renegades. Renegades he hadn't exactly gone out of his way to make friends with. They might find it more convenient to kill Cleo and himself and take the treasure anyway.

Just to test the waters, Evans shouted from behind the half-open door, "The treasure is here." There was no answer. "Do you want us to bring it out?"

He was answered by the sound of rifle fire. He slammed the door shut and heard a bullet ricochet off the brass door covering.

"Fool!" a deep voice shouted. "I ordered you

to wait until they came outside. Now you've made it harder to kill them."

Cleo put a hand on Evans's shoulder. "Fanatical, yes, but not too bright."

He looked up at her. "They did give away their intentions, didn't they?"

"So, waving a white flag at them, or pushing the box outside and hoping they'll go away, probably won't do us any good."

"It's logical for them not to leave any witnesses."

"We certainly can't reveal any ancient secrets if we're dead."

They spoke calmly, but he felt the slight trembling of her hand on his shoulder. He covered her hand with his. Then they both ducked to the floor as a bullet smashed through one of the overhead windows. They huddled close together and leaned their weight against the door. Evans thought it a pity that there was no way to lock the door from the inside, but he didn't suppose the future inhabitants of the place would feel any need to leave. If the Hoplites decided to rush the mausoleum, they were done for. It was only a matter of when.

"I'm not quite sure how we're going to get out of this," he admitted as he held Cleo close.

"Let's see," Cleo said. "Trapped in a crypt in an isolated cemetery with nothing but our weight to block the door, surrounded by an unknown number of armed assailants."

"We do have a gun. We might be able to shoot our way out."

"It's dark out there, Angel. They have cover and we don't."

"Right. We step outside and we're dead."

"Stay in here and we're dead, as well."

"Pity."

They shifted positions so that they were seated closely side by side, backs leaning against the door. Evans was glad of the metal sheeting that covered both the front and back of the door; the decorative brass was useful in deflecting bullets. Another of the small windows shattered from the impact of gunfire. This time the bullet ricocheted dangerously around the room and chipped a piece of marble from one of the coffin niches.

"Maybe they'll run out of bullets," Cleo suggested.

"We can only hope." He put his arm around her shoulder. Then he tilted her chin up and kissed her. If they had only a few minutes to live, he didn't want to waste a moment of it. She tasted of fire, and sweet memory, and of all the passions they'd shared for each other and life. He lifted his head and looked at Cleo as though seeing her for the first time. He could barely remember the lively, bright, pretty girl he'd seduced on the banks of the Nile. Yet he remembered vividly the woman who came so willingly and wonderfully into his arms and had been his lover, and every shared moment that led to right now. Looking at Cleo, being with her, touching her, laughing and fighting with her—he had never felt happier. Desire for her ran deep in him, was an integral part of him—he could not live without her. "We're going to die," he told her. "And I've never told you how much I love you."

Cleo blinked on tears. Oddly enough, under the circumstances, they were tears of complete, inexpressible joy. "You have," she told him as he kissed a tear off her cheek. His lips were soft against her skin, sending a sweet shiver through her. "Only a few moments ago." She smiled as she gazed into his eyes. "But I don't mind hearing you say it again."

"I love you," he said. "With all my heart and soul, and—everything."

"Everything." She sighed, and rested her forehead against his as more shots rang out and men began shouting outside. "That's how I love you," she whispered in his ear. "With everything I am. It's how I've always loved you," she admitted.

"When you weren't hating me."

"Even when I was hating you. I think I loved you the most the times I was furious with you."

"I know what you mean." He brushed his hands across her breasts. "You are so—alluring—when you're angry. Oh, what the hell." He kissed her throat and stroked her breasts while he talked. "I like getting you furious because you're so arousing when you're spitting like a hellcat."

"Arousing?" she questioned, letting her hand brush across the bulge of his trousers. "Me? Really?"

"We probably don't have time to make love, you know."

"I'm not sure I want to make love in a crypt, anyway. Think of the scandal when they find our bodies."

"At that point we'll be beyond scandal." He lifted his head from her breasts and looked around the dark little room. "At least it's an empty crypt. And quite clean, but for the broken glass."

The shouting outside was growing louder. "How many people are out there?" Cleo asked. "Sounds like a whole bloody Greek village." She closed her eyes and listened carefully, trying to discern what was going on out in the graveyard.

"Take that yon bloody *sassenach*!" a deep-voiced man with a distinctly Scottish accent shouted.

"That's not Greek."

She and Angel shared a hopeful look.

More shots, more shouts. Someone screamed. Someone let out a whoop of triumph. Angel helped Cleo to her feet, and they exchanged a tentative smile of hope. Then they both jumped back as someone banged loudly on the brass door.

"Hello?" a familiar voice called from outside. "Are you in there? Are you all right?"

"Sir Edward?" Cleo called back.

"Cleo?" another familiar voice shouted. "Thank heavens you're all right!"

"Father?"

"It's all right now. You can come out." The third voice was completely unexpected.

Cleo jerked open the crypt door and demanded, "Olympias Mary Fraser, what the devil are you doing here? Don't you know it's dangerous?"

She marched out of the mausoleum and confronted the men standing next to her little sister. Angel quickly followed her out, and stood with his hands on her shoulders. Sir Edward, her father, Mitchell, and Apolodoru were with Pia. In the background she noticed Spiros and a great many young men in kilts surrounding the men who'd attacked them.

"I saved your life," Pia said, justifying her presence amid the rescue party before Cleo could lecture her anymore. "Father let me come."

Cleo swung her gaze to her father. "You spoil her."

"Thank you, Pia," Angel said, and squeezed her shoulders. When Cleo looked at him, he was grinning. "I think Pia can be forgiven for staying up late just this once," he told her. "Don't you, Cleopatra?"

"Thank you, Pia," Cleo agreed. She turned her gaze to the others. "And thank you all. How did you find us?"

Dr. Apolodoru stepped forward to answer. He gestured toward the Hoplite prisoners. "As you know, I am with the Greek Bureau of Antiquities. My assistant Spiros and I—"

"But . . ." Cleo knew very well that Spiros was the son of an innkeeper on Amorgis and that he made his living fishing. And was a member of the Hoplite Order, she guessed, as was Dr. Apolodoru, who probably was also a legitimate member of the Bureau of Antiquities. "Go on," she urged him after a moment.

"Spiros and I have been on the trail of a group of Macedonian artifacts stolen from a museum storeroom in Athens. Artifacts that rightfully belong to the people of Greece," he added, with a dark look around from under heavy, lowered brows. No one tried to argue with him, not even her father.

In fact, Father said, "Shocking to discover that the relics we brought from Amorgis were stolen from a museum. Of course, they must be returned."

This made Cleo wonder what sort of conversation the head of the Hoplite Order, as Apolodoru must be, had had with Everett Fraser. She hoped it had been something along the lines of *"You want to see Alexander's grave? That can be arranged if you never reveal what you've seen."* Father would gleefully go along with that. It was finding Alexander that obsessed her father. In fact, Father was so brimming with joy at the moment that he took no notice that Cleo had been found in the company of his worst enemy.

"We knew we were not the only ones looking for this stolen treasure," Apolodoru went on. "It seems the treasure was stolen from the thieves and hidden away." He waved toward the renegade Hoplites again as he continued to spin his yarn. "The rest of the band followed the same clues Spiros and I did, all the way to Scotland. Only, once we arrived in Muirford we thought we were mistaken. No one spoke of these artifacts at the conference. They were not displayed at the museum. Dr. Fraser gave no indication that he had found anything of importance while working in Greece. We were confused. We watched and waited. Unfortunately, that gave the thieves the time to mount their own hunt for the missing treasure. Which led to this evening's unfortunate incidents." Dr. Apolodoru bowed and raised Cleo's hand to his lips when he straightened. "You have my sincerest apologies, Miss Fraser." His glance went to Angel. "Dr. Evans. And the gratitude of my people for having safeguarded some of our precious heritage."

Right now Cleo was too grateful to be alive and with the man she loved to care much about treasures or any of the other numerous complications of life. In fact, there *were* no complications in life. She loved Angel. He loved her. Anything beyond that was a minor matter and easily solved. She smiled over her shoulder at him, and the smile was returned. They stepped away from the entrance to the mausoleum and put their arms around each other's waists. She leaned on him, and he easily bore her weight. Lord, but that felt good.

"Your father led us here when Pia arrived with her tale of the attack on the museum and I explained the situation to him," Apolodoru went on.

"And my clansmen volunteered to come along for the fight," Sir Edward spoke up. He smiled proudly at the group of young local men wearing the Muir tartan.

"And I wouldn't have missed this for the world," Mitchell put in.

"We came to save a lady and protect our land," Sir Edward went on. "And because of the Stone of Scone," he added with a sideways look at Dr. Apolodoru. He clapped a hand on the other man's shoulder. "My thought at first was that since I financed the finding of this treasure, it was rightfully mine, to be displayed in the museum I built for the glory of my country. But Dr. Apolodoru reminded me that the English stole the national treasure of Scotland and display it as though they have a right to it, when it belongs to Scotland. How can I in good conscience deny a treasure to the Greeks when they ask for it back? It would make me no better than a *sassenach* Englishman."

"And we wouldn't want that," Mitchell said. Cleo wondered if she was the only one who noticed the irony in this, as Samuel Mitchell was an Englishman.

"So," Sir Edward said, gesturing Apolodoru toward the door of his bullet-riddled crypt. "Let us go and have a look at this treasure of yours."

"And see it safely away from this place," Apolodoru added.

Father and Mitchell accompanied Sir Edward and Apolodoru into the mausoleum. Pia flashed an anxious look at Cleo and followed the men inside—more to avoid a lecture than out of any interest in the Alexandrian treasure, Cleo supposed. Cleo had no interest in having a look herself. She was already holding on to all the treasure she wanted, and he was holding on to her.

"This is working out quite well," Angel whispered to her. "Especially if Apolodoru and your Aunt Jenny's romance works out, and Spiros and Annie. The Hoplites entrust their secret to their families."

After a glance at the gang of Hoplites, who were all neatly tied up and guarded by the brawny young Muirs and Spiros, Angel guided Cleo toward the other end of the churchyard. They stopped beneath the shadow of an ancient tree and kissed for a while.

She was as dizzy as a dervish when their lips parted, and infinitely happy. Molten honey flowed through her veins; slow, sweet desire. "Do that again, Angel."

"In a moment. Should I go down on my knee now, my dear?" He ran his hands slowly up and down her back.

"Why?" Cleo arched beneath his touch. Her eyes closed and her head tilted backward. He took this invitation to kiss her throat.

After another moment, he said, "We really must talk."

"Why?" she asked again. She considered

pulling him down onto the soft, mossy ground and having her way with him. "We should go back to your hotel."

"I'm afraid we can't."

Cleo's body straightened and her eyes snapped open. He laughed softly as she looked at him in shock, her heart sinking. "Can't? What do you mean, can't? I thought—"

"We can't make love to each other," Angel declared solemnly. He stepped back and put his hand over his heart. "It wouldn't be right. It would be scandalous."

"No, it wouldn't. Yes, it would. What's your point, Angel Evans?"

He threw back his head and laughed.

"Angel!" she demanded, hands on hips. "What are you up to now?"

"It's really quite simple," he answered. "Cleopatra Fraser, I know you have your heart set on living in sin, but would you mind settling for marriage?"

It took a moment for the word to sink in. *Marriage.* It was her turn to give a soft, breathy laugh. "And to one of the Hoplite Order, at that. What an elegant solution."

"Then you'll marry me? We can take Pia with us back to Egypt. Dr. DeClercq would be delighted to have your help on the expedition he wants me to head. It will be wonderful. You and me—together." He sounded anxious, as though for once in his life he wasn't confident of the outcome.

"Of course I'll marry you, Azrael David Evans." She didn't exactly have to mull the question over. "I love you with all my heart, and I'd quote Scripture about a woman leaving her father's house if I could remember the blasted verse. We shall go to Egypt and live together as man and wife, happily, for ever and ever." She tugged on the lapels of his jacket. Desire sizzled through her and she didn't want to deny it. "But why can't we go somewhere and make love right now?"

"Because this is a small town, and I will not have your name associated with any kind of scandal."

He sounded quite adamant. Quite the gentleman. Cleo loved him for his consideration, but she couldn't help but tease his newfound respectability. She brushed a hand through his hair as she said, "And you call yourself a scoundrel."

Coming next month from
Rita Award-winning author

Lorraine Heath

Never Marry a Cowboy
An Avon Romantic Treasure

Kit Montgomery is a rakish English aristocrat who's come to America to seek his fortune—but he is not looking for love. Ashton Robertson knew he was the man of her dreams the second she saw him.

Now, he's asked her to be his bride . . . but at what cost?

"(She writes) the most powerfully moving
love stories in romance today."
Jill Barnett

....